GW01191462

INTRUSIONS

INTRUSIONS

by

Robert Aickman

Tartarus Press

Intrusions
by Robert Aickman

First published Gollancz (London), 1980.

This edition is published by Tartarus Press, 2012 at Coverley House, Carlton-in-Coverdale, Leyburn, North Yorkshire, DL8 4AY, UK.

Intrusions © the Estate of Robert Aickman, 2012, c/o Artellus Limited, 30 Dorset House, Gloucester Place, London NW1 5AD, England.

'Introduction' © Reggie Oliver, 2012.

Cover illustration © Stephen J. Clark/
The Singing Garden, 2012.

ISBN 978-1-905784-48-6

The publishers would like to thank Jim Rockhill and Richard Dalby for their help in the preparation of this volume.

Printed and bound by
CPI Group (UK) Ltd, Croydon, CR0 4YY

Intrusions by Robert Aickman
is limited to 350 copies.

For
SARAH AND ELISABETH ANDERSON
Quos merito veneror pergrata mente, Penates
Vobis grata vicem me dare verba iubent.

CONTENTS

Introduction ... v

Hand in Glove ... 1
No Time Is Passing ... 32
The Fetch ... 61
The Breakthrough ... 116
The Next Glade ... 190
Letters to the Postman ... 234

Let us go hence—didst thou hear a sound?
A long, low lisped laughter—didst thou not hear?
A wicked whisper shuddering in mine ear,
And through the shuddering silence all around,
A growling as of wild beasts underground.
And lo, I know mine enemy is near,
Who dwelleth in the darkness, fraught with fear,
Tracking me ever as a silent hound.
—COUNT ERIC STENBOCK

INTRODUCTION
Reggie Oliver

Intrusions (Gollancz, 1980) was the last collection of Robert Aickman's stories to be published in his lifetime. If this is the first book by Aickman you have ever come across, it is as good a place as any to start, because the stories herein are entirely characteristic and among his best. My only advice to the Aickman novice would be that if you experience some initial bewilderment, do not be put off. The rewards of a little perseverance are great, because Robert Aickman was one of the most original and interesting short story writers of the late twentieth century.

Robert Aickman (1914-1981) was born in London. He was the grandson on his mother's side of Richard Marsh, a prolific writer whose horror novel *The Beetle* at one time exceeded *Dracula* in popularity. For a while he helped his father's architectural business, but had a passion for all the arts and pursued a desultory career, subsisting off private money, writing articles, essays and reviews for small journals and popular magazines.

He found some stability during the Second World War, in which for rather obscure reasons he was a conscientious objector, through his marriage to Edith Ray Gregorson. Together they set up the Richard Marsh Literary Agency, named after Aickman's grandfather.

Intrusions

He was a friend and later rival of L.T.C. Rolt with whom he ran the Inland Waterways Association. Besides an enthusiasm for canal boats they shared a love of ghost stories. In 1948, under the auspices of the Richard Marsh Agency, Rolt published a volume of ghost stories called *Sleep No More*. It is likely that Aickman began to write his 'strange stories' partly to compete with Rolt. Aickman coveted Rolt's position in the Inland Waterways Association; he coveted (according to Elizabeth Jane Howard) Rolt's wife; no doubt he also coveted Rolt's modest literary reputation as well. This last was the only area in which Aickman comprehensively overcame his rival.

Rolt's stories are well-crafted and atmospheric, but entirely conventional in form and content. Aickman, on the other hand, from the very first stories he published (in *We Are for the Dark*, 1951, with Elizabeth Jane Howard) discovers an entirely original vein. He writes like no-one else, but it would not be true to say that others have not occasionally written like him. Howard in *We Are for the Dark* produced tales that are uncannily like Aickman's. How, then, can we be sure that Aickman was not in fact imitating Howard who was, unlike him, already a successful writer of fiction when their collaboration was published?

The answer is simple. Howard's many books are nothing like the stories she wrote for *We Are for the Dark* whereas Aickman's are. Even Howard's themes in her stories—Inland Waterways, Opera, unrequited love for a woman, trains—are all Aickmanesque.

Such an adjective is justified. The distinctive quality of his writing is, of course, easier to experience than to describe, but some observations can be made.

In the first story of this collection 'Hand in Glove' two young women, one recovering from a failed relationship, go on a picnic in the country not far from a graveyard and a church.

Introduction

They encounter strangely prolific mushrooms, animals oddly gathered in a field, funeral wreaths, a church door without a handle or keyhole and a single black kid glove. But this is only the beginning. The incidents that occur have a dreamlike inconsequentiality and Aickman himself acknowledged that many of his stories were derived from dreams. But, like a dream, these objects and occurrences appear to have hidden resonances and connections. A pattern begins to emerge towards the end, but it is tentative and open to more than one interpretation.

I wonder if the adjective 'inconclusive', so often applied to Aickman, is quite the *mot juste*. His stories all have a beginning, a middle and an end. They conclude, but the conclusion is not absolute: puzzles remain. How like life! Aickman is both a realist and a surrealist: or, to put it another way, his surrealism is real.

His characters have the odd ordinariness of real people. He does not do 'characters' in the conventional Dickensian sense. Similarly, though he does give us at times a strong sense of place, he does not lay it on with vivid washes of colour; instead he gives us subtle hints, suggestions which dislocate as much as they locate. That overused critical term 'disturbing' is supremely appropriate to his writing. Like Housman he is a stranger and afraid in a world he never made, and which, in Aickman's case, he rather disapproves of.

One talent that gives him pre-eminence in his craft is that, like M.R. James, another eccentric conservative, he is a master of the disconcerting image. James has his mouths under pillows, his horrible faces of crumpled linen, Aickman has his—well, I won't spoil it for you, but if you can read, for example, 'The Fetch' in this volume and not be deeply troubled by the image of the woman coming up the stairs, then you are a stronger person than I am. The images in 'The Breakthrough' are even more

Intrusions

bizarre and remind me of the apparitions in Robert Graves's poem 'Welsh Incident':

> 'What were their colours?'
>   'Mostly nameless colours,
> Colours you'd like to see; but one was puce
> Or perhaps more like crimson, but not purplish.
> Some had no colour.'

Aickman thought a ghost story should be like a poem; and he derived inspiration from poetry. His images stay in the mind because they seem oddly significant, significantly odd.

An aspect of Aickman's method that has long puzzled me is his use of detail. Most writers tend to want to make detail count. If we say that someone wears a red sweater, it must signify something in the story. Aickman does not do this. He likes to proliferate detail apparently for its own sake. Do we *really* need to know, for example in 'The Fetch', that the narrator's second wife's grandfather was 'shot dead years before by thieves he had interrupted'? No, we don't. It is a quite gratuitous piece of information of no significance whatsoever. Aickman's stories often assume the aspect of a late Victorian parlour, so full of decoration and clutter that nothing immediately stands out. His fiction is curiously lacking in perspective: there is no obvious foreground and background.

The effect is disconcerting and I am not sure that it is always deliberate, but, after a while one begins to respond to it. In the first place it lends an extraordinary sense of verisimilitude to his odd narratives. We have entered a world full of detail as far as the eye can see and the strangeness of certain events is only part of an immensely complex pattern. Aickman was, in many ways, an alienated human being and his minute and obsessive use of particularities was, I think, his way of entering

Introduction

the lives of others. It is an unconventional device, but it works for him and, ultimately, for the sympathetic reader.

Aickman's methods are an expression of his profound discontent with life. His marriage had its compensations but it was not a love match. The great love of Aickman's life was Elizabeth Jane Howard and, though she was spellbound by him for a time, she was never in love as he was with her. Eventually she broke off the relationship, leaving him bereft, a feeling which is reflected in a number of his stories, notably a late masterpiece 'The Stains' (in *Night Voices*). One gets the impression that Aickman was someone who never quite got the hang of love, and its chief requirement: that at some stage the ego has to take a back seat.

Like many people with an unhappy childhood behind them Aickman was deeply nostalgic. Nostalgia is a disease which tends to afflict those who never inhabited a 'land of lost content' but who desperately want to believe it exists. In *Slipstream*, Elizabeth Jane Howard says of him:

> The main tenor of all our conversation—what everything came back to—was that everything had declined. Before the beginning of the century life had held more promise. . . . There had been nothing since those unspecified and halcyon days but a steady diminution in all standards. We were approaching the end of a civilisation.

Note that he harks back to a time *before* he was born.

Aickman was in many ways a conservative (as well as a conservationist) but he was also living proof that the words 'conservative' and 'conventional' are not synonyms. Nostalgia as such does not play a great part in his stories, but a general sense of the dismal arbitrariness of modern life does. Aickman was a man of strong spiritual and transcendentalist instincts, but no religious beliefs. His chief regret was, I suspect, like Matthew Arnold's, for the 'melancholy, long, withdrawing roar' of the Sea of Faith.

His stories, however dark, often contain an element of wish-fulfilment. Aickman was uneasy about his sketchy education and his family's social position. His narrators, Leith, in 'The Fetch' and van Goort in 'The Breakthrough', are in many ways what Aickman would have liked to have been but wasn't: university educated, cosmopolitan, well-born and discreetly wealthy. Aickman was an autodidact who became formidably well-read and well-informed about such things as opera, but the taint of insecurity remained, hence his need to dominate. In 'The Fetch', Leith's first wife, Shulie, has the elegance, sexuality and submissiveness that Aickman craved in his women but only fleetingly enjoyed. It is significant that he makes Shulie slightly disabled and homebound. I find this rather creepy—it reminds me of Dickens's treatment of Dora in *David Copperfield*—but the creepiness of Aickman the man enhances rather than mars his art.

Aickman also had the complementary gift of giving imaginative expression to the lack of sexual and emotional fulfilment in his life. This he expresses in images, such as the strikingly Freudian ones in 'Letters to the Postman', and often in spoken words. He excels in dialogue between two people who are on the verge of intimacy and yet not quite connecting. Take this from 'The Next Glade'—I have removed the non dialogue parts:

> 'I have sent the children away.'
> 'This is a boomerang.'
> 'It was my husband's.'
> 'Yours is a terrible loss for anyone. . . . Most of all for a woman as sensitive and highly strung as you. Your cheeks are wan and your lovely eyes are shadowed.'

Introduction

'I was very fond of my husband.'
'Of course. You have a warm heart and a tender soul.'
'In some ways he was not very grown up. I think he needed me.'
'Who would not need *you*?'
'Would you care for a glass of sherry?'
'If you will join me.'

This is as good as anything in Pinter: it could have come straight out of *The Lover*. It has the same rhythm, the sudden inconsequential turns, the same sexual charge and hidden menace, the same inherent silences. In fact the more I read of Aickman the more I am reminded of Pinter. I do not know whether they knew or liked each other's work—they certainly would not have cared for each other's politics—but they had a similarly bleak sense of humanity, trying desperately to communicate, thwarted by irrational forces, sinking forever back into isolation. Both also had the steely humour and the poetic imagination to make such visions strangely exhilarating.

HAND IN GLOVE

. . . that subtle gauzy haze which one only finds in Essex.
SIR HENRY CHANNON

WHEN MILLICENT FINALLY broke it off with Nigel and felt that the last tiny bit of meaning had ebbed from her life (apart, of course, from her job), it was natural that Winifred should suggest a picnic, combined with a visit, 'not too serious', as Winifred put it, to a Great House. Millicent realised that there was no alternative to clutching at the idea, and vouchsafed quite effectively the expected blend of pallor and gratitude. She was likely to see much more of Winifred in the future; provided always that Winifred did not somehow choose this precise moment to dart off in some new direction.

Everyone knew about Millicent and Nigel and took it for granted, so that now she was peacefully allotted an odd day or two off, despite the importance of what she did. After all, she had been linked with Nigel, in one way or another, for a long time; and the deceptively small gradations between the different ways were the business only of the two parties. Winifred, on the other hand, had quite a struggle to escape, but she persisted because she realised how much it must matter to Millicent. There are too many people about to make it sensible to assess most kinds of employment objectively. In one important respect, Winifred's life was simpler than Millicent's: 'I have never been in love,' she would say, 'I really don't understand about it.' Indeed, the matter arose but rarely, and less often now than ten or twelve years ago.

'What about Baddeley End?' suggested Winifred, attempting a black joke, inducing the ghost of a smile. Winifred had seldom supposed that the Nigel business would end other than as it had.

'Perfect,' said Millicent, entering into the spirit, extending phantom hands in gratitude.

'I'll look on the map for a picnic spot,' said Winifred. Winifred had found picnic spots for them in the Cévennes, the Appeninnes, the Dolomites, the Sierra de Guadarrama, even the Carpathians. Incidentally, it was exactly the kind of thing at which Nigel was rather hopeless. Encountering Nigel, one seldom forgot the bull and the gate.

'We'd better use my car,' continued Winifred. 'Then you'll only have to do what you want to do.'

And at first, upon the face of it, things had all gone charmingly as always. Millicent could be in no doubt of that. It is difficult at these times to know which to prefer: friends who understand (up to a point), or those who do not understand at all, and thus offer their own kind of momentary escape.

Winifred brought the car to a stand at the end of a long lane, perhaps even bridle-path, imperfectly surfaced, at least for modern traffic, even though they were no further from their respective flats than somewhere in Essex. She had been carrying a great part of their route in her head. Now she was envisaging the picnic site.

Hand in Glove

'It's a rather pretty spot,' she said with confidence. 'There's a right of way, or at least a footpath, through the churchyard and down to the river.'

'What river is it?' enquired Millicent idly.

'It's only a stream. Well, perhaps a *little* more than that. It's called the Waste.'

'Is it really?'

'Yes, it is. Can you please hand me out the rucksack?'

In hours of freedom, Winifred always packed things into a rucksack, where earlier generations would have prepared a luncheon basket or a cabin trunk.

'I'm sorry I've made no contribution,' said Millicent, not for the first time.

'Don't be foolish,' said Winifred.

'At least let me carry something?'

'All right, the half-bottle and the glasses. I couldn't get them in.'

'How sweet of you,' said Millicent. Potation was normally eschewed in the middle of the day.

'I imagine we go through the kissing gate.'

From even that accepted locution Millicent slightly shrank.

The iron kissing gate stood beside the wooden lych-gate, opened only on specific occasions. With the ancient church on their right, little, low, and lichened, they descended the track between the graves. The path had at one time been paved with bricks, but many of the bricks were now missing, and weeds grew between the others.

'It's very slippery,' said Millicent. 'I shouldn't like to have to hurry back up.' It was appropriate that she should make a remark of some kind, should show that she was still alive.

'It can't really be slippery. It hasn't rained for weeks.'

Millicent had to admit the truth of that.

Intrusions

'Perhaps it would be better if I were to go first?' continued Winifred. 'Then you could take your time with the glasses. Sorry they're so fragile.'

'*You* know where we're going,' responded Millicent, falling into second place.

'We'll look inside the church before we leave.'

Though ivy had begun to entangle the mossy little church like a stealthily encroaching octopus, Millicent had to admit that the considerable number of apparently new graves suggested the continuing usefulness of the building. On the other hand, the plastered rectory or vicarage to their left, behind a dangerous-looking hedge, was stained and grimed, and with no visible open window on this almost ideal day.

Whatever Winifred might say, the churchyard seemed very moist. But then much of Essex is heavy clay. Everyone in the world knows that.

At the far end was another kissing gate, very creaky and arbitrary, and, beyond, a big, green, sloping field. There were cows drawn together in the far, upper corner: 'a mixed lot of animals', as Millicent's stepfather would have put it in the old days—the very old days they seemed at that moment.

Down the emerald field ran no visible track, but Winifred, with the dotted map in the forefront of her mind, pursued a steady course. Millicent knew from experience that at the bottom of Winifred's rucksack was a spacious groundsheet. It seemed just as well.

Winifred led the way through an almost non-existent gate to the left, and along a curious muddy passage between rank hedges down to the brink of the river.

Here there were small islands of banked mud with tall plants growing on them that looked almost tropical, and, to the right, a crumbling stone bridge, with an ornament of some kind upon the central panel. Rich, heavy foliage shaded the scene, but early dragonflies glinted across vague streaks of sunlight.

'The right of way goes over the bridge,' remarked Winifred, 'but we might do better on this side.'

Sedgy and umbrous, the picnic spot was romantic in the extreme; most unlikely of discovery even at so short a distance from the human hive, from their own north side of the Park. After the repast, one might well seek the brittle bones of once-loitering knights; or one might aforetime have done that, when one had the energy and the faith. Besides, Millicent had noticed that the bridge was obstructed from end to end by rusty barbed wire, with long spikes, mostly bent.

In repose on the groundsheet, they were a handsome pair: trim; effective; still, despite everything, expectant. They wore sweaters in plain colours, and stained, familiar trousers. In the symphony of Millicent's abundant hair were themes of pale grey. Winifred's stout tow was at all times sturdily neutral. A poet lingering upon the bridge might have felt sad that life had offered them no more. Few people can pick out, merely from the lines on a map, so ideal a region for a friend's grief. Few people can look so sensuous in sadness as Millicent, away from the office, momentarily oblivious to its ambiguous, paranoid satisfactions.

It had indeed been resourceful of Winifred to buy and bring the half-bottle, but Millicent found that the noontide wine made no difference. How could it? How could anything? Almost anything?

But then—

'Winifred! Where have all these mushrooms come from?'

'I expect they were there when we arrived.'

'I'm quite certain they were not.'

Intrusions

'Of course they were,' said Winifred. 'Mushrooms grow fast but not *that* fast.'

'They were not. I shouldn't have sat down if they had been. I don't like sitting among a lot of giant mushrooms.'

'They're quite the normal size,' said Winifred, smiling and drawing up her legs. 'Would you like to go?'

'Well, we *have* finished the picnic,' said Millicent. 'Thanks very much, Winifred, it was lovely.'

They rose: two exiled dryads, the poet on the bridge might have said. On their side of the shallow, marshy, wandering river were mushrooms as far as the eye could see, downstream and up; though it was true that in neither direction could the eye see very far along the bank, being impeded one way by the bridge and the other by the near-jungle.

'It's the damp,' said Millicent. 'Everything is so terribly damp.'

'If it is,' said Winifred, 'it must be always like this, because there's been very little rain. I said that before.'

Millicent felt ashamed of herself, as happened the whole time now. 'It was very clever of you to find such a perfect place,' she said immediately. 'But you always do. Everything was absolutely for the best until the mushrooms came.'

'I'm not really sure that they *are* mushrooms,' said Winifred.

'Perhaps merely fungi.'

'Let's not put it to the test,' said Millicent. 'Let's go. Oh, I'm so sorry. You haven't finished repacking.'

Duly, the ascent was far more laborious. 'Tacky' was the word that Millicent's stepfather would have applied to the going.

'Why do all the cows stay clustered in one corner?' asked Millicent. 'They haven't moved one leg since we arrived.'

Hand in Glove

'It's to do with the flies,' said Winifred knowledgeably.

'They're not waving their tails about. They're not tossing their heads. They're not lowing. In fact, they might be stuffed or modelled.'

'I expect they're chewing the cud, Millicent.'

'I don't think they are.' Millicent of course really knew more of country matters than Winifred.

'I'm not sure they're there at all,' said Millicent.

'Oh, hang on, Millicent,' said Winifred, without, however, ceasing to plod, and without even looking back at Millicent over her shoulder, let alone at the distant cows.

Millicent knew that people were being kind to her, and that it was an unsuitable moment for her to make even the smallest fuss, except perhaps a fun-fuss, flattering to the other party.

They reached the wilful kissing gate at the bottom of the churchyard. It made its noise as soon as it was even touched, and clanged back spitefully at Millicent when Winifred had passed safely through it.

Millicent had not remembered the gate's behaviour on their outward trip. Probably one tackled things differently according to whether one was descending or ascending.

But—

'Winifred, look!' Millicent, so carefully self-contained the entire day, had all but screamed.

'None of that was there just now.'

She could not raise her arm to point. Ahead of them, to the left of the ascending, craggy path through the churchyard, was a pile of wreaths and sprays, harps wrought from lilies, red roses twisted into hearts, irises concocted into archangel trumpets. Commerce and the commemorative instinct could hardly collaborate further.

Intrusions

'You didn't notice it,' replied Winifred upon the instant. She even added, as at another time that day she certainly would not have done, 'Your mind was on other things.' She then looked over her shoulder at Millicent and smiled.

'They weren't there,' said Millicent, more sure of her facts than of herself. 'There's been a funeral while we were by the river.'

'I think we'd have heard something.' replied Winifred, still smiling. 'Besides; you don't bury people in the lunch hour.'

'Well, something's happened.'

'Last time you just didn't notice,' replied Winifred, turning away, and looking ahead of her at the weedy path. 'That's all.'

The challenge was too much for Millicent's resolutions of mousiness. 'Well, did *you?*' she enquired.

But Winifred had prepared herself. 'I'm not sure whether I did or didn't, Millicent. Does it matter?'

Winifred took several steps forward and then asked, 'Would you rather give the church a miss?'

'Not at all,' replied Millicent. 'Inside there might be an explanation of some kind.'

Millicent was glad she was in the rear, because at first she had difficulty in passing the banked-up tributes. They all looked so terribly new. The oblong mound beneath them was concealed, but one could scarcely doubt that it was there. At first, the flowers seemed to smell as if they were unforced and freshly picked; not like proper funerary flowers at all, which either smell not, or smell merely of accepted mortality. But then, on second thoughts, or at a second intake of Millicent's breath, the smell was not exactly as of garden, or even of hedgerow flowers either. After a few seconds, the smell seemed as unaccountable as the sudden apparition of the flowers themselves. Certainly it was not in the least a smell that Millicent would have expected, or could ever much care for.

She noticed that Winifred was stumping along, still looking at the battered bricks beneath her feet.

Millicent hesitated. 'Perhaps we ought to inspect some of the cards?' she suggested.

That must have been a mischievous idea, because this time Winifred just walked on in silence. And, as a matter of fact, Millicent had to admit to herself that she could in any case see no cards attached to the flowers, and whatever else might be attached to them.

Winifred walked silently ahead of Millicent right up to the church porch. As she entered it, a sudden bird flopped out just above her head and straight into Millicent's face.

'That's an owl,' said Millicent. 'We've woken him up.'

She almost expected Winifred to say that for owls it was the wrong time of day, or the wrong weather, or the close season; but Winifred was, in fact, simply staring at the wooden church door.

'Won't it open?' enquired Millicent.

'I don't really know. I can see no handle.'

The awakened owl had begun to hoot mournfully, which Millicent fancied really was a little odd of it in the early afternoon.

Millicent in turn stared at the door.

'There's nothing at all.'

'Not even a keyhole that we can look through,' said Winifred.

'I suppose the church has simply been closed and boarded up.'

Intrusions

'I'm not sure,' said Winifred. 'It looks like the original door to me. Old as old, wouldn't you say? Built like that. With no proper admittance offered.'

Gazing at the door, Millicent could certainly see what Winifred meant. There were no church notices either, no local address of the Samaritans, no lists of ladies to do things.

'Let's see if we can peep in through a window,' proposed Winifred.

'I shouldn't think we could. It's usually pretty difficult.'

'That's because there are usually lookers-on to cramp one's style. We may find it easier here.'

When they emerged from the porch, Millicent surmised that there were now two owls hooting, two at least. However, the once-bright day was losing its lustre, becoming middle-aged and overcast.

'God, it's muggy,' said Millicent.

'I expect there's rain on the way. You know we could do with it.'

'Yes, but not here, not now.'

Winifred was squeezing the tips of her shoes and her feet into places where the mortar had fallen out of the church wall, and sometimes even whole flints. She was adhering to ledges and small projections. She was forcing herself upwards in the attempt to look first through one window, and then, upon failing and falling, through another. 'I simply can't imagine what it can look like inside,' she said.

They always did things thoroughly and properly, whatever the things were, but it was not a day in her life when Millicent felt like any kind of emulation. Moreover, she did not see how she could even give assistance to Winifred. They were no longer two school-girls, one able to hoist up the other as easily as Santa Claus's sack.

Unavailingly, Winifred had essayed two windows on the south side of the nave and one on the south side of the chancel; which three offered clear glass, however smudgy. In the two remaining windows on that side of the church, the glass was painted, and so it was with the east window. Winifred went round to the north side, with Millicent following. Here the sun did not fall, and it seemed to Millicent that the moping owls had eased off. En route the churchyard grasses had been rank and razory.

But here the masonry was further gone in decomposition and Winifred could jump up quite readily at the first attempt.

For a surprisingly long time, or so it seemed, Winifred stared in through the easternmost window on the north side of the nave, but speaking no word. Here many of the small panes were missing. Indeed, one pane fell into the church from somewhere with a small, sharp clatter even while Winifred was still gazing and Millicent still standing. The whole structure was in a state of moulder.

At her own rather long last, Winifred descended stiffly.

She began trying to remove the aged, clinging rubble from the knees of her trousers, but the dust was damp too: on this side of the church particularly damp.

'Want to have a look?' Winifred asked.

'What is there to see?'

'Nothing in particular.' Winifred was rubbing away, though almost certainly making matters worse. 'Really, nothing. I shouldn't bother.'

'Then I won't,' said Millicent. 'You look like a pilgrim: more on her knees than on her back, or whatever it is.'

'Most of the things have been taken away,' continued Winifred informatively.

Intrusions

'In that case, where did the funeral happen? Where did they hold the service?'

Winifred went on fiddling with her trousers for a moment before attempting a reply. 'Somewhere else, I suppose. That's quite common nowadays.'

'There's something wrong,' said Millicent. 'There's something very wrong with almost everything.'

They ploughed back through the coarse grass to the brick path up to the porch. The owls seemed indeed to have retired once more to their carnivorous bothies.

'We must get on with things or we shall miss Baddeley,' said Winifred. 'Not that it hasn't all been well worth while, as I hope you will agree.'

But—

On the path, straight before them, between the church porch and the other, by now almost familiar, path, which ran across the descending graveyard, right in the centre of things, lay a glove.

'That wasn't there either,' said Millicent immediately.

Winifred picked up the glove and they inspected it together. It was a left-hand glove in black leather or kid, seemingly new or almost so, and really rather elegant. It would have been a remarkably small left hand that fitted it, Millicent thought. People occasionally remarked upon the smallness of her own hands; which was always something that pleased her. The tiny but expensive-looking body of the glove terminated in a wider gauntlet-like frill or extension of rougher design.

'We'd better hand it in,' said Winifred.

'Where?'

'At the rectory, I suppose, if that is what the place is.'

'Do you think we must?'

'Well, what else? We can't go off with it. It looks costly.'

Hand in Glove

'There's someone else around the place,' said Millicent. 'Perhaps more than one of them.' She could not quite have said why she thought there might be such a crowd.

But Winifred again remained silent and did not ask why.

'I'll carry the glove,' said Millicent. Winifred was still bearing the rucksack and its remaining contents, including the empty half-bottle, for which the graveyard offered no litter basket. The carriage gate, which had once been painted in some kind of blue and was now falling apart, crossbar from socket, and spikework from woodwork, offered no clue as to whether the abode was, or had been, rectory or vicarage. The short drive was weedy and littered. Either the trees pre-dated the mid-Victorian building, or they were prematurely senile.

The front-door bell rang quite sharply when Winifred pushed it, but nothing followed. After a longish, silent pause, with Millicent holding the glove to the fore, Winifred rang again. Again, nothing followed.

Millicent spoke: 'I believe it's open.'

She pushed and together they entered; merely a few steps. The hall within, which had originally been designed more or less in the Gothic manner, was furnished, though not abundantly, and seemed to be 'lived in'. Coming towards them, moreover, was a bent figure, female, hirsute, and wearing a discoloured apron, depending vaguely.

'We found this in the churchyard,' said Winifred in her clear voice, pointing to the glove.

'I can't hear the bell,' said the figure. 'That's why the door's left open. I lost my hearing. You know how.'

Millicent knew that Winifred was no good with the deaf: so often a matter not of decibels, but presumably of psychology.

'We found this glove,' she said, holding it up, and speaking quite naturally.

Intrusions

'I can't hear anything,' said the figure, disappointingly. 'You know why.'

'We don't,' said Millicent. 'Why?'

But of course that could not be heard either. It was no good trying further.

The retainer, if such she was, saved the situation. 'I'll go for madam,' she said, and withdrew without inviting them to seat themselves on one of the haphazard sofas or uncertain-looking chairs.

'I suppose we shut the door,' said Winifred, and did so.

They stood about for a little. There was nothing to look at apart from a single coloured print of lambs in the Holy Land. At each corner of the frame, the fretwork made a cross, though one of the crosses had been partly broken off.

'None the less, I don't think it's still the rectory,' said Winifred. '*Or* the vicarage.'

'You're right.' A middle-aged woman had appeared, wearing a loose dress. The colour of the dress lay between oatmeal and cream, and round the oblong neck and the ends of the elbow-length sleeves ran wide strips of a cherry hue. The woman's shoes were faded, and she had taken little trouble with her bird's-nest hair. 'You're perfectly right,' said the woman. 'Hasn't been a clergyman here for years. There are some funny old rectories in this county, as you may have heard.'

'Borley, you mean,' said Millicent, who had always been quite interested in such things.

'That place and a number of other places,' said the woman. 'Each little community has its speciality.'

'This was a *rectory*,' Winifred enquired in the way she often did, politely elevating her eyebrows; 'not a vicarage?'

'They would have found it even more difficult to keep a vicar,' said the woman in the most matter-of-fact way. Millicent could see there was no wedding ring on her hand. Indeed, there was no ring of any kind on either of her rather massive, rather unshaped hands. For that matter, there were no gems in her ears, no gewgaws round her neck, no Castilian combs in her wild hair.

'Sit down,' said the woman. 'What can I do for you? My name's Stock. Pansy Stock. Ridiculous, isn't it? But it's a perfectly common name in Essex.'

Winifred often went on in that very same way about 'Essex', had indeed already done so more than once during the journey down, but Millicent had always supposed it to be one of Winifred's mild fancies, which it was up to her friends to indulge. She had never supposed it to have any objective metaphysic. Nor had she ever brought herself to address anyone as Pansy, and was glad that the need was unlikely to arise now.

They sat, and, because it seemed to be called for, Winifred introduced herself and then Millicent. Miss Stock sat upon the other sofa. She was wearing woolly mid-green stockings.

'It's simply about this glove,' went on Winifred. 'We explained to your servant, but we couldn't quite make her understand.'

'Lettice has heard nothing since it happened. That was the effect it had on her.'

'Since *what* happened?' asked Winifred. 'If we may ask, that is.'

'Since she was jilted, of course,' answered Miss Stock.

'That sounds very sad,' said Winifred, in her affable and emollient way. Millicent, after all, had not exactly been jilted, not exactly. Technically, it was she who was the jilt. Socially, it still made a difference.

'It's the usual thing in this place. I've said that each community had its speciality. This is ours.'

'How extraordinary!' said Winifred.

Intrusions

'It happens to all the females, and not only when they're still girls.'

'I wonder they remain,' responded Winifred smilingly.

'They don't remain. They come back.'

'In what way?' asked Winifred.

'In what is known as spirit form,' said Miss Stock.

Winifred considered. She was perfectly accustomed to claims of that kind, to the many sorts it takes to make a world.

'Like the Wilis in *Giselle*?' she enquired helpfully.

'I believe so,' said Miss Stock. 'I've never been inside a theatre. I was brought up not to go, and I've never seen any good reason for breaking the rule.'

'It's become so expensive too,' said Winifred, if only because it was what she would have said in other, doubtless more conventional, circumstances.

'This glove,' interrupted Millicent, actually dropping it on the floor, because she had no wish to hold it any longer. 'We saw it lying by itself on the churchyard path.'

'I daresay you did,' said Miss Stock. 'It's not the only thing that's been seen lying in and around the churchyard.'

Winifred politely picked up the glove, rose, and placed it on Miss Stock's sofa. 'We thought we should hand it in locally.'

'That's good of you,' said Miss Stock. 'Though no one will claim it. There's a room half full of things like it. Trinkets, knicknacks, great gold hearts the size of oysters, souvenirs of all kinds, even a pair of riding boots. Things seem to appear and disappear just as they please. No one ever enquires again for them. That's not why the females come back. Of course it was a kind action on your part. Sometimes people benefit, I suppose. They say that if one finds something, or sees something, one will come back anyway.' Miss Stock paused for half a second. Then she asked casually, 'Which of you was it?'

Hand in Glove

At once Millicent replied: 'It was I who saw the glove first, and several other things too.'

'Then you'd better take the greatest possible care,' said Miss Stock, still quite lightly. 'Avoid all entanglements of the heart, or you may end like Lettice.'

Winifred, who was still on her feet, said: 'Millicent, we really must go, or we shall *never* get to Baddeley End.'

Miss Stock said at once: 'Baddeley End is closed all day on Thursdays, so wherever else you go, there's no point in going *there*.'

'You're right about Thursdays, Miss Stock,' said Winifred, 'because I looked it up most carefully in the book before we left. But this is Wednesday.'

'It's not,' said Millicent. 'It's Thursday.'

'Whatever else it may be,' confirmed Miss Stock, 'it indubitably is Thursday.'

There was an embarrassing blank in time, while an angel flitted through the room, or perhaps a demon.

'I now realise that it is Thursday,' said Winifred. She had turned pale. 'Millicent, I *am* so sorry. I must be going mad.'

'Of course there are many, many other places you can visit,' said Miss Stock. 'Endless places. Almost every little hamlet has something of its own to offer.'

'Yes,' said Winifred. 'We must have a look round.'

'What, then, *do* they come back for,' asked Millicent, interrupting again, 'if it's not for their property?'

'I didn't say it wasn't for their property. It depends *what* property. Not for their gloves or their rings or their little false thises and thats, but for their property none the less. For what they *regard* as their property, anyway. One's broken heart, if it can be mended at all, can be mended only in one way.'

Intrusions

'And yet at times,' said Millicent, 'the whole thing seems so trivial, so unreal. So absurd, even. Never really there at all. Utterly not worth the melodrama.'

'Indubitably,' said Miss Stock. 'And the same is true of religious faith, of poetry, of a walk round a lake, of existence itself.'

'I suppose so,' said Millicent. 'But personal feeling is quite particularly—' She could not find the word.

'Millicent,' said Winifred. 'Let's go.' She seemed past conventions with their hostess. She looked white and upset. 'We've got rid of the glove. Let's go.'

'Tell me,' said Millicent. 'What is the one way to mend a broken heart? If we are to take the matter so seriously, we need to be told.'

'Millicent,' said Winifred, 'I'll wait for you in the car. At the end of the drive, you remember.'

'I'm flattered that you call it a drive,' said Miss Stock.

Winifred opened the front door and walked out. The door flopped slowly back behind her.

'Tell me,' said Millicent. 'What is the one way to mend a broken heart?' She spoke as if in capital letters.

'You know what it is.' said Miss Stock. 'It is to kill the man who has broken it. Or at least to see to it that he dies.'

'Yes, I imagined it was that,' said Millicent. Her eyes were on the Palestinian lamblets.

'It is the sole possible test of whether the feeling is real,' explained Miss Stock, as if she were a senior demonstrator.

'Or *was* real?'

'There can be no *was*, if the feeling's real.'

Millicent withdrew her gaze from the gambolling livestock. 'And have you yourself taken the necessary steps? If you don't mind my asking, of course?'

Hand in Glove

'No. The matter has never arisen in my case. I live here and I look on.'

'It doesn't seem a very jolly place to live.'

'It's a very instructive place to live. Very cautionary. I profit greatly.'

Millicent again paused for a moment, staring across the sparsely endowed room at Miss Stock in her alarming clothes.

'What, Miss Stock, would be your final words of guidance?'

'The matter is probably out of your hands by now, let alone of mine.'

Millicent could not bring herself to leave it at that.

'Do girls—women—come here from outside the village? If there really is a village? My friend and I haven't seen one and the church appears to be disused. It seems to have been disused for a very long time.'

'Of course there's a village,' said Miss Stock, quite fiercely. 'And the church is not *entirely* disused, I assure you. And there are cows and a place where they are kept; and a river and a bridge. All the normal things, in fact, though, in each case, with a local emphasis, as is only right and proper. And, yes, females frequently come from outside the village. They find themselves here, often before they know it. Or so I take it to be.'

Millicent rose.

'Thank you, Miss Stock, for bearing with us, and for taking in our glove.'

'Perhaps something of your own will be brought to me one day,' remarked Miss Stock.

'Who knows?' replied Millicent, entering into the spirit, as she regularly tried to do.

Millicent detected a yellow collecting box on a broken table to the right of the front door. In large black letters, a label proclaimed JOSEPHINE BUTLER AID FOR UNFORTUNATES.

Intrusions

From her trousers pocket, Millicent extracted a contribution. She was glad she did not have to grope ridiculously through a handbag, while Miss Stock smiled and waited.

Miss Stock had risen to her feet, but had not advanced to see Millicent out. She merely stood there, a little dimly.

'Goodbye, Miss Stock.'

In the front door, as with many rectories and vicarages, there were two large panes of glass, frosted overall but patterned *en clair* round the edge, so that in places one could narrowly see through to the outer world. About to pull open the door, which Winifred had left unlatched, Millicent apprehended the shape of a substantial entity standing noiselessly without. It was simply one thing too many. For a second time that day, Millicent found it difficult not to scream. But Miss Stock was in the mistiness behind her, and Millicent drew the door open.

'Nigel, my God!'

Millicent managed to pull fast the door behind her. Then his arms enveloped her, as ivy was enveloping the little church.

'I'm having nothing more to do with you. How did you know I was here?'

'Winifred told me, of course.'

'I don't believe you. She's sitting in her car anyway, just by the gate. I'll ask her.'

'She's not,' said Nigel. 'She's left.'

'She can't have left. She was waiting for me. Please let me go, Nigel.'

'I'll let you go, and then you can see for yourself.'

They walked side by side in silence down the depressing, weedy drive. Millicent wondered whether Miss Stock was watching them through the narrow, distorting streaks of machine-cut glass.

Hand in Glove

There was no Winifred and no car. Thick brown leaves were strewn over the place where the car had stood. It seemed to Millicent for a moment as if the car had been buried there.

'Never mind, my dear. If you behave yourself, I'll drive you home.'

'I can't see your car either.' It was a notably inadequate rejoinder, but at least spontaneous.

'Naturally not. It's hidden.'

'Why is it hidden?'

'Because I don't want you careering off in it and leaving me behind. You've tried to ditch me once, and once is enough for any human being.'

'I didn't *try* to ditch you, Nigel. I completed the job. You were smashing up my entire life.'

'Not your life, sweet. Only your idiot career, so-called.'

'*Not* only.'

'Albeit, I shan't leave you to walk home.'

'Not home. Only to the station. I know precisely where it is. Winifred pointed it out. She saw it on the map. She said there are still trains.'

'You really can't rely on Winifred.'

Millicent knew that this was a lie. Whatever had happened to Winifred, Nigel was lying. Almost everything he said was a lie, more or less. Years ago it had been among the criteria by which she had realised how deeply and truly she loved him.

'You can't always rely on maps either,' said Nigel.

'What's happened to Winifred?' How absurd and schoolgirlish she always seemed in her own eyes when trying to reach anything like equal terms with Nigel! The silly words leapt to her lips without her choosing or willing them.

Intrusions

'She's gone. Let's do a little sight-seeing before we drive home. You can tell me about the crockets and finials. It will help to calm us down.'

Again he put his arm tightly round her and, despite her half-simulated resistance, pushed and pulled her through the kissing gate into the churchyard. Her resistance was half simulated because she knew from experience how useless with Nigel was anything more. He knew all the tricks by which at school big boys pinion and compel small ones, and he had never hesitated to use them against Millicent, normally, of course, upon a more or less agreed basis of high spirits, good fun, and knowing better than she what it would be sensible for them to do next. His frequent use of real and serious physical force had been another thing that had attracted her.

He dragged her down the uneven path. 'Beautiful place. Peaceful. Silent as the grave.'

And, indeed, it *was* quiet now: singularly different in small ways from when Millicent had been there with Winifred. Not only the owls but all the hedgerow birds had ceased to utter. One could not even detect an approaching aircraft. The breeze had dropped, and all the long grass looked dead or painted.

'Tell me about the architecture,' said Nigel. 'Tell me what to look at.'

'The church is shut,' said Millicent. 'It's been closed for years.'

'Then it shouldn't be,' said Nigel. 'Churches aren't meant to be shut. We'll have to see.'

He propelled her up the path where earlier she had first seen the glove. The hand that belonged to it must be very nearly the hand of a child: Millicent realised that now.

In the porch, Nigel sat her down upon the single, battered, wooden bench, perhaps at one time borrowed from the local school; when there had been a local school. 'Don't move, or I'll catch you one. I'm not having you leave me again, yet awhile.'

Nigel set about examining the church door, but really there was little to examine. The situation could be taken in very nearly at a glance and a push.

Nigel took a couple of steps back, and massed himself sideways. Wasting no time, he had decided to charge the door, to break it down. Quite possibly it was already rickety, despite appearances.

But that time, Millicent really did scream.

'No!'

The noise she had made seemed all the shriller when bursting upon the remarkable quietness that surrounded them. She could almost certainly have been heard in the erstwhile rectory, even though not by poor Lettice. Millicent had quite surprised herself. She was an unpractised screamer.

She had even deflected Nigel for a moment.

She expostulated further. 'Don't! Please don't!'

'Why not, chicken?' Almost, beyond doubt, his surprise was largely real.

'If you want to, climb up outside and look in through the window, first.' The volume and quality of her scream had given her a momentary ascendancy over him. 'The other side of the church is easier.'

He was staring at her. 'All right. If you say so.'

They went outside without his even holding on to her.

'No need to go round to the back,' said Nigel. 'I can manage perfectly well here. So can you, for that matter. Let's jump up together.'

'No,' said Millicent.

'Please yourself,' said Nigel. 'I suppose you've seen the bogey already. Or is it the black mass?' He was up in a single spring, and adhering to nothing visible, like an ape. His head was sunk between his shoulders as he peered, so that his red curls made him resemble a larger Quasimodo, who, Millicent recollected, was always clinging to Gothic walls and descrying.

Nigel flopped down in silence. 'I see what you mean,' he said upon landing. 'Not in the least a sight for sore eyes. Not a sight for little girls at all. Or even for big ones.' He paused for a moment, while Millicent omitted to look at him. 'All right. What else is there? Show me. Where do we go next?'

He propelled her back to the path across the churchyard and they began to descend towards the river.

It was, therefore, only another moment or two before Millicent realised that the pile of wreaths was no longer there: no sprays, no harps, no hearts, no angelic trumpets; only a handful of field flowers bound with common string. For a moment, Millicent merely doubted her eyes yet again, though not only her eyes.

'Don't think they use this place any longer,' said Nigel. 'Seems full up to me. That would explain whatever it is that's been going on in the church. What happens if we go through that gate?'

'There's a big meadow with cows in it, and then a sort of passage down to the river.'

'*What* sort of passage?'

'It runs between briars, and it's muddy.'

'We don't mind a little mud, do we, rooster? What's the river called, anyway?'

'Winifred says it's called the Waste.'

'Appropriate,' said Nigel. 'Though not any more, I hasten to add, not any more.'

It was exactly as he said it that Millicent noticed the headstone. *Nigel Alsopp Ormathwaite Ticknor. Strong, Patient, and*

True. Called to Higher Service. And a date. No date of birth: only the one date. That day's date.

The day that she had known to be a Thursday when Winifred had not.

The stone was in grey granite, or perhaps near-granite. The section of it bearing the inscription had been planed and polished. When she had been here last, Millicent had been noticing little, and on the return from the picnic the inscription would not have confronted her in any case, as was shown by its confronting her now.

'Not any more,' said Nigel a third time. 'Let's make it up yet again, henny.'

At last, Millicent stopped. She was staring at the inscription. Nigel's hands and arms were in no way upon or around her or particularly near her.

'I love you, chickpeas,' said Nigel. 'That's the trouble, isn't it? We got on better when I didn't.'

Seldom had Nigel been so clear-sighted. It was eerie. Still, the time of which he spoke was another thing that had been long, long ago.

'I don't know what to say,' said Millicent. What other words were possible? No longer were they children, or young people, or anything at all like that.

They went forward a few paces, so that the headstone now stood behind Millicent. She did not turn to see whether there were words upon the back of it.

Nigel went through the second kissing gate ahead of her. 'Don't you bother,' he said. 'I expect you've been down to the river with Winifred. I know you won't run away now. I'll just take a quick peek at the fishing.'

However, there seemed by now no point in not following him, and Millicent pushed back the gate in her turn.

Intrusions

'Please yourself,' said Nigel.

But Millicent had become aware of a development. The animals formerly in the far and upper corner were now racing across the open space towards Nigel and her, and so silently that Nigel had not so much as noticed them; 'cows', she had described them, when speaking of them to Winifred; 'stock', as her stepfather might have termed them. There is always an element of the absurd about British domestic animals behaving as if they were in the Wild West. Still, this time it was an element that might be overlooked.

'Nigel!' exclaimed Millicent, and drew back through the gate, which clanged away from her.

'Nigel!!'

He went sturdily on. We really should not be frightened of domestic animals in fields. Moreover, so quiet were these particular fields that Nigel still seemed unaware of anything moving other than himself.

'Nigel!!!'

The animals were upon him and leaving little doubt of their intentions, in so far as the last word was applicable. In no time, on the grass and on the hides, there was blood; and worse than blood. Before long, there was completely silent, but visibly most rampageous, trampling. Tails were raised now, and eyes untypically stark. But the mob of beasts, by its mere mass, probably concealed the worst from Millicent.

Seek help. That is what one is called upon to do in these cases. At the least, call for help. Millicent, recently so vocal, found that she could make no noise. The grand quietness had taken her in as well.

'Oh, Nigel, love.'

But soon the animals were merely nuzzling around interestedly. It was as if they had played no part in the consummation towards which they were sniffing and over which they were slobbering.

Millicent clung to the iron gate. Never before that day had she screamed. Never yet in her life had she fainted.

Then she became aware that the churchyard had somehow filled with women: or, at least, that women were dotted here and there among the mounds and memorials; sometimes in twos, threes, and fours, though more commonly as single spies.

These women were not like the Wilis in Winifred's favourite ballet. They were bleak, and commonplace, and often not young at all. Millicent could not feel herself drawn to them. But she realised that they were not merely in the churchyard, but in the meadow too; from which the tempestuous cattle seemed to have withdrawn while for a second her back had been turned. In fact, at that moment the women were just about everywhere.

Absurd, absurd. Even now, Millicent could not overlook that element. The whole business simply could not be worth all this, and, in the world around her, everyone knew that it was not. Sometimes one suffered acutely, yes, but not even the suffering was ever quite real, let alone the events and experience supposedly suffered over. Life was not entirely, or even mainly, a matter of walking round a lake, if one might adopt Miss Stock's persuasive analogy.

None the less, it must have been more or less at this point that Millicent somehow lost consciousness.

Winifred was looking from above into her face. Winifred was no longer pale, but nearly her usual colour, and renewed in confidence.

'My dear Millicent, I should have put you to bed instead of taking you out into the country! How on earth did you come to fall asleep?'

Intrusions

'Where are the cows?'

Winifred looked through the ironwork of the gate into the field behind her. 'Not there, as far as I can see. I expect they've gone to be milked.'

'They're not really cows at all, Winifred. Not ordinary cows.'

'My dear girl!' Winifred looked at her hard, then seemed more seriously concerned. 'Have you been attacked? Or frightened?'

'Not *me*,' said Millicent.

'Then who?'

Millicent gulped, and drew herself together.

'It was a dream. Merely a dream. I'd rather not talk about it.'

'Poor sweet, you must be worn out. But how did you get down here? Have you been sleepwalking?'

'I was taken. That was part of the dream.'

'It was shocking that Stock woman going on as she did. You should have closed your ears.'

'And eyes,' said Millicent.

'I expect so,' said Winifred, smiling. 'It was a hideous place. If you're fully awake now, I expect you'd like to go? I've made a mess of the whole day.'

'I couldn't see the car. I was looking for it.'

'I moved it. I wanted to be out of sight. You couldn't have supposed I'd driven it through the churchyard.'

'Anything seems possible,' said Millicent, as they walked up the slope. 'Anything. For example, you saw all those flowers. You saw them with your own eyes. Where are they?'

'They've been taken off to some hospital. It's what people do after funerals nowadays.'

'And the mushrooms down by the river?'

Hand in Glove

'They were there from the first, as I told you.'

'And Miss Stock's stories?'

'She just needs a man. Oh, I'm sorry, Millicent.'

'And the inside of the church?'

'That was really rather nasty. I'm not going to talk about it, I'm not even going to think about it, and I'm certainly not going to let you look at it.'

'Oughtn't whatever it is to be reported somewhere?'

'Not by me,' said Winifred with finality.

As they had passed for the last time through the gate leading out of the churchyard, Winifred had said, 'We're going home as quickly as possible, I'm taking you to my place, and I'm putting you to bed with a sedative. I don't really know about this kind of trouble, but I've seen what I've seen, and what you need in the first place is a good, long sleep, I'm sure of it.'

Millicent herself knew that grief, especially repressed grief, was said to induce second sight, let alone second thoughts.

None the less, Millicent woke up at just before half-past eleven. Long ago, in the early days with Nigel, one of them had each night telephoned the other at that time and often they had conversed until midnight, when it had been agreed that the closure be applied. Such simplicities had come to an end years and years before, but on no evening since she had given up Nigel had Millicent gone to bed before that particular hour.

There was little chance of Nigel even remembering the old, sentimental arrangement, and less chance of his now having anything easeful to say to her. Still, Millicent, having looked at her watch, lay there sedated and addled, but awake; and duly the telephone rang.

Intrusions

An extension led to the bedside in Winifred's cosy spare room. Winifred herself could not relax in a room without a telephone.

Millicent had the receiver in her hand at the first half-ping of the delicate little bell.

'Hullo,' said Millicent softly to the darkness. Winifred had drawn all the curtains quite tight, since that was the way Winifred liked her own room at night.

'Hullo,' said Millicent softly, a second time. At least it could hardly now be a call for Winifred. It was all the more important not to waken her.

On the line, or at the other end of it, something seemed to stir.

There could be little doubt of it. It was not a mere reflex of the mechanism.

'Hullo,' repeated Millicent softly.

Third time lucky, because at last there was a reply.

'Hullo, feathers,' said Nigel.

In all the circumstances, Millicent could not possibly just ring off, as rationally she should have done. 'Are you all right?' she asked.

'What a sight you look in Winifred's nightwear. Not your style at all, crop.'

Every inch of Millicent's flesh started simultaneously to fall inwards. 'Nigel! Where are you?'

'I'm right outside your door, gizzard. Better come at once. But do wear your own pyjamas. The scarlet ones. The proper ones.'

'I'm not coming, Nigel. I've told you that. I mean it.'

'I'm sure you mean it since you left me to be trodden upon by a lot of bloody heifers without doing one thing except grin. It makes no difference. Less difference than ever, in fact. I want you and I'm waiting outside your door now.'

She simply couldn't speak. What could she possibly say?

'You come to me, three toes,' said Nigel, '*and* wearing your own clothes. Or, make no mistake, I'm coming to you.'

The receiver fell from Millicent's hand. It crashed to the bedroom floor, but the carpet in Winifred's guest bedroom was substantial. And Winifred heard nothing. In any case, Winifred herself had just passed a trying day also, and needed her rest, before the demands of life on the morrow, the renewed call of the wild.

A group of concerned friends, male and female, clustered round Winifred after the inquest; for which a surprising number had taken time off.

'I have never been in love,' said Winifred. 'I really don't understand about it.'

People had to accept that, and get on with things, routine and otherwise. What else could they do?

NO TIME IS PASSING

> Assises dans le sang du soleil moribond,
> Près des noirs cygnes nés de l'ombre des carènes,
> Plus d'une fois j'ai vu les divines Sirènes
> Et j'ai miré mon rêve en leur regard profond.
> GABRIELE D'ANNUNZIO

I

TRUTH TO TELL, Delbert Catlow was at first scarcely even surprised that he had not previously noticed the wide river behind the thick hedge at the bottom of their garden; let alone startled.

By no means was this because he had been long oppressed by cares. Perhaps, on the contrary, it was because everything had been so seraphically right and perfect. One does not turn aside from angels in order to count dustbins.

They occupied the ground floor and basement of the nineteenth-century house, solid and dependable as Angkor Wat, which it somewhat resembled; and, before that afternoon, Delbert had hardly entered the garden, first, because always he had so many other things to do, many of them pleasant things, and, second, because it had been crackly, cosy winter ever since they had moved in. One could hear and smell the holly burning everywhere.

It was an evergreen hedge at the far end of the medium-sized lawn. Perhaps the occupants of the flats upstairs might have seen over it; but there had been no occupants of the flats upstairs, though one sometimes heard noises. The Catlows supposed the flats upstairs were too expensive for occupants, and smiled ruefully at one another, and at most others.

That day, Gregory Barfield, the most responsible partner at the office where Delbert worked, had departed at about midday for a friend's wedding in the country; after which everything had run swiftly into the sand, until all concerned yawned and upped, especially as the weather was so absolutely ideal. No longer draughty, but not yet too hot. No longer blustery, but not too still. No longer overcast, but not too glary. A day such as one finds only in England; and unlikely to recur that year, or the year after.

At that hour, Hesper was, of course, working still. She had been filling in at the Town Hall, of all places, until the birth of their child. She had reported that there was almost nothing to do and a crowd to do it; but that it was often difficult actually to leave the building. As for the child, Delbert was not quite sure what the position was. Probably it would work out in the end.

There were no fewer than nine composition steps to the front door. Delbert sprang up them, lugged forth his bunch of keys, darted lightly through the house, and, for the first time, he thought, that year, unlocked the door on the other side. Quite possibly he was singing slightly; or, certainly, whistling. He saw the river at once. It was impossible not to see it.

Eleven alternative steps in highly ornamental iron descended to the lawn. The grass was in need of its first seasonal haircut. Hesper used to work purposefully in the garden from time to time, even in winter; but to Delbert she seemed nearly a stranger when she was among trugs and slugs. Assuredly, she looked different. He might never have embraced her had she always looked like that, so impersonal, so committed, so like others, so undemonstrative.

Delbert went down and on in order to investigate. The ancient rust on the steps abraded the feet, even through shoes. The grass tinkled as the feet passed. These were not frail stems, lucky to be alive. They were the hardy and exclusive survivors. Delbert rose upon his toes, as he had been trained to do, every day, again and again, in his echoing school gymnasium. He gazed across the top of the evergreen hedge. The long rainfall had turned the familiar dust on the thick leaves into something rather different. Delbert's suit was in danger.

It was a fairly bleak scene; though, on this quite perfect day, beautiful too, if one cared for things like that. On any other day, many people might look away. The water was unexpectedly low, especially as it was the end of a hard winter. No doubt the river was tidal, and, at the moment, the tide had turned again home. There was much mud, and not a seabird to scratch at it anywhere. Delbert, a male, was already becoming preoccupied with the working, practical details.

All the same, there was nowadays very little open country east of Gunnersbury, and though the Thames figured considerably in the maps of the district, the Catlows did not dwell upon its brink. Delbert was certain of that. Of course he was. Nor was this river particularly like the Thames, as far as Delbert had inspected the Thames. There was no sign at all of what Eric de Maré used to call 'the Thames vernacular'. There were few works of man to which a name could be put; that or any other. There was not even much litter; scarcely a transistor radio, living or dead.

No Time is Passing

But there were steps; downwards: and at the bottom of them was a small blue boat with small green sculls.

This time, the steps were of enduring Portland; not of precarious timber, or of make-believe. They led from a gate in his garden that Delbert had not previously noticed; in the very far corner.

Delbert sank upon his full two feet. He had learned to feel little pain at those times. He wondered if the gate were locked. He had no wish that Hesper be suddenly confronted with cadging, lusting beachcombers, their feet and shins red and bare beneath tattered, rolled-up sea trousers.

The gate was a delicate affair which would hardly have held back such characters in any case; and it opened widely at the first touch, so that Delbert was beyond it without having to make a decision. On this side, the evergreen hedge was smeared with mud up to its top; as if winter tides swept through it and six or seven feet over the Catlows' lawn, which could hardly have been the case, and assuredly had not been for the last six months.

Or could it sometimes have happened when they had both been out at work? Delbert looked back over the gate at the windows in the three upper floors of the house. Could there be more dependable observers? At least no one was close enough to the glass to be visible from where he stood. The gate was designed to close itself, as if the Fire Officer had intervened. No matter: it could be reopened very easily indeed. Delbert had just learned that for himself.

He descended this further flight of steps, looking carefully where he trod. Not until he had reached the bottom did he properly re-examine the whole landscape. . . . Or seascape, perhaps. For Delbert now felt doubts whether this water was properly to be described as a river at all. It looked saline and sullen.

It was true that on his side of things were many of the familiar suburban landmarks. Or Delbert supposed they were familiar: he had really spent little of his time staring at them. He had always had something better to do. On the other side were dark green trees, flat-topped and rather low. There was a certain amount of couch grass. There were black hulks, where ships of different kinds had been wrecked, whether by tempests or by failure to pay their way. Some were sprawled on the wet mud. Some were crumbling much further inshore. Beyond doubt, the spot had its own melancholy appeal. On the far side, there was no sign of human life in the present tense. Perhaps, for the moment, that added to the appeal. The land over there rose gently. Possibly beyond the low ridge things were different.

The boat at Delbert's feet looked charming and tempting. Her short painter was tied to a ring in the bottom but one step. In his time, Delbert had come upon ferries that people were trusted to use with discretion and to look after on their own; though, in the nature of things, such accommodations must become rarer, as must, indeed, ferries of all kinds. Delbert peered at the name of the boat, painted upon the stern in slightly cramped letters. It appeared to be SEE FOR YOURSELF. Delbert almost guffawed and looked at his watch.

Unfortunately, his watch had stopped, as that particular watch often did, when brought to unexpected places, or otherwise disturbed in its ways. Delbert looked at the sun instead. At camp on the Plain, he had been trained to assess time and place. He estimated that it would be an hour and a half before Hesper could be back. Even if he were not there, it would not matter, because Hesper could have little idea of what partner Gregory's absence had brought about. At that very moment, partner

Gregory could be drawing on the bridal Bollinger; perhaps even rehearsing a gloriously facetious toast, tapping his feet the while, like Jack Buchanan, whom he often imitated from films, quite unconsciously.

    Delbert loved all boats, as he loved so many things. With at least ninety minutes for pure play, he could not be expected to hold back. He knew well how to handle oars and sculls. At school he had risen to first reserve for the second eight. He and his associate had all but won a double-sculling plate. All the same, as he embarked this time, he distinctly heard a voice speaking for a moment, though not what the precise words were. In a general way, the silence was little less than heavenly; especially while so much else was heavenly.

    Very soon, the only sound at all was the chatter of the water. It was delightful, but unusually rapid, like the voice he had heard. Delbert realised that the current was running faster than he had supposed. Nothing could be plainer than that he must not allow himself to go with it; not, if possible for a single yard. He must scull diligently against it, for as long as seemed worthwhile; or as directly as possible to the opposite shore. It was not, however, that the current was strong enough to cause the slightest actual alarm. Delbert had seen for himself, before setting out, that it was not. He could never have been as mistaken as that. For example, he was not concerned about any possibility of difficulty in returning to the steps and leaping ashore. Such trouble as there was related to his being unsuitably dressed for real exertion. If he were to land on the other shore, wellingtons would be desirable, possibly high waders. After all, the best thing might be simply to make a circuit of some kind, and then return sooner than he had originally planned.

    He set about pushing his way sturdily upstream—if that was the proper term of reference. The little shallop was pleasingly spick and span, a delectable miniature of the true boatbuilder's craft, but Delbert began to wonder if the sculls might not split apart in his hands, or the whole construction suddenly disintegrate in the swirl. It had been driven into him that courage was always the very first thing in life, not least during periods of recreation, and of course he had found it true. One trouble was that there were so often others to think of: his mother and stepfather (who had long been a second father to him); Hesper; the elusive unborn child; the chaps who depended on him at work, many of them less well placed than he was. As Delbert reflected in this way, taking very short strokes, feathering industriously, pressing his City shoes against the tiny adjustable stretcher, a flat grey mist, like a soiled lace curtain, passed before the sun, though only for moments, and even then by no means blotting out the placid disc. Delbert, who, in the nature of sculling, was looking backward towards his home, saw that a uniformed lad stood behind the delicate gate waving a telegraphic envelope.

Now was the real test, and well Delbert knew it. In his conspicuous clothes, he had to bring the almost uncontrollable cockleshell to a smooth and perfect landing at one single, special spot. Furthermore, he had first to turn the said cockleshell in the swift and stubborn stream, and then discern the landfall with eyes in the back of his head. While not exposing himself to jocosity and ensuing hostility, he had to accomplish all swiftly lest the boy filter away. Hesper and he often sent one another telegrams, because both of them were much of the time away from a telephone. The local Post Office had instructions, for what they amounted to, to put telegrams through the letter box if no one answered either bell or knocker. Other things commonly eventuated; as now.

No Time is Passing

II

As it happened, Delbert both came in and stepped out perfectly. Nothing so far that day had given him greater pleasure. He even stood there and waved to the boy to come down.

But the boy shook his head and dangled the orange envelope over the gate. Delbert ascended the stone steps with dignity and took it from him. It was never worth complaining about anything, even jocularly, or referring to anyone's short measure or lack of enterprise; and, in any case, the boy seemed particularly eager to be on his way. He was a shrimpish boy with overlong arms, and his face was pale as a mushroom.

Delbert read the telegram: DELAYED BY INSPECTION AUDIT SORRY DARLING BACK BY NINE HESPER. It was unusual, but not unprecedented.

The boy was almost back at the dank passage alongside the house. To communicate, Delbert had to shout.

'What's the name of this river?'

'Dunno.' The boy sounded as if he had little wish to know, or to speak either, let alone to bellow. But he did stop for a moment; possibly from surprise or shock.

'Or is it a creek?'

The boy said nothing. Perhaps he might not know what a creek was; might think it was some kind of Chinaman.

'Or a straits?'

At which word the boy looked very scared, too scared even to say something rude or obscene, and scampered down the passage as if from the copper. Delbert could not think how he had come to ask such a question, to use such a term.

He shoved the telegram into his pocket, and stared out once more at the equivocal prospect. He would be without defined

Intrusions

occupation for the next five and a half hours: longer if Hesper's estimate were insufficient. The crowd at the Town Hall were at once the servants and the masters of democracy. Despite all the protocol, their behaviour was inevitably unpredictable, even to themselves.

Delbert saw that on the far side of the water a figure of some kind was waving, much as the telegraph boy had just done, but more lustily.

For the moment, from the top of the steps which he was beginning to think of as 'his', Delbert could make out mainly a mass of unusually bright yellow hair. The sun, no longer curtained, glinted on it, and at the same time dazzled Delbert. He began once more to descend, for no particular reason, except possibly that the figure was summoning him. He saw too that a strip of matting now descended the muddy opposite slope from the low ridge. It was as if the figure had unrolled a dun carpet behind it; somewhat after the manner of a snail.

Back at the water's edge, Delbert realised something else. The number of steps had diminished by one, and the little boat was floating more freely to its painter. Somewhere, the tide had turned. Possibly the mist before the sun had related to this.

At this level, one could see more than hair across the flood. A squat, square, but probably masculine figure dwelt beneath the yellow, and was beckoning to Delbert personally and urgently.

When Delbert did not at once respond, but merely stood staring, the figure began to make vivid movements indicating the need for Delbert to re-embark and scull over. Delbert seemed to be confronted with a competent natural mime, but he wondered why, if the man needed his company so badly, he did not himself make the passage; why he had no visible vessel in which to do so, or to go anywhere else. Delbert himself was already settling down as an established boat owner. One day he might hope to own something larger and more spectacular than this almost childish little pram.

Delbert had no wish to be disobliging, so he stepped gingerly aboard and settled to the crossing. Different reflexes were required from the last occasion, but Delbert deemed that he handled himself well. First, the telegraph boy; now the yellow-haired person: perhaps Delbert shaped up best when under strong observation. Within the exigencies of the sculling process across a wilful flood, Delbert could see no more of the man on the far side until at the very last moment he was confronted with the entirety of him.

The man had seized the painter from far off. Everyone seemed to have very long arms that afternoon, young and old. The man dragged in the dory a little too roughly (Delbert simply did not know the exact and best name for the tiny ship); but as if habituated to such ploys.

In a second, his hand was outstretched to Delbert, big and hard as the largest of crabs.

'Petrovan,' he said. His voice was unexpectedly high.

His face was flat, his eyes were flat. His general coloration was rubicund or umber. His hair was as the flames round the sun. His height was as restricted as had been thought; his breadth as boundless. Moreover, the name was known.

'Catlow.' Delbert took the hand with such circumspection as could be applied.

'We're neighbours,' said the man.

'I suppose so,' said Delbert, trying to smile. The man had been smiling most broadly from the very first.

'So we may as well be neighbourly,' said the man, gleaming at Delbert's entirety as if waiting instantly to stamp hard upon the slightest exception taken.

Intrusions

'As far as all this water between us permits,' said Delbert, establishing a small advance, and now himself smiling quite noticeably.

'When it's there,' said the man. 'Come and have a drink, a smoke, a yarn.'

'A drink would be very pleasant,' said Delbert.

'Very well then,' said the man, and led the way.

The wide strip of matting ran upwards among the curious, flat-topped trees and the black wrecks. It gave little sign of having been trodden upon. Delbert was convinced that it really had been unrolled while he had been back in his garden for a few moments. The man's feet were bare in any case, and his trousers rolled to the knees. Here was just such ship of passage as Delbert had feared might invade. Moreover, there was an extreme inconsistency between the present appearance of the two of them.

As he ascended, Delbert became aware of shapes standing motionless beneath the trees. The shapes were black too. They frightened Delbert. Since returning to his home that afternoon, he had not been exactly frightened: not until now. Before he had reached the ridge, he had come to realise that under each tree was at least one of these shapes.

Perhaps they guarded the path from the shore. Perhaps they were not to be found further inland—if one might put it like that. Perhaps they lived in the wrecks, and had crept out for some warmth.

The long-armed man with the yellow hair said nothing as they climbed. Nor did he once look back encouragingly. Nor, for that matter, did he glance from side to side, verifying the black residents.

But Delbert knew perfectly well who he was; or who he was claiming to be. There were probably impostors; notoriety seekers and attention demanders. The real Petrovan (so to speak) had often received attention in the newspapers. He was good copy. The items about Petrovan and his kind were of no particular interest to Delbert. He could not remember even discussing them with Hesper. He did know that Petrovan refused to appear on television. Prominence was always given to that eccentricity. Petrovan claimed that television waves disintegrated the enduring soul. His face, therefore, was less familiar than many. What he said about the television seemed to be very likely, Delbert had always thought. But there his concern had ended.

Beneath the ridge stood a red hut; square as Petrovan (if he it really was). The planks had been flushed again and again with ox blood. Thick grass rotted on the roof. Delbert passed his hand slowly over his head, as he often did; confirming that his hair was still smooth and even silky.

And beyond the hut was nothing at all: nothing but a muddy waste extending to the sky and, afar off, indistinguishable from it. The flat trees were confined to the slope up which Delbert had climbed, though there they had seemed to grow abundantly and uniformly. On this flat muddy plain were only occasional trunks and stumps; struggling amid tangles of dead weeds. Nor beyond the ridge were there any of the wrecks. Presumably the ridge acted as a barrier even to the very highest tides; to those tides which must have engulfed the Catlows' lawn when they had not been there, and so much else, no doubt.

Delbert looked back. He could see his home quite plainly, and the other semi-familiar suburban landmarks. He was almost surprised that they were still there. All the same, he could see also that the tide was now racing ahead. So small a boat as his should probably be withdrawn from the water, temporarily but soon. He could see it bobbing and flopping.

'I ought to go back,' he cried. 'While I still can.'

Intrusions

'There's no need,' said Petrovan in his high voice, but still without turning, or even looking over his shoulder.

He had nearly reached the hut. On this side of the ridge, the mud looked viscous and bottomless. Perhaps the ridge was man-made: a vast sea wall. Perhaps men of old had directed colossi in the building of it. Perhaps it was an ultimate precinct.

'Where am I?' cried Delbert to the man's unturning back. 'What is this place?'

'My little humble burrow,' squeaked Petrovan. 'I'm sorry it's not gaudier.' He had opened the crimson door: gaudy enough for any six ordinary folk.

'But where are we?' persisted Delbert. 'I have never been here before.'

'You live here,' squeaked Petrovan, and began to giggle.

'But all this open space—' began Delbert interrogatively.

However, he was inside the red hut, whatever the thought. Petrovan was piling bottles on to a table: three or four at a time in each of his hands. The oblong wooden table, very thick and solid, was marked with geometrical shapes: some table game that had not before come Delbert's way. Certain of the pictures on the walls were impossible to look at; others were merely inexplicable. There were caged animals everywhere; all so strangely silent that Delbert could not at first make out whether they were animate or stuffed. The wooden floor was marked out also.

'What shall it be?' asked Petrovan. 'You name it.'

Delbert tried to take in the numerous bottles; to discriminate.

'Try this,' said Petrovan.

Delbert had not seen him pour it, but Petrovan was holding out a triangular glass on a polygonal stem. The fluid within was colourless but clouded. Delbert supposed it to be ouzo. One is supposed in the West to like ouzo nowadays; even to select it.

'What is it?' enquired Delbert, as affably as he could.

'Ambrosia,' said Petrovan. 'Down with it.'

Delbert had realised that the smell was quite different from the smell of ouzo. This smell was as rare and heavenly as the day outside. The smell must have inebriated Delbert, or liberated him. He drank down the little draught as if upon doctor's orders, and as if the doctor were present to watch him.

'That's a remarkable drink,' he cried. 'What's it made of?'

'Beeswing, among other things. Moonstone. Edelweiss.'

'Do you make it yourself?'

'To the old recipe.'

'Where did you find that?'

The truth was that Delbert would eagerly have accepted a refill, but Petrovan showed no sign of offering one.

'In one of the old books,' he said. 'I forget which.'

There were many old books in the hut, in among the animals and weird sketches.

Petrovan himself was not drinking at all, despite the profusion. Delbert began to suspect that somehow the display of bottles, many of them entirely familiar, was fake.

'Better sit down,' said Petrovan, and again giggled shortly. Delbert had to admit that he was glad of the invitation.

All the seats were solid wood and all but one were backless. All but the one with the back bore deep marks on the seats. The one with the back was plain and worn as Charlemagne's throne. There seemed to be provision for more people than the hut could hold. Still, the inside of the hut seemed far larger than the outside had suggested. Delbert saw that there were even doors. But perhaps they merely led to cupboards; or perhaps they provided for apartments that had not yet been added, and very

Intrusions

likely never would be. Such situations were common enough, after all.

'I still don't know where this is,' said Delbert.

'Where is anywhere?' replied Petrovan. 'What do the words mean? What answer can be given? You are on the far side. It is always strange on the far side to begin with.'

'This place feels like an island.'

'This place is an island,' said Petrovan. 'I live on an island, though I don't recommend you to walk all the way round it, because you'll never come back.' From somewhere he picked up a grapefruit, tore it apart, and sinking his reddy-brown face into the two shards, began to suck riotously.

Delbert looked at him.

'I think I know who you are,' he said. The matter had to be raised sooner or later. Delbert was not prepared to be taken for a ninny or an unread ignoramus.

'*Think* you know!' gurgled Petrovan. 'Of course you know. Everyone knows.'

But over Petrovan's shoulder, Delbert had noticed something. In one of the wired cages was an animal that no one thought possible. It was a very small white sphinx, and its two vague eyes were gazing at him.

'Have an apple!' squeaked Petrovan, and pitched it at him. 'Or would you prefer a very big pear?'

Delbert slowly shook his head.

'Let's gossip,' said Petrovan. 'I'll have to start, I see. Eat your apple. I'll ask you a series of questions. First question: what do you make of me? Decide for yourself. Ignore what is written.'

Delbert looked at the floor, covered with intersecting trapezia and spirals: more of them, he fancied, than when just now he had entered.

No Time is Passing

'I imagine that it is hypnosis you go in for. I don't know much about that.' As he spoke, the apple seemed to throb in his hands.

Petrovan threw away the sucked-out grapefruit skin and began to eat a long banana, skin and all. The skin was bright as his hair. Delbert simply could not see where all this fruit was coming from. He had not seen where the bottles had come from. It was these things that had given him his clue. Perhaps cross-headings in the various news items also: absorbed subliminally.

'Second question: what do you think is going to happen to you?'

'In a few minutes, I am leaving and crossing the water before it rises much further.'

'Third question: what do you suppose the world is doing?'

'Going to the dogs, mainly.' Really, he did absolutely need another drink. Perhaps an addiction had been established. That seemed quite likely. But possibly it was only the sudden warmer weather. Delbert tried to concentrate his mind upon when he had previously drunk anything at all, but he simply could not remember. No mere apple would quench such a thirst. In any case, he had mislaid the apple.

'Fourth question: what were you doing that you noticed so little in all the time you've lived here?'

'We've only just arrived. I'm quite newly married. I have my career to think of. My wife may be expecting a baby.'

'Last question: would you rather be living or dead?'

'Oh, living. I've had a topping life so far, and mean to go on while the luck lasts.'

'Do you feel ready for bed?' asked Petrovan.

'I thought you'd asked your last question.'

Intrusions

To that Petrovan said nothing. Perhaps Delbert had caught the demon by its tail. That is said only to happen inadvertently. None the less, it had to be admitted that the day seemed to have grown very overcast, especially as, properly speaking, it was but teatime; pleasant in the office, and pleasanter still in the home. Spacious though the interior of Petrovan's hut was, the windows were few, small, and irregular. Jewelled lights had come on here and there inside the hut without Delbert noticing the actual moment. But it had been such an adorable day, while it lasted! One was bound to regret it.

'There is nothing to worry about,' said Petrovan, chortling. 'It's only the sunset.'

But it was not a proper sunset at all. It was much more as if the heaviest of sea mists had descended upon the land. Delbert could see that mist was even seeping into the hut. The little lights were as markers in the mouth of a huge dark harbour; or in the mouth of Behemoth himself.

'Busy people have no time for twilight,' remarked Petrovan.

'It's the time you're most likely to see a ghost,' rejoined Delbert. He had remembered that ever since his infant school: a private kindergarten; no subsequent place like it.

'Busy people have no time for ghosts,' asserted Petrovan.

It was upon this surprising observation that Delbert acquired insight. The normal and average idea was that the press took every opportunity to exaggerate frenziedly. The truth was that, in any matter of consequence, the press was bound to act with great caution, to diminish, to belittle, to concede. Else the press would go unread by normal and average people.

Petrovan appeared now to be laying into a whole green pineapple, hair, spikes, and all; but the interior of the hut had assumed the blackness of the empyrean, with just a few misty, twinkling, and multicoloured stars.

No Time is Passing

'Release me!'

Delbert had purposed a commanding shout. He had achieved but a foggy mutter.

'Sleep for you now,' said Petrovan. One could hear his fangs rending through the fibrous flesh.

In the other room, there was no mist at all, though a single stout candle provided the only direct light. Painted upon the walls were dim glistening angels with wings and mantles. From his recollections of the outside, Delbert could not see how there could be another room of this shape at all. But it hardly mattered: he had been very far from sure that he really wished what he had demanded. Freedom might be all very well for Petrovan and his kind—a rare kind.

'My wife!' exclaimed Delbert; theatrically, though throatily. But he was looking with longing at the mysterious couch.

'No time is passing,' squeaked Petrovan.

'In that case, will you please blow out the candle?'

'You'll need a light of some kind.'

This tempted Delbert to boldness. 'I'd like another drink.'

'One is enough before sleep.'

'Am I going to die?'

'Of course not.'

'Shall I see my home again?'

'In a matter of minutes.'

'The candle's like a headlight. It's like the Dungeness lighthouse.' All through his and his sister's childhood, Delbert's family had stayed each year at an hotel in Hythe. He and Hesper still went there whenever they could; despite the enormously increased costs. It was a really good place; especially for young children, when one was one.

'It'll calm down when you're alone with it,' said Petrovan.

Intrusions

III

Petrovan had been wrong about one thing, even if about nothing else. He had twice spoken of sleep; and so far Delbert had failed to sleep at all. Winds from all quarters were converging upon the hut. Every now and then, objects from the night sky fell heavily on the earthy, grassy roof. The candlelight was now small, as Petrovan had promised, and startlingly distant: light at the end of the tunnel, Delbert could not help thinking. The mantled and aerial angels gleamed ambiguously on all sides. The protection proffered by sexless angels can be terrifying. None the less, Delbert no longer knew when or whether he was frightened or not. Physically, he was most comfortable. As was to be expected, he had never before known so cosy a crib.

Hesper! Oh, Hesper and their lovely life together! Lovely even when they were apart!

Now Delbert was not only longing for another wonderful elixir. He would have been grateful for a drink of pure water. Perhaps there was no acceptable source on Petrovan's island. Delbert was as parched as the man in the last sequence of Erich von Stroheim's film, but he suspected that multiform thirst was the explanation of his managing to remain awake.

From the far dream world beyond the tiny light of the candle, a figure was gliding; totally imprecise except that it was carrying a flat bowl. The angels stirred slightly as the figure passed; like shapes in the Wayang. Delbert knew that the bowl contained water and stretched forth both his arms, so considerably shorter than Petrovan's arms, or even the arms of the boy from the Telegraph Office.

No Time is Passing

The figure was standing by Delbert's couch. Delbert prepared to take the receptacle. He was not used to drinking from a wide bowl; so first he looked.

There was a picture in the water; at the bottom of it; on the surface of the bowl itself: a moving picture in a half-light.

Delbert saw Gregory Barfield, the most responsible partner at the office, enjoying the wedding, which must of course be going on at that moment. There was no doubt about the locality: Gregory was togged out as when Delbert had last seen him; and nuptial accessories were discernible on all sides, though not the white bride and beflowered groom, Siamese twins at such a time. At the moment of viewing, Gregory Barfield, with his familiar grin, was holding the hand of another guest, a lady of course; and, in fact, the lady was Hesper.

She had never said a word to Delbert about going to any wedding; and what about the wording of her telegram? Delbert realised that he had not checked the Office of Transmission. He was so perfectly accustomed to Hesper's telegrams; almost always from the one Office, a sub-department of the Town Hall itself.

Delbert forgot to drink, even to attempt to drink; and the figure glided on without his noticing.

However, he reached a decision, quickly and without difficulty: he had just seen his own thoughts, an occurrence not remarkable in such a place as this, and two things uppermost in his mind had become blended. There is no certainty in anything, only likelihood; and if we lose hold of likelihood, we never cease worrying.

As soon as he was comparatively settled in his mind, Delbert felt thirstier than ever. First came the thirst for water. Then was likely to return the craving for Petrovan's fluid speciality. To end that, a protracted, costly, and unpleasant professional cure might be necessary. Probably the recipe had not come from an

Intrusions

old book at all. People often made statements of that kind; figments of conversation; reasonable responses.

Delbert realised that a second figure was approaching.

He sat right up; as far as was possible on so delectable a divan.

This time, however thirsty he might be, Delbert still looked first. It was a bigger bowl, but the picture filled it.

He saw the garden side of his home, but his home was surrounded by figures whom he took to be a new kind of police. All the windows were tightly shut, and the structure exceedingly disconsolate. Rather curiously, there was no crowd of inquisitive, hostile people outside the cordon. No one seemed to care what was happening; to be curious.

Delbert addressed the figure bearing the bowl. 'What is it? What is happening?'

The figure replied in the gentlest, sweetest voice, though the words were few.

'You are wanted by the Enforcement.'

'What do they wish to enforce?'

But the figure had glided on. Perhaps one sentence only was possible—or was permitted. Delbert saw that the mantled angels, one and all, had altogether ceased to shine. He was alone with the one, faint candle in the unbounded dark; though still comfortable enough in the muscular sense; a consideration never by a wise man to be disregarded.

There was too little light for the third figure to be seen at all; or possibly Delbert was too distraught.

'I'm not looking. I'm not drinking.'

He was aware that the figure continued to stand there, none the less. He was too paralysed positively to turn his back. He perceived that the water in this third bowl was flecked with darting, internal lights, as from very tiny phosphorescent tiddlers.

The figure went on standing. The lights in the bowl became more razory all the time, hurting Delbert's eyes. He tightened his eyelids, as when in earlier days his hideous grandmother had entered the room; but now it seemed to make no difference. The lambent fish were swimming through the intermediate void.

Not in the bowl at all, but in the black though flecky air before him, Delbert saw himself. It is always alarming to see oneself, and said by many to be a presage of one's death; but what Delbert saw was himself in some public security office, surrounded by democratic interrogators, even though the actual instruments of their task were omitted from the picture, presumably left by request in the next room, the first of the rooms with blood on the floor, ceiling, and walls, like the walls of this hut.

The sharp lights had gone. The bowl had gone. The figure had gone. Ultimately, Delbert clutched at comfort: among the interrogators, none of them in uniform, had been, most unmistakably, Gregory Barfield, the responsible one; which alone suggested, in all probability, that confusion and bald nightmare reigned still. But Gregory's apparition was *not*, as it happened, alone as evidence. Delbert had identified the room also. It was a room at the Town Hall; adjacent, actually, to the room in which Hesper mostly worked.

IV

'Call it a day, if you wish.'

Petrovan was standing there. He had come silently in from behind Delbert's head. He was now wearing a grey, knee-length

Intrusions

garment of ancient Hellenic pattern. His legs and huge feet remained bare. It struck Delbert that Petrovan's legs were as short as his arms were long.

'Call it tomorrow, if you prefer,' continued Petrovan.

'What time is it really?' Delbert enquired feebly.

'Look at your watch. I see you carry one.'

'My watch has stopped. It stopped long ago.'

'It has not stopped.'

Delbert looked up, then held the watch to his right ear, already the better one. The watch was ticking frenziedly. Delbert had never known it make so much din. Of course Petrovan had heard it. The whole oddly-shaped room could hear it. Delbert looked at the dial. The two hands crudely underlined the fact that the time was four or five minutes later than the time at which they had recently ceased to move. This particular watch was always behaving peculiarly; always saying less than it should.

'Do you want to go?' asked Petrovan. He expelled a prune stone on to the floor, and kicked it neatly into a corner with his bare toes. Then he inserted another prune. He appeared to have a stock of them in his garment, even though ancient Hellenic dress included no pockets. That was something else Delbert had learned at one school or another.

To his own surprise, Delbert could not at once answer.

'It's entirely for you to say,' observed Petrovan, always open-handed.

'What if I remain?' enquired Delbert in a low voice. He had been having trouble with his voice for some time.

'You can have anything you wish. Pretty well.'

'But only an imitation of it? A facsimile?'

Petrovan giggled. 'You would hardly want the reality of it.'

No Time is Passing

Delbert continued to reflect. He needed to be entirely fair to all parties.

'Why me?' he asked. 'Why do you make this offer to me?'

'We're neighbours.' Petrovan put in two prunes simultaneously; at least two. 'Besides,' he added, 'not everyone is fit to serve.'

That really settled it. Delbert was upon his feet in a jiffy. Those words had set the old school bell tinkling and clanging like a fire alarm.

'I wasn't being serious,' Delbert said; hoping to score in a tiny way against a conversationalist so absurdly over-weaponed. 'I have my wife to think of. She must come first.'

Petrovan's merriment might have split the roof timbers, and brought down the earth on their two heads.

'You remind me of Nietzsche, who had no wife,' he gasped out. 'At one time, he was always speaking like that about women. I can hear him now. It was before he took the pox, of course, and went off his clever little balance. Do you know what Nietzsche could never keep his tiny hands off?'

Delbert shook his head. He had scarcely heard of Nietzsche, or of any other deep Teutonic thinker.

'Sweet cream cakes at the Konditorei. The floppier and fluffier and featherier the better. You know what Nietzsche said about women in the end? Or rather about Woman?'

'It's not my line of country,' replied Delbert firmly. 'I'm not interested in such things. I prefer to take life exactly as it comes. I'm going to trot off and catch my boat.'

He noted, again to his surprise, that he could not now manage even a conventional Thank you. How glad he was that, since he had had to lie down, he had done so fully dressed! He was quite tired of all funny business. He would consult his usual doctor, and, in all other ways too, resume his proper beliefs and optimism.

'I told you that you were free to choose,' was all Petrovan had to say. He inserted more prunes. 'Everyone is free to choose.'

In his heart, Delbert doubted that last; but Petrovan's line of talk was as much beyond him as he had always assumed it would be. It was impossible not to succumb at the outset, but enduring attitudes and values soon made a comeback, as they always do.

In confirmation whereof, Delbert saw that the sun was again shining brightly, though not too brightly. 'I'm going to skip,' he said.

Petrovan spat once more. 'Do you know what Soloviev told me?'

Really, Delbert felt, the old fellow with the hair was becoming a mere bore! Quoting another wordy Continental he had met somewhere, or said he had!

If he were to be honest, Delbert would have had to admit that he did not know how exactly he had emerged from the hut. It was something else that didn't seem to matter much.

Now he was scrambling in his City suit up the less familiar side of the low ridge. At the top, he was pleased to note that the long strip of matting was still in position, though now smeared from side to side with mud, as if whole damp legions had marched up and down it again and again; or been marched. In many places, the matting was now positively driven into the basic mud beneath it, and rapidly merging. As far as Delbert could see while he ran, all the black shapes were still in position under the umbrella trees, watching and guarding, or else merely sunbathing. Fortunately, Delbert had often run on matting. It had been put down when the grass tracks had become quagmires in which immature ankles and knees twisted and tangled like spaghetti. Each year it had very soon become too soppy and deliquescent to use.

Delbert could hear Petrovan pelting down the course behind him; though upon what rationale it would be difficult to say. Delbert had experience enough neither to slacken nor to quicken, and in no time he had leapt lightly aboard and cast skilfully off. Only when his hands were on the sculls and the blades in the briny did he look back. By then he had no choice, in the nature of the sculling process.

Petrovan was dancing about like a Numidian, with both long arms waving in the air, and his garment shivering preposterously.

'Come again whenever you like. Think again whenever you wish.'

'Farewell, old cock.'

Actually, Petrovan was more like a cockatoo, but to have called him that would have been ruder than Delbert proposed.

V

But all was again familiar; in so far as a hideous screaming main road with no one thing to be said for it, even as a mere utility, with nothing to distinguish it from any other hideous screaming main road, could be described as familiar. For a moment, Delbert looked around at the structures and creations and graffiti on this side of things; all familiar enough too, even though never previously inspected as individual exhibits, thank God.

Delbert strolled through the traffic, recovering his breath and full composure.

Intrusions

A thicket of weeds and junk, all more truly and personally familiar, lay at the bottom of his garden, as he had always known it, or at least believed. He plunged in. The thicket had once itself been a garden, but now the squatters were in and out of the homestead, now one, now the other. Everyone remarked upon how well they behaved, how considerate they were. The homestead belonged to a very old lady, who was said still to hang out precariously in one of the rooms, entirely dependent upon the kindness of strangers. Seldom, as will have been gathered, did Delbert make use of this particular plunging route, but the present seemed hardly the moment for squeamishness.

He found that the delicately ornamental gate at the corner of the evergreen hedge had been bound with a brand-new padlock. He sprang over the obstacle. On the other side of his lawn, by the house, stood a police officer; but one only, and in accepted garb.

'Who are you?' asked the police officer, stepping towards him.

'I live here,' said Delbert.

'Can you prove that?' enquired the police officer.

'Very easily,' said Delbert, producing his credit card, his driving licence, an insurance certificate, and three fully addressed envelopes from foreign parts.

'I have bad news for you,' said the police officer. 'You've had housebreakers.'

Delbert gazed upwards. The whole building looked smashed to pieces and wan to a degree. The weather was again going off, too.

'Do you mean we've been burgled?'

'Housebroken. We don't think they've taken much. Often they don't these days. Probably just pop records and things they think too personal. They don't like personal things. Sharing

No Time is Passing

should be the word for all. That's what they say. Better go in and see.'

Delbert went down the dark passage without a word. Another police officer was on guard by the front door. His was a doubly significant service, because the front door had been blown apart as in wartime. This second officer saluted Delbert gravely. There could be no question of his being other than a normal respectful constable.

Inside it was much as had been predicted. The authorities acquire experience of these cases and can often analyse at a glance. Here everything possible had been wrecked or despoiled, but little removed beyond what the first officer had said. The main positive demonstration was that two separate people had done business upon two separate areas of the new carpet in the living room. Two separate people there really must have been; two at the minimum. Also something suggestive had taken place on, in, around, and even beneath Hesper's once pretty bed.

Among the main things not taken were seven demands, applications, and interrogations from public bodies. They were piled neatly in the hall; probably by the police. One had come from Gateshead, one from Galashiels, one from somewhere in Wales that not merely began with a G but was almost all Gs: job creative, in every case. Delbert sat down immediately and opened them in succession, breathing heavily the while.

There seemed to be no other correspondence; but perhaps other correspondence had been deemed suitable for censorship, at present informal. Oh, here was a new wedding invitation; for 'Hesper and Delbert Catlow and Jimmy', whoever he might be.

Delbert went to the sink and downed glass after glass of water, as if it had been the end of the house match. The police officers waited without; cleaving to protocol; survivors. Delbert waited within. In the end, another of Petrovan's special foggy sunsets made itself felt: even over here. Not that anything had so far taken place that directly lent support to those three terrifying visions. If a last ditch were ever to come into sight, coincidence could be called upon. There are coincidences everywhere, and likelihood is often linked with them.

Hesper showed up little more than an hour later than her telegram had promised. She was wearing a silk dress, which Delbert did not think he had seen before. Whether or not he had seen it in the vision, he simply could not remember. Probably he had never noticed. Few men really take heed of what women are wearing at any particular moment; least of all their own women.

By that hour, the police officers were long departed: 'We'll have to go now, sir. You'll be perfectly all right.' Happily, many of the lights still worked, and even some of the other gadgets. Everything could have been far worse.

Furthermore, Hesper explained herself at once.

'Sorry to be so late, darling. The Assistant Borough Treasurer's daughter threw a birthday party.' Hesper then shrank away from Delbert's arms. She stared around. 'Why, whatever's happened?'

She seemed terribly shaken; even more, Delbert thought for a moment, than the admittedly grim situation quite warranted.

But in the end she pulled herself together wonderfully and was effective and efficient in every relevant direction. Whatever could be done at that rather late hour, she immediately did; and that which had to be left till the morrow, she faultlessly planned. Delbert was a cipher by comparison, but not for one moment did she allow him to feel this.

Tomorrow is always another day, take it or leave it.

THE FETCH

I

IN ALL THAT matters, I was an only child. There was a brother once, but I never saw him, even though he lived several years. My father, a Scottish solicitor or law agent, and very much a Scot, applied himself early to becoming an English barrister, and, as happens to Scots, was made a Judge of the High Court, when barely in middle age.

In Court, he was stupendous. From the first, I was taken once every ten days by Cuddy, my nurse, to the public gallery in order to behold him and hearken to him for forty minutes or so. If I made the slightest stir or whimper, it was subtly but effectively repaid me; on those and all other occasions. Judges today are neither better nor worse than my father, but they are different.

At home, my father, only briefly visible, was as a wraith with a will and power that no one available could resist. The will and power lingered undiminished when my father was not in the house, which, in the nature of things, was for most of the time. As well as the Court, and the chambers, there were the club and the dining club, the livery company and the military historical society, all of which my father attended with dedication and sacrifice. With equal regularity, he pursued the cult of self-defence, in several different branches, and with little heed for the years. He was an elder of a Scottish church in a London suburb, at some distance from where we lived. He presided over several successive Royal Commissions, until one day he threw up his current presidency in a rage of principle, and was never invited again. After his death, I realised that a further centre of his interest had been a club of a different kind, a very expensive and sophisticated one. I need not say how untrue it is that Scots are penny-scraping in all things.

I was terrified of my father. I feared almost everything, but there was nothing I feared more than to encounter my father or to pick up threads from his intermittent murmurings in the corridors and closets. We lived in a huge house at the centre of Belgravia. No Judge could afford such an establishment now. In addition, there was the family home of Pollaporra, modest, comfortless, and very remote. Our ancestry was merely legal and commercial, though those words have vastly more power in Scotland than in England. In Scotland, accomplishments are preferred to graces. As a child, I was never taken to Pollaporra. I never went there at all until much later, on two occasions, as I shall unfold.

I was frightened also of Cuddy, properly Miss Hester MacFerrier; and not least when she rambled on, as Scottish women do, of the immense bags and catches ingathered at Pollaporra by our ancestors and their like-minded acquaintances. She often emphasised how cold the house was at all times and how far from a 'made road'. Only the elect could abide there, one gathered; but there were some who could never bear to leave, and who actually shed tears upon being compelled by the advancing winter to do so. When the snow was on the ground, the house could not be visited at all; not even by the factor to the estate, who lived down by the sea loch, and whose name was Mason. Cuddy had her own methods for compelling the attention of any child to every detail she cared to impart. I cannot recall

The Fetch

when I did not know about Mason. He was precisely the man for a Scottish nursemaid to uphold as an example.

My father was understood to dislike criminal cases, which, as an advanced legal theorist and technician, he regarded with contempt. He varied the taking of notes at these times by himself sketching in lightning caricature the figures in the dock to his left. The caricatures were ultimately framed, thirty or forty at a time; whereafter Haverstone, the odd-job man, spent upwards of a week hanging them at different places in our house, according to precise directions written out by my father, well in advance. Anybody who could read at all, could at any time read every word my father wrote, despite the millions of words he had to set down as a duty. Most of the other pictures in our house were engravings after Landseer and Millais and Paton. Generations of Scottish aunts and uncles had also contributed art works of their own, painstaking and gloomy.

I was afraid of Haverstone, because of his disfigurements and his huge size. I used to tiptoe away whenever I heard his breathing. I never cared or dared to ask how he had come to be so marked. Perhaps my idea of his bulk was a familiar illusion of childhood. We shall scarcely know; in that Haverstone, one day after my seventh birthday, fell from a railway bridge into the main road beneath and was destroyed by a lorry. Cuddy regarded Haverstone with contempt, and never failed to claim that my father employed him only out of pity. I never knew what he was doing on the railway bridge, but later I became aware of a huge mental hospital near by and drew obvious conclusions.

My mother I adored and revered. For better or for worse, one knows the words of Stendhal: 'My mother was a charming woman, and I was in love with my mother. . . . I wanted to cover my mother with kisses and wished there weren't any clothes. . . . She too loved me passionately. She kissed me, and I

Intrusions

returned those kisses sometimes with such passion that she had to leave me.' Thus it was with me; and, as with Stendhal, so was the sequel.

My mother was very dark, darker than me, and very exotic. I must suppose that only the frenzy of Scottish lust brought my father to marrying her. At such times, some Scots lose hold on all other considerations; in a way never noticed by me among Englishmen. By now, my father's fit was long over. At least he did not intrude upon us, as Stendhal's father did. I am sure that jealousy was very prominent in my father, but perhaps he scorned to show it. He simply kept away from his wife entirely. At least as far as I could see. And I saw most things, though facing far from all of them, and acknowledging none of them.

Day after day, night after night, I lay for hours at a time in my mother's big bed, with my head between her breasts, and my tongue gently extended, as in infancy. The room was perfumed, the bed was perfumed, her nightdress was perfumed, she was perfumed. To a child, it set the idea of Heaven. Who wants any other? My mother's body, as well as being so dark, was softer all over than anyone else's, and sweeter than anything merely physical and fleeting, different and higher altogether. Her rich dark hair, perfumed of itself, fell all about me, as in the East.

There was no social life in our home, no visiting acquaintances, no family connections, no chatter. My father had detached himself from his own folk by his marriage. My mother loved no one but me. I am sure of that. I was in a position to know. The only callers were her hairdresser, her dressmaker, her maker of shoes and boots, her parfumier, her fabricator of lingerie, and perhaps one or two others of the kind. While she was shorn, scented, and fitted, I sat silently in the corner on a little grey hassock. None of the callers seemed to object. They knew the world and what it was like; and would soon enough be like for me. They contained themselves.

I was there whatever my mother did; without exception.

Cuddy dragged me off at intervals for fresh air, but not for very long. I could see for myself that Cuddy, almost familiar with my father, was afraid of my mother. I never knew why, and am far from certain now, but was glad of the fact. It was the key circumstance that transformed the potential of utter wretchedness for me into utter temporary bliss.

My mother taught me all I know that matters; smiling and laughing and holding me and rewarding me, so that always I was precocity incarnate; alike in concepts, dignity, and languages. Unfortunately, my mother was often ill, commonly for days, sometimes for weeks; and who was there to care, apart from me, who could do nothing—even if there was something that others could have done? My lessons ceased for a spell, but as soon as possible, or sooner, were bravely resumed.

Later, I strayed through other places of education, defending myself as best I could, and not unsuccessfully either; and, of what I needed, learning what I could. It was not my father who dispatched me. He regarded me without interest or expectation. To him I was the enduring reminder of a season's weakness. The ultimate care of me lay with Trustees, as often in Scotland; though only once did I see them as individuals, and hardly even then, because the afternoon was overcast, and all the lights were weak, for some reason that I forget.

Before all that formal education, I had encountered the woman on the stairs. This brief and almost illusory episode was the first of the two turning points in my life and I suspect the more important.

I had been playing on the landing outside the door of my mother's room. I do not know how long she had been ill that time. I feared to count the days, and never did so. I am sure that it was longer than on various previous occasions. I was alarmed, as always; but not especially alarmed.

My mother had been instrumental in my being given a railway, a conjuring outfit, and a chemical set: those being the things that small boys were supposed to like. My father should have given me soldiers, forts, and guns; possibly a miniature, but accurate, cricket bat: but he never once gave me anything, or spoke at all in our house if he could avoid it—except, on unpredictable occasions, to himself, memorably, as I have hinted.

I mastered the simple illusions, and liked the outfit, but had no one to awe. Even my mother preferred to hug me than for me to draw the ace of spades or a tiny white rabbit from her soft mouth. The chemical effects, chlorine gas and liquid air, I never mastered at that time, nor wished to. The railway I loved (no other word), though it was very miniature: neither 1 gauge (in those days) nor 0 gauge, but something smaller than 00. The single train, in the Royal Bavarian livery of before the First World War, clinked round a true circle; but *en route* it traversed a tunnel with two cows painted on top and one painted sheep, and passed through two separate stations, where both passengers and staff were painted on the tin walls, and all the signs were in Gothic.

That day, I had stopped playing, owing to the beating of my heart; but I had managed to pack everything into the boxes. I needed no bidding to do that, and never had done. I was about to lug the heap upstairs, which by then I could perfectly well do. I heard the huge clock in the hall strike half-past three. The clock had come from Pollaporra, and reached to the ceiling. I looked at my watch, as I heard it. I was always doing that. It was very late autumn, just before Christmas, but not yet officially winter. There is nothing in this world I know better than exactly what day of the year it was. It is for ever written in the air before me.

My ears were made keen by always listening. Often, wherever I was, even at the top of the house, I waited motionless for the enormous clock to strike, lest the boom take me by surprise. But the ascending woman was upon me before I had heard a footfall. I admit that all the carpets were thickest Brussels and Wilton. I often heard footfalls, none the less, especially my father's strangely uneven tread. I do not think I heard the woman make a sound from first to last. But last was very close to first.

She had come up the stairs, beyond doubt, even though I had neither heard nor seen anything; because by the time I did observe her, she was still two or three steps from the top of the flight. It was a wide staircase; but she was ascending in a very curious way, far further from the rail than was necessary and far nearer to the wall, and with her head and face actually turned to the wall.

At that point, I did hear something. I heard someone shut the front door below; which could not be seen from where I stood. I was surprised that I had not heard the door being opened, and the words of enquiry and caution. I remember my surprise. All these sounds were unusual in our house at that time.

I felt the cold air that the woman had brought in with her from the December streets and squares, and a certain cold smell; but she never once turned towards me. She could easily have been quite unaware of me; but I was watching her every motion. She had black hair, thin and lank. She was dressed in a dirty red and blue plaid of some kind, tightly wound. I was of course used to pictures of people in plaids. The woman's shoes were cracked and very unsuited to the slush outside. She moved with short steps, and across the carpet she left a thin trail of damp, though I knew that it was not raining. It was one of the things I always

Intrusions

knew. Everything about the woman was of a kind that children particularly fear and dislike. Women, when frightening, are to children enormously more frightening than any man or men.

I think I was too frightened even to shrink back. As the woman tottered past, I stood there with my boxes beside me. My idea of her motion was that she had some difficulty with it, but was sustained by extreme need. Perhaps that is a fancy that only came to me later.

I never had any doubt about where the woman was going but, even so, I was unable to move or to speak or to do anything at all.

As she traversed the few yards of the landing, she extended her right arm and grimy hand from out of her plaid, the hand and arm nearer to me, still without in any degree turning her head. In no time at all, and apparently without looking, she had opened the door of my sweet mother's room, had passed within, and had shut the door behind her.

I suppose it is unnecessary for me to say that when my mother was ill, her door was never locked; but perhaps it is not unnecessary. I myself never entered at such times. My mother could not bear me to see her when she was ill.

There was no one sympathetic to whom I could run crying and screaming. In such matters, children are much influenced by the facilities available. For me, there was only my mother, and, in fact, I think I might actually have gone in after the woman, though not boldly. However, before I was able to move at all, I heard Cuddy's familiar clump ascending the stair behind me as I gazed at the shut door.

'What are you doing now?' asked Cuddy.

'Who was that?' I asked.

'Who was who?' Cuddy asked me back. 'Or what?'

'The woman who's gone in there.'

The Fetch

'Whist! It's time *you* were in bed with Christmas so near.'
'It *wasn't* Father Christmas,' I cried.
'I daresay not,' said Cuddy. 'Because it wasn't anybody.'
'It was, Cuddy. It *was*. Go in and look.'

It seems to me that Cuddy paused at that for a moment, though it may only have been my own heart that paused.

It made no difference.

'It's bed for you, man,' said Cuddy. 'You're overexcited and we all know where that ends.'

Needless to say, it was impossible for me to sleep, either in the dark or in the light: the choice being always left to me, which was perhaps unusual in those days. I heard the hours and the half-hours all through the night, and at one or two o'clock my father's irregular step, always as if he were dodging something or someone imperfectly seen, and his periodical mutterings and jabberings as he plodded.

All was deeply upsetting to a child, but I must acknowledge that by then I was reasonably accustomed to most of it. One explanation was that I had no comparisons available. As far as I knew, all people behaved as did those in my home. It is my adult opinion that many more, in fact, do so behave than is commonly supposed, or at least acknowledged.

Still, that night must have proved exceptional for me; because when Cuddy came to call me in the morning, she found that I was ill too. Children, like adults, have diseases that it is absurd to categorise. Most diseases, perhaps all, are mainly a collapse or part-collapse of the personality. I daresay a name for that particular malady of mine might in those days have been brain fever. I am not sure that brain fever is any longer permitted to be possible. I am sure that my particular malady went on for weeks, and that when I was once more deemed able to make sense out of things, I learned that my mother was dead, and, indeed, long buried. No one would tell me where. I further gathered that there was no memorial.

About four weeks after that, or so it now seems to me, but perhaps it was longer, I was told that my father was proposing to remarry, though he required the consent of the Trustees. A Judge was but a man as far as the Trustees were concerned, a man within the scope of their own settlement and appointment. Thus it was that I acquired my stepmother; *née* Miss Agnes Emily Fraser, but at the moment a widow, Mrs Johnny Robertson of Baulk. To her the Trustees had no objection, it seemed.

I still have no idea of why my father married Agnes Robertson, or why he remarried at all. I do not think it can have been the motive that prompted his earlier marriage. From all that, since his death, I have learned of his ways, the notion would seem absurd. It was true that the lady had wealth. In the end, the Trustees admitted as much; and that much of it was in Burmah Oil. I doubt whether this was the answer either. I do not think that more money could have helped my father very much. I am not sure that by then anything could have helped him. This is confirmed by what happened to him, conventional in some ways though it was.

Moreover, the marriage seemed to me to make no difference to his daily way of life: the bench, the chambers, the club, the dining club, the livery company, the military historical society, the self-defence classes, the kirk; or, I am sure, to those other indulgences. On most nights, he continued to ponder and by fits and starts to cry out. I still tiptoed swiftly away and, if possible, hid myself when I heard his step. I seldom set eyes upon my stepmother, though of course I am not saying that I never did. I took it for granted that her attitude to me was at

The Fetch

least one thing that she shared with my father. That seemed natural. I found it hard to see what else she had any opportunity of sharing. It had, of course, always been Cuddy to whom I was mainly obliged for information about my father's habits and movements, in so far as she knew them. Cuddy was much less informative about my stepmother.

One new aspect of my own life was that my lessons had stopped. I believe that for more than a year I had nothing to do but keep out of the way and play, as far as was possible. Now there seemed to be no callers at all, and assuredly not parfumiers and designers of lingerie. No doubt my stepmother's circle was entirely in Scotland, and probably to the north of the Forth and Clyde Canal. She would not have found it easy to create an entirely new circle in Belgravia. I suppose there were two reasons why I suffered less than I might have done from the unsatisfactory aspects of my situation. The first was that I could hardly suffer more than I was suffering from my sweet mother's death. The second reason was my suspicion that any other life I might be embarked upon would be even more unsatisfactory.

In the end, the Trustees intervened, as I have said; but, before that, Cuddy had something to impart, at long last, about my stepmother. She told me that my stepmother was drinking.

It debarred her, Cuddy informed me in a burst of gossip, from appearing in public very often. That was exactly how Cuddy expressed it; with a twinkle or a glint or whatever may be the Scottish word for such extra intimations. I gathered that my stepmother seldom even dressed herself, or permitted herself to be dressed by Cuddy. One thing I was not told and do not positively know is whether or not the poor lady was drinking as hard as this before her second marriage. It is fair to her to say that the late Johnny Robertson was usually described as a scamp or rogue. Certainly my stepmother's current condition was something that would have had to be concealed by everyone as far as possible at that time in Belgravia, and with her husband a High Court Judge.

In any case, after the Trustees had taken me away and sent me to an eminent school, I began to hear tales. At first, I knocked about those who hurled and spat them at me. I discovered a new strength in the process; just as the grounding (to use the favoured word) provided by my mother enabled me to do better than most in class, not so much by knowing more as by using greater imagination and ingenuity, qualities that tell even in rivalry among schoolboys. The jibes and jeers ceased, and then I began cautiously to enquire after the facts. The school was of the kind attended by many who really know such things. I learned that my father too had long been drinking; and was a byword for it in the counties and the clubs. No doubt in the gaols also, despite my father's dislike of criminal jurisdiction.

One morning, Jesperson, who was the son of a Labour ex-minister and quite a friend of mine, brought me *The Times* so that I could see the news before others did. I read that my father had had to be removed from his Court and sent for treatment. *The Times* seemed to think that if the treatment were not successful, he might feel it proper to retire. There was a summary of the cases over which he had presided from such an unusually early age (some of them had been attended by me, however fleetingly); and a reference to his almost universal popularity in mainly male society.

I was by then in a position at school to take out any chagrin I might feel upon as many other boys as I wished, but I was too introspective for any such easy release, and instead began for the first time to read the *Divine Comedy*.

There was nothing particularly unusual in what had happened to my father so far, but the treatment seems, as far as one

The Fetch

can tell, to have been the conclusive ordeal, so that he died a year later in a mental hospital, like poor Haverstone, though not in the same one. My father returned in spirit to his sodden, picturesque wilderness, and is buried in the kirkyard four or five miles by a very rough road from Pollaporra. It was the first instruction in his will, and the Trustees heeded it, as a matter of urgency, to the last detail.

I could not myself attend the funeral, as I was laid low by a school epidemic, though by then in my last term, and older than any of my *confrères*. My stepmother also missed the funeral, though she had returned to Scotland as soon as she could. She had resolved to remain there, and, for all I know, she is there still, with health and sobriety renewed. Several times I have looked her up in directories and failed to find her, despite reference to all three of her known surnames; but I reflect that she may well have married yet again.

My father had left her a moiety of his free estate, in equal part with the various organisations he wished to benefit, and which I have already listed. She possessed, as I have said, means of her own. My father left me nothing at all, but he lacked power, Judge though he was, and a Scots solicitor also, to modify the family settlement. Therefore, I, as only surviving child, inherited a life interest in Pollaporra, though not in the house in Belgravia, and a moderate, though not remarkable, income for life. Had my brother survived, he would have inherited equally. Thinking about him, I wondered whether the demon drink, albeit so mighty among Scotsmen, had not rather been a symptom of my father's malady than the cause of it. Thinking of that, I naturally then thought about my own inwardness and prospects. Eugene O'Neill says that we become like our parents of the same sex, even when we consciously resolve not to. I wept for my mother, so beloved, so incomparable.

Intrusions

II

Immediately, the question arose of my going to a university. The idea had of course been discussed before with the Trustees, but I had myself rejected it. While my father had been alive, my plan had been simply to leave the country as soon as I could. Thanks to my mother, I had made a good start with two European languages, and I had since advanced a little by reading literature written in them: *Die Räuber* and *Gerusalemme liberata*. The other boys no longer attacked or bullied me when they found me doing such things; and the school library contained a few basic texts, mostly unopened, both in the trade sense and the literal sense.

Now I changed my mind. The Trustees were clamant for Edinburgh, as could be expected; but I scored an important victory in actually going to Oxford. Boys from that school did not proceed to Edinburgh University, or did not then. It had never been practicable to send me to Fettes or Loretto. My friend, Jesperson, was at Oxford already. Oxford was still regarded by many as a dream, even though mainly in secret and in silence.

I read Modern Languages and Modern History, and I graduated reasonably, though not excitingly. I surprised myself by making a number of friends. This brought important benefits, in the short term and the long.

I now had no home other than Pollaporra, which, as will be recalled, could not always be visited during the winter, in any case. I spent most of the vacations with new friends; staying in their homes for astonishingly generous periods of time, or travelling with them, or reading with them. With the Second World War so plainly imminent and so probably apocalyptic,

The Fetch

everyone travelled as much as he could. I met girls, and was continually amazed by myself. My closest involvement was with a pretty girl who lived in the town; who wrote poetry that was published; and who was almost a cripple. That surprised me most of all. I had learned something about myself, though I was unsure what it was. The girl lived, regardless, at the top of the house, which taught me something further. Her name was Celia. I fear that I brought little happiness to her or to any of the others, do what I would. I soon realised that I was a haunted man.

As for the main longer-term benefit, it was simple enough, and a matter of seemingly pure chance. My friend, Jack Oliver, spoke to his uncle, and as soon as I went down, modestly though not gloriously endorsed, I found myself *en route* to becoming a merchant banker. I owe Jack a debt that nothing can repay. That too is somehow a property of life. Nothing interlocks or properly relates. Life gives, quite casually, with one hand, and takes away rather more with the other hand, equally unforeseeably. There is little anyone can do about either transaction. Jack Oliver was and is the kindest man I have known, and a splendid offhand tennis player. He has a subtle wit, based on meiosis. From time to time, he has needed it. I have never climbed or otherwise risen to the top of the banking tree, but the tree is tall, and I lived as a child in a house with many stairs.

It was Perry Jesperson who came with me on my first visit to Pollaporra. He had borrowed one of his father's cars.

Even on the one-inch map, the topography was odd. It had struck me as odd many years before. I had always thought myself good with maps, as solitary children so often are; but now that I had been able to travel frequently, I had come to see that one cannot in every case divine from a map a feature of some kind that seems central when one actually arrives and inspects. In that way, I had made a fool of myself on several occasions, though sometimes to my own knowledge only. When it comes to Scotland, I need hardly say that many one-inch maps are sometimes needed for a journey from one place to another, and that some of the maps depict little but heaving contours and huge hydroelectric installations.

Pollaporra stood isolated amid wild altitudes for miles around. Its loneliness was confirmed by its being marked at all. I knew very well that it was no Inveraray or even Balmoral. It stood about three and a half miles from the sea loch, where Mason lived. That of course was as the crow flies, if crows there were. I had miled out the distance inaccurately with thumb and forefinger when I had still been a child. I had done it on many occasions. The topographical oddity was that the nearest depicted community was eight miles away in the opposite direction, whereas in such an area one would expect it to be on the sea, and to derive its hard living therefrom. It was difficult to think of any living at all for the place shown, which was stuck down in a hollow of the mountains, and was named Arrafergus. An uncoloured track was shown between Pollaporra and Arrafergus; the rough road of which I had heard so much, and along which my father's corpse had passed a few years before. One could see the little cross marking the kirk and kirkyard where he lay. It was placed almost halfway between the two names, which seemed oddest of all. For much of the year, no congregation could assemble from either house or village. A footpath was shown between Pollaporra and the sea loch, but one could hardly believe in more than a technical right of way, perhaps initiated by smugglers and rebels.

I had commented upon all this to Jesperson before we left. He had said: 'I expect it was an effect of the clearances.'

The Fetch

'Or of the massacres,' I had replied, not wishing to become involved in politics with Jesperson, even conversationally.

The roads were already becoming pretty objectionable, but Jesperson saw it all as progress, and we took it in turns to drive. On the third morning, we were advancing up the long road, yellow on the map, from the dead centre of Scotland to little Arrafergus. By English standards, it should not have been shown in yellow. Even Jesperson could hardly achieve more than a third of his normal speed. We had seen no other human being for a very long time, and even animals were absent, exactly as I had expected. Why was Arrafergus placed where it was, and how could it survive? Long ago, the soaking mist had compelled us to put up the hood of the roadster. I admit that it was April.

In the early afternoon, the road came to an end. We were in a deep cleft of the rock-strewn hills, and it would have been impossible for it to go further. There was a burn roaring, rather than gurgling, over the dark stones. There was no community, no place, not even a road sign saying where we were or prohibiting further progress, not a shieling, not a crow. I speculated about what the funeral cortège could have done next.

'Do you want to get out and look for the foundations?' enquired Jesperson. 'There's probably the odd stone to be found. The landlords razed everything, but I'm told there are usually traces.'

'Not for the moment,' I said. 'Where do you suppose is the track to Pollaporra?'

'Up there,' said Jesperson immediately, and pointed over my head.

How had I missed it? Despite the drizzle, I could now see it quite plainly. Nor must I, or anyone, exaggerate. The track was exceedingly steep and far from well metalled, but, apart from the angle of incline, hardly worse to look at than the yellow

Intrusions

road. Obviously, it must be difficult to keep the maps up to date, and in certain areas hardly worth while at present prices.

'Are we game?' I asked Jesperson. 'It's not your car, and I don't want to press.'

'We've got to spend the night somewhere,' said Jesperson, who had not even stopped the engine.

After that, all went surprisingly well. Cars were tougher and more flexible in those days. We ascended the mountain without once stopping, and there were no further major gradients until we came within sight of Pollaporra itself. I had feared that the track would die out altogether or become a desert of wiry weeds, such as spring up vengefully on modern roads, if for a moment neglected.

The little kirk was wrapped in rain which was now much heavier. There were a few early flowers amid and around the crumbling kirkyard walls. By June there would be more.

Jesperson drew up and this time stopped the engine reverently.

'It's all yours,' he said, glancing at me sideways.

I stepped out. The huge new monument dominated the scene.

I scrambled across the fallen stones.

My father's full name was there, and his dates of birth and death. And then, in much smaller lettering, A JUST MAN A BRAVE MAN AND A GOOD. That was it: the commemorated was no one's beloved husband or beloved father; nor were any of his honours specified; nor was confident hope expressed for him, or, by implication, for anyone, he having been so admirable.

Around were memorials, large and small, to others among my unknown ancestors and collaterals; all far gone in chipping, flaking, and greening, or all that I studied. Among us we seemed to cram the entire consecrated area. Perhaps the residue from

The Fetch

other families had no mementoes. I was aware of the worms and maggots massed beneath my feet; crawling over one another, as in a natural history exhibit. At any moment, the crêpe rubber soles of my shoes might crack and rot. Moreover, did the Church of Scotland ritually consecrate any place? I did not know. I turned round and realised that in the distance I could see Pollaporra also.

The house, though no more than a grey stone, slate-roofed rectangle, neither high nor particularly long, dominated the scene from then on, probably because it was the only work of man visible, apart from the bad road. Also it seemed to stand much higher than I had expected.

Jesperson wisely refused to set his father's car at the final ascent. We went up on foot. From the ridge we could make out the sea loch, green and phantasmal in the driving drizzle.

Cuddy was living in the house now; virtually pensioned off by the Trustees, and retained as caretaker: also as housekeeper, should the need arise, as it now did, almost certainly for the first time.

'Cuddy,' I cried out in my best English university style, and with hand outstretched, as we entered. It was desirable to seem entirely confident.

'Brodick,' she replied, not familiar perhaps, but independent.

'This is Mr Jesperson.'

'It's too late for the shooting and too early for the fishing,' said Cuddy. I think those were her words. I never quite remember the seasons.

'Mr Leith has come to take possession,' said Perry Jesperson.

'It's his for his life,' said Cuddy, as if indicating the duration of evening playtime.

Intrusions

'How *are* things?' I asked in my English university way. I was trying to ignore the chill, inner and outer, which the place cast.

'Wind and watertight as far as this house is concerned. You can inspect it at once. You'll not find one slate misplaced. For the rest you must ask Mr Mason.'

'I shall do so tomorrow,' I replied. 'You must set me on the way to him.'

'It is a straight road,' said Cuddy. 'You'll not go wrong.'

Of course it was not a road at all, but a scramble over rocks and stones all three miles; slow, slippery, and tiring. I could see why Mason spent little of his time visiting. None the less, the way was perfectly straight to the sea; though only from the top could one discern that. Jesperson had volunteered to look for some sport. Cuddy had been discouraging, but the house was as crammed with gear as the kirkyard with ancestral bones.

Mason lived in a small, single-storeyed house almost exactly at the end of the path, and at the edge of the sea. The local letter-box was in his grey wall, with a single collection at 6.30 a.m. each day, apart from Saturdays, Sundays, and Public Holidays. There were a few other small houses, too small for the map but apparently occupied, and even a shop, with brooms in the window. The shop was now closed, and there was no indication of opening hours. A reasonably good, though narrow, road traversed the place, and in both directions disappeared along the edge of the loch. It ran between the path from Pollaporra and Mason's house. There was no detectable traffic, but there was a metal bus-stop sign, and a timetable in a frame. I looked at it. If Jesperson's father's car were to break up, as seemed quite likely, we should need alternative transport. I saw that the bus appeared at 7 a.m. on the first Wednesday in each month between April and September. We had missed the April bus. I persisted and saw that the bus returned as early as 4.30 p.m. on the same day, and then went on to Tullochar at the head of the loch. Despite the length of the inlet, the waves were striking the narrow, stony beach sharply and rapidly. A few small and broken boats were lying about, and some meshes of sodden net, with shapeless cork floats. There was even a smell of dead crustaceans.

I realised that all these modest investigations were being observed by Mason himself. He had opened the faded brown door of his house and was standing there.

'Brodick Leith,' he said, in the Scottish manner.

'Mr Mason,' I replied. 'I am very glad to meet you. I have heard about you all my life.'

'Ay,' said Mason, 'you would have. Come indoors. We'll have a drop together and then I'll show you the books. I keep them to the day and hour. There's not as much to do as once there was.'

'That was in my father's time?'

'In the Judge's time. Mr Justice Leith. Sir Roderic Leith, if you prefer. A strong man and a mysterious.'

'I agree with what you say.'

'Come inside,' said Mason. 'Come inside. I live as an unmarried man.'

Mason opened a new bottle, and before I left, we had made our way through all of it, and had started on the remains of the previous one. Though I drank appreciably less than half, it was still, I think, more spirit than I had drunk on any previous occasion. The books were kept in lucid and impersonal handwriting, almost as good as my father's, and were flawless, in so far as I could understand them; my career in banking having not yet begun. Mason left me to go through them with the bottle at my elbow, while he went into the next room to cook us steaks, with his own hands. I could see for myself that the amounts brought out as surplus or profit at the end of each account were not large. I had never supposed they would be, but the costs and responsibilities of land ownership were brought home to me, none the less. Until then, I had been a baby in the matter, as in many others. Most people are babies until they confront property ownership.

'I know you attended my father's funeral, Mr Mason,' I said. 'How was it? Tell me about it.' The steak was proving to be the least prepared that I had ever attempted to munch. No doubt the cooking arrangements were very simple. I had not been invited to inspect them.

'Ay,' said Mason, 'and the funeral was the least of it.' He took a heavier swig than before and stopped chewing altogether, while he thought.

'How many were there?' I had always been curious about that.

'Just me, and Cuddy MacFerrier, and the Shepstones.'

The Shepstones were relatives. I had of course never set eyes upon even one of them. I had never seen a likeness. Millais had never painted a single Shepstone, and if one or more of them had appeared upon a criminal charge, my father would hardly have been the Judge.

'How many Shepstones?' I asked, still essaying to devour.

'Just the three of them,' replied Mason, as if half-entranced. I am making little attempt to reproduce the Scottishness of his speech, or of anyone else's. I am far from being Sir Walter or George Douglas.

'That is all there are?'

'Just the three. That's all,' said Mason. 'Drink up, man.'

'A minister was there, of course?'

The Fetch

'Ay, the minister turned out for it. The son was sick, or so he said.'

'I am the son,' I said, smiling. 'And I *was* sick. I promise you that.'

'No need to promise anything,' said Mason, still motionless. 'Drink up, I tell you.'

'And no one else at all?' I persisted.

'Maybe the old carlin,' said Mason. 'Maybe her.'

For me that was a very particular Scottish word. I had in fact sprung half to my feet, as Mason spoke it.

'Dinna fash yoursel'. She's gone awa' for the noo,' said Mason.

He began once more to eat.

'I saw her once myself,' I said, sitting right down again. 'I saw her when my darling mother died.'

'Ay, you would,' said Mason. 'Especially if maybe you were about the house at the time. Who let her in?'

'I don't know,' I replied. 'Perhaps she doesn't have to be let in?'

'Och, she does that,' said Mason. 'She always has to be let in.'

'It was at the grave that you saw her?'

'No, not there, though it is my fancy that she was present. I saw her through that window as she came up from the sea.'

I know that Mason pointed, and I know that I did not find it the moment to look.

'Through the glass panes or out on the wee rocks you can view the spot,' said Mason. 'It's always the same.' Now he was looking at nothing and chewing vigorously.

'I saw no face,' I said.

'If you'd seen that, you wouldn't be here now,' said Mason. He was calm, as far as I could see.

Intrusions

'How often have you seen her yourself?'

'Four or five times in all. At the different deaths.'

'Including at my mother's death?'

'Yes, then too,' said Mason, still gazing upon the sawn-up sections of meat. 'At the family deaths she is seen, and at the deaths of those, whoever they be, that enter the family.'

I thought of my brother whom I had never known. I wasn't even aware that there had been any other family deaths during Mason's likely lifetime.

'She belongs to those called Leith, by one right or another,' said Mason, 'and to no one at all else.'

As he spoke, and having regard to the way he had put it, I felt that I saw why so apparently alert a man seemed to have such difficulty in remembering that I was presumably a Leith myself. I took his consideration kindly.

'I didn't see anyone when the Judge died,' I remarked.

'Perhaps in a dream,' said Mason. 'I believe you were sick at the time.'

That was not quite right of course, but it was true that I had by no means been in the house.

We dropped the subject, and turned once more to feu duties, rents, and discriminatory taxes; even to the recent changes in the character of the tides and in the behaviour of the gannets.

I have no idea how I scrambled back to dismal Pollaporra, and in twilight first, soon in darkness. Perhaps the liquor aided instead of impeded, as liquor so often in practice does, despite the doctors and proctors.

The Fetch

III

After the war, Jack Oliver was there to welcome me back to the office off Cornhill. He was now a colonel. His uncle had been killed in what was known as an incident, when the whole family house had been destroyed, including the Devises and De Wints. The business was now substantially his.

I found myself advanced very considerably from the position I had occupied in 1939. From this it is not to be supposed, as so many like to suppose, that no particular aptitude is required for success in merchant banking. On the contrary, very precise qualities both of mind and of temperament are needed. About myself, the conclusion I soon reached was that I was as truly a Scottish businessman as my ancestors in the kirkyard, whether I liked it or not, as O'Neill says. I should have been foolish had I not liked it. I might have preferred to be a weaver of dreams, but perhaps my mother had died too soon for that to be possible. I must add, however, that the business was by no means the same as when I had entered it before the war. No business was the same. The staff was smaller, the atmosphere tenser. The gains were illusory, the prospects shadowy. One worked much less hard, but one believed in nothing. There was little to work for, less to believe in.

It was in the office, though, that I met Shulie. She seemed very lost. I was attracted by her at once.

'Are you looking for someone?' I asked.

'I have just seen Mr Oliver.' She had a lovely voice and a charming accent. I knew that Jack was seeking a new secretary. His present one had failed to report for weeks, or to answer her supposed home telephone number.

'I hope that all went well.'

Intrusions

Shulie shook her head and smiled a little.

'I'm sorry about that.'

'Mr Oliver had chosen a girl who went in just before me. It always happens.'

'I'm sure you'll have better luck soon.'

She shook her head a second time. 'I am not English.'

'That has advantages as well as disadvantages,' I replied firmly.

It struck me that she might be a refugee, with behind her a terrible story. She was small, slender, and dark, though not as dark as my mother. I could not decide whether or not she looked particularly Jewish. I daresay it is always a rather foolish question.

'No advantages when you are in England,' she said. 'Can you please tell me how to get out of this place?'

'I'll come with you,' I said. 'It's difficult to explain.'

That was perfectly true. It matters that it was true, because while we were winding through the corridors, and I was holding swing doors, I was successful in persuading Shulie to have lunch with me. Time was gained for me also by the fact that Shulie had a slight limp, which slowed her down quite perceptibly. I am sure she was weary too, and I even believe that she was seriously underfed, whatever the exact reason. I perceived Shulie as a waif from the start; though also from the start I saw that it was far from the whole truth about her. I never learned the whole truth about her. Perhaps one never does learn, but Shulie refused, in so many words, to speak about it.

It was February, and outside I could have done with my overcoat. Jack Oliver still went everywhere in a British warm. He had several of them. There was snow on the ground and on the ledges. We had been under snow for weeks. Though do I imagine the snow? I do not imagine the cold. Shulie, when the blast struck her, drew into herself, as girls do. She was certainly not dressed for it; but few girls then were. The girlish image was still paramount. I myself actually caught a cold that day, as I often did. I was laid up for a time in my small flat off Orchard Street, and with no one in any position to look after me very much. Later, Shulie explained to me that one need never catch cold. All that is necessary is a firm resolution against it: faith in oneself, I suppose.

On most days, Jack and I, together or apart, went either to quite costly places or to certain pubs. That was the way of life approved, expected, even enforced; and, within the limits of the time, rewarded. I, however, had kept my options more open than that. I took Shulie to a near-by tea shop, though a somewhat superior tea shop. We were early, but it was filling fast. Still, we had a table to ourselves for a time.

'What's your name?'

'Shulie.'

Her lips were like dark rose petals, as one imagines them, or sometimes dreams of them.

I have mentioned how lamentably sure I am that I failed to make Celia happy; nor any other girl. During the war, I had lived, off and on, with a woman married to another officer, who was never there when I was. I shall not relate how for me it all began. There was a case for, and a case against, but it had been another relationship inconducive to the ultimate happiness of either party.

When I realised that I was not merely attracted by Shulie, but deeply in love with her, and dependent for any future I might have upon marrying her, I applied myself to avoiding past errors. Possibly in past circumstances, they had not really been errors; but now they might be the difference between life and

Intrusions

death. I decided that, apart from my mother, I had never previously and properly loved anyone; and that with no one else but my mother had I been sufficiently honest to give things a chance. When the time came, I acted at once.

Within half an hour of Shulie tentatively accepting my proposal of marriage, I related to her what Mason had told me, and what I had myself seen. I said that I was a haunted man. I even said that she could reverse her tentative decision, if she thought fit.

'So the woman has to be let in?' said Shulie.

'That's what Mason told me.'

'A woman who is married does not let any other woman in, except when her husband is not there.'

'But suppose you were ill?'

'Then you would be at home looking after me. It would not be a time when you would let in another woman.'

It was obvious that she was not taking the matter seriously. I had been honest, but I was still anxious.

'Have you ever heard a story like it before?'

'Yes,' said Shulie. 'But it is the message that matters more than the messenger.'

After we married, Shulie simply moved into my small flat. At first we intended, or certainly I intended, almost immediately to start looking for somewhere much larger. We, or certainly I, had a family in mind. With Shulie, I wanted that very much, even though I was a haunted man, whose rights were doubtful.

But it was amazing how well we seemed to go on living exactly where we were. Shulie had few possessions to bring in, and even when they were increased, we still seemed to have plenty of room. It struck me that Shulie's slight infirmity might contribute to her lack of interest in that normal ambition of any

The Fetch

woman: a larger home. Certainly, the trouble seemed at times to fatigue her, even though the manifestations were very inconspicuous. For example, Jack Oliver, at a much later date, denied that he had ever noticed anything at all. The firm had provided me with a nice car and parking was then easier than it is now. Shulie had to do little walking of the kind that really exhausts a woman; pushing through crowds, and round shops at busy hours.

As a matter of fact, Shulie seldom left the flat, unless in my company. Shulie was writing a book. She ordered almost all goods on the telephone, and proved to be skilful and firm. She surprised me continually in matters like that. Marriage had already changed her considerably. She was plumper, as well as more confident. She accompanied me to the Festival Hall, and to picnics in Kew Gardens. The picnics were made elegant and exciting by her presence, and by her choice of what we ate and drank, and by the way she looked at the flowers, and by the way people and flowers looked at her. Otherwise, she wrote, or mused upon what she was about to write. She reclined in different sets of silk pyjamas on a bright blue daybed I'd bought for her, and rested her square, stiff-covered exercise book upon her updrawn knees. She refused to read to me what she had written, or to let me read it for myself. 'You will know one day,' she said.

I must admit that I had to do a certain amount of explaining to Jack Oliver. He would naturally have preferred me to marry a woman who kept open house and was equally good with all men alike. Fortunately, business in Britain does not yet depend so much upon those things as does business in America. I was able to tell Jack that setting a wife to attract business to her husband was always a chancy transaction for the husband. For better or for worse, Jack, having lately battled his way through a very complex divorce, accepted my view. The divorce had ended in a most unpleasant situation for Jack financially, as well as in some public ridicule. He was in no position even to hint that I had married a girl whom he had rejected for a job. His own wife had been the daughter of a baronet who was also a vice-admiral and a former Member of Parliament. Her name was Clarissa. Her mother, the admiral's wife, was an M.F.H.

After my own mother's death, I should never have thought possible the happiness that Shulie released in me. There was much that remained unspoken to the end, but that may have been advantageous. Perhaps it is always so. Perhaps only madmen need to know everything and thus to destroy everything. When I lay in Shulie's arms, or simply regarded her as she wrote her secret book, I wished to know nothing more, because more would diminish. This state of being used to be known as connubial bliss. Few, I believe, experience it. It is certainly not a matter of deserts.

Shulie, however, proved to be incapable of conception. Possibly it was a consequence of earlier sufferings and endurances. Elaborate treatments might have been tried, but Shulie shrank from them, and understandably. She accepted the situation very quietly. She did not seem to cease loving me. We continued to dwell in the flat off Orchard Street.

I asked Shulie when her book would be finished. She replied that the more she wrote, the more there was to be written. Whenever I approached her, she closed the exercise book and lifted herself up to kiss me. If I persisted at all, she did more than kiss me.

I wanted nothing else in life than to be with Shulie, and alone with her. Everything we did in the outside world was incorporated into our love. I was happy once more, and now I was happy all the time, even in the office near Cornhill. I bought a bicycle to make the journey, but the City men laughed, and nicknamed me, and ragged me, so that Jack Oliver and the others suggested that I gave it up. Jack bought the bicycle himself, to use at his place in the country, where, not necessarily on the bicycle, he was courting the divorced daughter of the local High Sheriff, a girl far beyond his present means. She was even a member of a ladies' polo team, though the youngest. When one is happy oneself, everyone seems happy.

Our flat was on the top floor in a small block. The block had been built in more spacious days than the present, and there were two lifts. They were in parallel shafts. Above the waistline, the lifts had windows on three sides; the gate being on the fourth. They were large lifts, each *Licensed to carry 12 people*; far more than commonly accumulated at any one time. The users worked the lifts themselves, though, when I had first taken the flat, the lifts in Selfridges round the corner had still been worked by the famous pretty girls in breeches, among whom an annual competition was held. The two lifts in the flats were brightly lit and always very clean. Shulie loved going up and down in them; much as she loved real traffic blocks, with boys ranging along the stationary cars selling ice cream and evening newspapers. None the less, I do not think she used the lifts very much when I was not there. Travelling in them was, in fact, one tiny facet of our love. When Shulie was alone, I believe she commonly used the stairs, despite her trouble. The stairs were well lighted and well swept also. Marauders were seldom met.

Tenants used sometimes to wave to their neighbours through the glass, as the two lifts swept past one another, one upwards, one downwards. It was important to prevent this becoming a mere tiresome obligation. One morning I was alone in the descending lift. I was on my way to work: Bond Street Underground station to Bank Underground station. There had been a wonderful early morning with Shulie, and I was full of joy; thinking about nothing but that. The other lift swept upwards past me. In it were four people who lived in the flats, three women and one man; all known to me by sight, though no more than that. As a fifth, there was the woman whom I had seen when my mother died.

Despite the speed with which the lifts had passed, I was sure it was she. The back was turned to me, but her sparse hair, her dirty plaid, her stature, and somehow her stance, were for ever unmistakable. I remember thinking immediately that the others in the lift must all be seeing the woman's face.

Melted ice flowed through me from the top of my head to the soles of my feet. There was a device for stopping the lift: *To be used only in Emergency*. And of course I wanted to reverse the lift also. I was so cold and so shaky that I succeeded merely in jamming the lift, and neatly between floors, like a joke in *Puck* or *Rainbow*, or a play by Sartre.

I hammered and raved, but most of the tenants had either gone to work or were making preparations for coffee mornings. The other lift did not pass again. As many as ten minutes tore by before anyone took notice of me, and then it was only because our neighbour, Mrs Delmer, wanted to descend from the top, and needed the lift she always used, being, as she had several times told us, frightened of the other one. The caretaker emerged slowly from his cubicle and shouted to me that there was nothing he could do. He would have to send for the lift company's maintenance men. He was not supposed to be on duty at that hour anyway, he said. We all knew that. Mrs Delmer made a detour as she clambered down the staircase, in order to tap on the glass roof of my lift and give me a piece of her mind, though in refined phrases. In the end, I simply sank upon the floor and tried to close myself to all thought or feeling, though with no success.

The Fetch

I must acknowledge that the maintenance men came far sooner than one could have expected. They dropped from above, and crawled from below, even emerging from a trap in the lift floor, full of cheerful conversation, both particular and general. The lift was brought slowly down to the gate on the floor immediately below. For some reason, that gate would not open, even to the maintenance men; and we had to sink, slowly still, to the ground floor. The first thing I saw there was a liquid trail in from the street up to the gate of the other lift. Not being his hour, the caretaker had still to mop it up, even though it reeked of seabed mortality.

Shulie and I lived on the eighth floor. I ran all the way up. The horrible trail crossed our landing from the lift gate to under our front door.

I do not know how long I had been holding the key in my hand. As one does at such times, I fumbled and fumbled at the lock. When the door was open, I saw that the trail wound through the tiny hall or lobby and entered the living room. When the woman came to my mother, there had been a faint trail only, but at that time I had not learned from Mason about the woman coming from the sea. Fuller knowledge was yielding new evidence.

I did not find Shulie harmed, or ill, or dead. She was not there at all.

Everything was done, but I never saw her again.

IV

The trail of water soon dried out, leaving no mark of any kind, despite the rankness.

Intrusions

The four people whom I had seen in the lift, and who lived in the flats, denied that they had ever seen a fifth. I neither believed nor disbelieved.

Shulie's book was infinitely upsetting. It was hardly fiction at all, as I had supposed it to be, but a personal diary, in the closest detail, of everything we had done together, of everything we had been, of everything she had felt. It was at once comprehensive and chaste. At one time, I even thought of seeking a publisher for it, but was deterred, in an illogical way, by the uncertainty about what had happened to Shulie. I was aware that it had been perfectly possible for her to leave the building by the staircase, while I had been caged between floors in the lift. The staircase went down a shaft of its own.

The book contained nothing of what had happened to Shulie before she met me.

Shulie's last words were: 'So joyful! Am I dreaming, or even dead? It seems that there is no external way of deciding either thing.' Presumably, she had then been interrupted. Doubtless, she had then risen to open the door.

I had been married to Shulie for three years and forty-one days.

I wrote to the Trustees suggesting that they put Pollaporra on the market, but their law agent replied that it was outside their powers. All I had done was upset both Cuddy and Mason.

I sold the lease of the flat off Orchard Street, and bought the lease of another one, off Gloucester Place.

I settled down to living with no one and for no one. I took every opportunity of travelling for the bank, no matter where, not only abroad, but even to Peterhead, Bolton, or Camborne. Previously, I had not wished or cared to leave Shulie for a single night.

The Fetch

I pursued new delights, such as they were, and as they came along. I joined a bridge club, a chess club, a ma-jong society, and a mixed fencing group. Later, I joined a very avant-garde dance club, and went there occasionally.

I was introduced by one of the people in my firm to a very High Anglican church in his own neighbourhood, and went there quite often. Sometimes I read one of the lessons. I was one of the few who could still do that in Latin.

Another partner was interested in masonics, but I thought that would be inconsistent. I did join a livery company: it is expected in the City.

I was pressed to go in for regular massage, but resisted that too.

I was making more paper money than I would ever have thought possible. Paper money? Not even that. Phantom wealth, almost entirely: taxes took virtually the whole of it. I did not even employ a housekeeper. I did not wish for the attentions of any woman who was not Shulie. All the same, I wrote to Celia, who replied at once, making clear, among very many other things, that she was still unmarried. She had time to write so long and so prompt a letter. She had hope enough to think it worthwhile.

It is amazing how full a life a man can lead without for one moment being alive at all, except sometimes when sleeping. As Clifford Bax says, life is best treated as simply a game. Soon enough one will be bowled middle stump, be put out of action in the scrum, or ruled offside and sent off. As Bax also says, it is necessary to have an alternative. But who really has?

None the less, blood will out, and I married again. Sometime before, Shulie's death had been 'presumed'. Mercifully, it was the Trustees who attended to that.

I married Clarissa. I am married to her now.

Intrusions

The Court had bestowed upon Clarissa a goodly slice of Jack's property and prospects, and Jack was recognised by all as having made a complete fool of himself, not only in the area of cash; but Clarissa never really left at all. Even though Jack was now deeply entangled with Suzanne, herself a young divorcee, Clarissa was always one of Jack's house party, eager to hear everything, ready to advise, perhaps even to comfort, though I myself never came upon her doing that. She might now be sleeping in the room that had once been set aside for the visits of her sister, Naomi, but of course she knew the whole house far more intimately than Jack did, or than any normal male knows any house. She continued being invaluable to Jack; especially when he was giving so much of his time to Suzanne. One could not know Jack at all well, let alone as well as I knew him, without continuing to encounter Clarissa all the time.

The word for Clarissa might be deft—the first word, that is. She can manage a man or a woman, a slow child or a slow pensioner, as effortlessly as she can manage everything in a house, at a party, in a shop, on a ship. She has the small but right touch for every single situation—the perfect touch. Most of all, she has the small and perfect touch for every situation, huge or tiny, in her own life. Few indeed have *that* gift. No doubt Clarissa owes much to her versatile papa. On one occasion also, I witnessed Clarissa's mother looking after a difficult meet. It was something to note and remember.

Clarissa has that true beauty which is not so much in the features and body, but around them: nothing less than a mystical emanation. When I made my proposal to Clarissa, I naturally thought very devoutly of Shulie. Shulie's beauty was of the order one longs from the first to embrace, to be absorbed by. Of course, my mother's dark beauty had been like that also. Clarissa one hardly wished or dared to touch, lest the vision fade. A man who felt otherwise than that about Clarissa would be a man who could not see the vision at all. I imagine that state of things will bear closely upon what happens to Clarissa. There is little that is mystical about Clarissa's detectable behaviour, though there must be *some* relationship between her soul and the way she looks. It is a question that arises so often when women as beautiful as Clarissa materialise in one's rose garden. I myself have never seen another woman as beautiful absolutely as Clarissa, or certainly never spoken to one.

Clarissa has eyes so deep as to make one wonder about the whole idea of depth, and what it means. She has a voice almost as lovely as her face. She has a slow and languorous walk: beautiful too, but related, I fear, to an incident during her early teens, when she broke both legs in the hunting field. Sometimes it leads to trouble when Clarissa is driving a car. Not often. Clarissa prefers to wear trousers, though she looks perfectly normal in even a short skirt, indeed divinely beautiful, as always.

I fear that too much of my life with Clarissa has been given to quarrelling. No one is to blame, of course.

There was a certain stress even at the proposal scene, which took place on a Saturday afternoon in Jack's house, when the others were out shooting duck. Pollaporra and its legend have always discouraged me from field sports, and all the struggling about had discouraged Clarissa, who sat before the fire, looking gnomic.

But she said Yes at once, and nodded, and smiled.

Devoted still, whether wisely or foolishly, to honesty, I told her what Mason had told me, and what I had myself seen on two occasions, and that I was a haunted man.

Clarissa looked very hostile. 'I don't believe in things like that,' she said sharply.

'I thought I ought to tell you.'

Intrusions

'Why? Did you want to upset me?'

'Of course not. I love you. I don't want you to accept me on false pretences.'

'It's got nothing to do with my accepting you. I just don't want to know about such things. They don't exist.'

'But they do, Clarissa. They are part of me.'

From one point of view, obviously I should not have persisted. I had long recognised that many people would have said that I was obsessed. But the whole business seemed to me the explanation of my being. Clarissa must not take me to be merely a banker, a youngish widower, a friend of her first husband's, a faint simulacrum of the admiral.

Clarissa actually picked up a book of sweepstake tickets and threw it at me as I sat on the rug at her feet.

'There,' she said.

It was a quite thick and heavy book, but I was not exactly injured by it, though it had come unexpectedly, and had grazed my eye.

Clarissa then leaned forward and gave me a slow and searching kiss. It was the first time we had kissed so seriously.

'There,' she said again.

She then picked the sweepstake tickets off the floor and threw them in the fire. They were less than fully burnt ten minutes later, when Clarissa and I were more intimately involved, and looking at our watches to decide when the others were likely to return.

The honeymoon, at Clarissa's petition, was in North Africa, now riddled with politics, which I did not care for. For centuries, there has been very little in North Africa for an outsider to see, and the conformity demanded by an alien society seemed not the best background for learning to know another person.

The Fetch

Perhaps we should have tried Egypt, but Clarissa specifically demanded something more rugged. With Shulie there had been no honeymoon.

Before marrying me, Clarissa had been dividing her life between her flat and Jack's country house. Her spacious flat, very near my childhood home, was in its own way as beautiful as she was, and emitted a like glow. It would have been absurd for me not to move into it. The settlement from Jack had contributed significantly to all around me, but by now I was able to keep up, or nearly so. Money is like sex. The more that everyone around is talking of little else, the less it really accounts for, let alone assists.

Not that sex has ever been other than a problem with Clarissa. I have good reason to believe that others have found the same, though Jack never gave me one word of warning. In any case, his Suzanne is another of the same kind, if I am any judge; though less beautiful, and, I should say, less kind also. Men chase the same women again and again; or rather the same illusion; or rather the same lost part of themselves.

Within myself, I had of course returned to the hope of children. Some will say that I was a fool not to have had that matter out with Clarissa before marrying her, and no doubt a number of related matters also. They speak without knowing Clarissa. No advance terms can be set. None at all. I doubt whether it is possible with any woman whom one finds really desirable. Nor can the proposal scene be converted into a businesslike discussion of future policy and prospects. That is not the atmosphere, and few would marry if it were.

With Shulie, the whole thing had been love. With Clarissa, it was power; and she was so accustomed to the power being hers that she could no longer bother to exercise it, except indirectly. This was and is true even though Clarissa is exceedingly good-hearted in many other ways. I had myself experienced something of the kind in reverse with poor Celia, though obviously in a much lesser degree.

Clarissa has long been impervious to argument or importunity or persuasion of any kind. She is perfectly equipped with counterpoise and equipoise. She makes discussion seem absurd. Almost always it is. Before long, I was asking myself whether Clarissa's strange and radiant beauty was compatible with desire, either on her part or on mine.

There was also the small matter of Clarissa's black maid, Aline; who has played her little part in the immediate situation. On my visits to the flat before our marriage, I had become very much aware of Aline, miniature and slender, always in tight sweater and pale trousers. Clarissa had told me that Aline could do everything in the place that required to be done; but in my hearing Aline spoke little for herself. I was told that often she drove Clarissa's beautiful foreign car, a present from Jack less than a year before the divorce. I was also told, as a matter of interest, that Jack had never met Aline. I therefore never spoke of her to him. I was telling him much less now, in any case. I certainly did not tell him what I had not previously been told myself: that when I was away for the firm, which continued to be frequently, Aline took my place in Clarissa's vast and swanlike double bed. I discovered this in a thoroughly low way, which I do not propose to relate. Clarissa simply remarked to me that, as I knew, she could never sleep well if alone in the room. I abstained from rejoining that what Clarissa really wanted was a nanny; one of those special nannies who, like dolls, are always there to be dominated by their charges. It would have been one possible rejoinder.

Nannies were on my mind. It had been just then that the Trustees wrote to me about Cuddy. They told me that Cuddy

The Fetch

had 'intimated a wish' to leave her employment at Pollaporra. She wanted to join her younger sister, who, I was aware, had a business on the main road, weaving and plaiting for the tourists, not far from Dingwall. I could well believe that the business had become more prosperous than when I had heard about it as a child. It was a business of the sort that at the moment did. The Trustees went on to imply that it was my task, and not theirs, to find a successor to Cuddy. They reminded me that I was under an obligation to maintain a property in which I had merely a life interest.

It was a very hot day. Clarissa always brought the sun. She had been reading the letter over my shoulder. I was always aware of her special nimbus encircling my head and torso when she did this. Moreover, she was wearing nothing but her nightdress.

'Let's go and have a look,' she said.

'Are you sure you want to?' I asked, remembering her response to my story.

'Of course I'm sure. I'll transform the place, now I've got it to myself.'

'That'll be the day,' I said, smiling up at her.

'You won't know it when I've finished with it. Then we can sell it.'

'We can't,' I said. 'Remember it's not mine to sell.'

'You must get advice. Jack might be able to help.'

'You don't know what Pollaporra's like. Everything is bound to be totally run down.'

'With your Cuddy in charge all these years, and with nothing else to do with herself? At least, you say not.'

I had seen on my previous visit that this argument might be sound, as far as it went.

'You can't possibly take on all the work.'

'We'll have Aline with us. I had intended that.'

Intrusions

By now, I had seen for myself also that Aline was indeed most competent and industrious. It would have been impossible to argue further: Clarissa was my wife and had a right both to accompany me and to take someone with her to help with the chores. If I were to predecease her, she would have a life interest in the property. Moreover, Clarissa alone could manage very well for us when she applied herself. I had learned that too. There were no sensible, practical objections whatever.

'Aline will be a help with the driving as well,' added Clarissa.

There again, I had seen for myself how excellent a driver little Aline could be. She belongs to just the sort of quiet person who in practice drives most effectively on the roads of today.

'So write at once and say we're arriving,' said Clarissa.

'I'm not sure there's anyone to write to,' I replied. 'That's the point.'

I had, of course, a set of keys. For whatever reason, I did not incline to giving Mason advance notice of my second coming, and in such altered circumstances.

'I'm not sure how Aline will get on with the Highlanders,' I remarked. There are, of course, all those stories in Scotland about the intrusion of huge black men, and sometimes, I fancy, of black females. They figure in folklore everywhere.

'She'll wind each of them three times round each of her fingers,' replied Clarissa. 'But you told me there were no Highlanders at Pollaporra.'

Clarissa, when triumphing, looks like Juno, or Diana, or even Minerva.

Aline entered to the tinkling of a little bell. It is a pretty little bell, which I bought for Clarissa in Sfax; her earlier little bell having dropped its clapper. When Aline entered in her quiet way, Clarissa kissed her, as she does every morning upon first sighting Aline.

'We're all three going into the wilderness together,' said Clarissa. 'Probably on Friday.'

Friday was the day after tomorrow. I really could not leave the business for possibly a week at such short notice. There was some tension because of that, but it could not be helped.

When we did reach Pollaporra, the weather was hotter than ever, though there had been several thunderstorms in London. Aline was in her element. Clarissa had stocked up the large car with food in immense quantity. When we passed through an outlying area of Glasgow, she distributed two pounds of sweets to children playing in the roads of a council estate. The sweets were melting in their papers as she threw them. The tiny fingers locked together.

When we reached the small kirkyard, Clarissa, who was driving us along the rough road from Arrafergus, categorically refused to stop.

'We're here to drive the bogies out,' she said, 'not to let them in.'

Clarissa also refused to leave the car at the bottom of the final slope, as Perry Jesperson had done. My friend Jesperson was now a Labour M.P. like his father, and already a Joint Parliamentary Secretary, and much else, vaguely lucrative and responsible. Clarissa took the car up the very steep incline as if it had been a lift at the seaside.

She stood looking at and beyond the low grey house. 'Is that the sea?' she asked, pointing.

'It's the sea loch,' I replied. 'A long inlet, like a fjord.'

'It's a lovely place,' said Clarissa.

I was surprised, but, I suppose, pleased.

Intrusions

'I thought we might cut the house up into lodges for the shooting and fishing,' said Clarissa. 'But now I don't want to.'

'The Trustees would never have agreed,' I pointed out. 'They have no power to agree.'

'Doesn't matter. I want to come here often. Let's take a photograph.'

So, before we started to unpack the car, Clarissa took one of Aline and me; and, at her suggestion, I took one of Aline and her. Aline did not rise to the shoulders of either of us.

Within the house, the slight clamminess of my previous visit had been replaced by a curiously tense airlessness. I had used my key to admit us, but I had not been certain as to whether or not Cuddy was already gone, and Clarissa and I went from room to room shouting for her, Clarissa more loudly than I. Aline remained among the waders and antlers of the entrance hall, far from home, and thinking her own thoughts. There was no reply anywhere. I went to the door of what I knew to be Cuddy's own room, and quietly tapped. When there was no reply there either, I gently tried the handle. I thought the door might be locked, but it was not. Inside was a small unoccupied bedroom. The fittings were very spare. There were a number of small framed statements on the walls, such as *I bow before Thee*, and *Naught but Surrender*, and *Who knows All* without a mark of interrogation. Clarissa was still calling from room to room. I did not care to call back but went after her on half-tiptoe.

I thought we could conclude we were alone. Cuddy must have departed some time ago.

Dust was settling everywhere, even in that remote spot. The sunlight made it look like encroaching fur. Clarissa seemed undeterred and undaunted.

'It's a lost world and I'm queen,' she said.

The Fetch

It is true that old grey waders, and wicker fish baskets with many of the withies broken, and expensive guns for stalking lined up in racks, are unequalled for suggesting loss, past, present, and to come. Even the pictures were all of death and yesterday; stags exaggeratedly virile before the crack shot, feathers abnormally bright before the battle, men and ancestors in bonnets before, behind, and around the ornamentally piled carcases, with the lion of Scotland flag stuck in the summit. When we reached the hall, I noticed that Aline was shuddering in the sunlight. I myself had never been in the house before without Cuddy. In practice, she had been responsible for everything that happened there. Now I was responsible—and for as long as I remained alive.

'We'll paint everything white and we'll put in a swimming pool,' cried Clarissa joyously. 'Aline can have the room in the tower.'

'I didn't know there was a tower,' I said.

'*Almost* a tower,' said Clarissa.

'Is there anything in the room?' I asked.

'Only those things on heads. They're all over the walls and floor.'

At that, Aline actually gave a little cry. Perhaps she was thinking of things on walls and floors in Africa.

'It's all right,' said Clarissa, going over to her. 'We'll throw them all away. I promise. I never ask you to do anything I don't do myself, or wouldn't do.'

But, whatever might be wrong, Aline was uncomforted. 'Look!' she cried, and pointed out through one of the hall windows, all of them obstructed by stuffed birds in glass domes, huge and dusty.

'What have you seen this time?' asked Clarissa, as if speaking to a loved though exhausting child.

Intrusions

At that moment, it came to me that Clarissa regularly treated Aline as my mother had treated me.

Aline's hand fell slowly to her side, and her head began to droop.

'It's only the car,' said Clarissa. '*Our* car. You've been driving it yourself.'

I had stepped swiftly but quietly behind the two of them. I admit that I too could see nothing but the car, and, of course, the whole of Scotland.

I seldom spoke directly to Aline, but now was the moment.

'What was it?' I asked, as sympathetically as I could manage. 'What did you see?'

But Aline had begun to weep, as by now I had observed that she often did. She wept without noise or any special movement. The tears just flowed like thawing snow; as they do in nature, though less often on 'Change.

'It was nothing,' said Clarissa. 'Aline often sees nothing, don't you, Aline?' She produced her own handkerchief, and began to dry Aline's face, and to hug her tightly.

The handkerchief was from an enormous casket of objects given us as a wedding present by Clarissa's grandmother (on the mother's side), who was an invalid, living in Dominica. Clarissa's grandfather had been shot dead years before by thieves he had interrupted.

'Now,' said Clarissa after a few moments of tender reassurance. 'Smile, please. That's better. We're going to be happy here, one and all. Remember. Happy.'

I suppose I was reasonably eager, but I found it difficult to see how she was going to manage it. It was not, as I must in justice to her make clear, that normally I was unhappy with Clarissa. She was too beautiful and original for that to be the word at any time. The immediate trouble was just Pollaporra

The Fetch

itself: the most burdensome and most futile of houses, so futile as to be sinister, even apart from its associations, where I was concerned. I could not imagine any effective brightening; not even by means of maquillage and disguise: a pool, a discothéque, a sauna, a black-jack suite. To me Pollaporra was a millstone I could never throw away. I could not believe that modern tenants would ever stop there for long, or in the end show us a profit. For all the keep nets and carcase sleighs in every room, I doubted whether the accessible sport was good enough to be marketed at all in contemporary terms. Nor had I started out with Clarissa in order that we should settle down in the place ourselves. When I can get away from work, I want somewhere recuperative. About Pollaporra, I asked the question all married couples ask when detached from duties and tasks: what should we do all day? There was nothing.

'I have never felt so free and blithe,' said Clarissa later that evening, exaggerating characteristically but charmingly. She was playing the major part in preparing a quite elaborate dinner for us out of tins and packets. In the flat, Aline had normally eaten in her own pretty sitting room, but here she would be eating with us. Clarissa would be tying a lace napkin round her neck, and heaping her plate with first choices, and handing her date after date on a spike. Employees are supposed to be happier when treated in that way, though few people think it is true, and few employees.

'We'll flatten the roof and have li-los,' said Clarissa, while Aline munched with both eyes on her plate, and I confined myself to wary nibblings round the fringe of Rognons Turbigo, canned but reinvigorated. The plates at Pollaporra depicted famous Scots, such as Sawney Bean and Robert Knox, who employed Burke and Hare, the body-snatchers. Mr Justice Leith, who despised the criminal law, had never been above such likenesses, as we know; nor had he been the only sporting jurist in the family, very far from it.

'I think to do that we'd have to rebuild the house,' I remarked.

'Do try not to make difficulties the whole time. Let yourself go, Brodick.'

It is seldom a good idea, according to my experience, and especially not in Scotland, but of course I could see what Clarissa meant. There was no reason why we should not make of the trip as much of a holiday as was possible. It would be a perfectly sensible thing to do. If Clarissa was capable of fun at Pollaporra, I was the last person with a right to stand in her way.

'We might build a gazebo,' I said, though I could feel my heart sinking as I spoke.

Aline, with her mouth full of prunes (that day), turned her head towards me. She did not know what a gazebo was.

'A sort of summerhouse,' explained Clarissa. 'With cushions and views. It would be lovely. So many things to look at.'

I had never known Clarissa so simple-minded before; in the nicest sense, of course. I realised that this might be a Clarissa more real than the other one. I might have to consider where I myself stood about that. On the other hand, Pollaporra instead of bringing out at long last the real woman, might be acting upon her by contraries, and have engaged the perversity in her, and to no ultimately constructive end. I had certainly heard of that too, and in my time seen it in action among friends.

'I don't want to look,' said Aline, expelling prune stones into spoons.

'You will by tomorrow. You'll feel quite different. We're going to drive all the banshees far, far away.'

I am sure that Aline did not know what a banshee was either, but Clarissa's general meaning was clear, and the word

The Fetch

has an African, self-speaking sound in itself, when one comes to think about it. Words for things like that are frightening in themselves the world over.

Only Clarissa, who believed in nothing she could not see or imagine, was utterly undisturbed. I am sure that must have played its part in the row we had in our room that night.

There were small single rooms, of course, several of them. There were also low dormitories for body servants and sporting auxiliaries. All the rooms for two people had Scottish double beds. Clarissa and I had to labour away in silence making such a bed with sheets she had brought with us. Blankets we should have had to find in drawers and to take on trust, but on such a night they were unnecessary. Aline, when not with Clarissa, always slept in a striped bag, which that night must have been far too hot. Everything, everywhere, was far too hot. That contributed too, as it always does. Look at Latin America!

I admit that throughout the evening I had failed to respond very affirmatively to Clarissa's sequence of suggestions for livening up the property and also (she claimed) increasing its market value; which, indeed, cannot, as things were and are, be high. I could see for myself how I was leading her first into despondency, then into irritation. I can see that only too well now. I was dismayed by what was happening, but there was so little I could conscientiously offer in the way of encouragement. All I wished to do with Pollaporra was patch up some arrangement to meet my minimum obligations as a life tenant, and then, if possible, never set eyes upon the place again. One reason why I was cast down was the difficulty of achieving even a programme as basic as that. I daresay that Clarissa's wild ideas would actually be simpler to accomplish, and conceivably cheaper also in the end. But there is something more than reason that casts me down at Pollaporra. Shall I say that the house brings into consciousness the conflict between my hereditament and my identity? Scotland herself is a land I do well to avoid. Many of us have large areas of danger which others find merely delightful.

There was no open row until Clarissa and I went upstairs. One reason was that after doing the washing-up, Aline had come into the sitting room, without a word, to join us. I was not surprised that she had no wish to be alone; nor that she proved reluctant to play a game named Contango, of which Clarissa was very fond, and which went back to her days with Jack, even though Jack had always won, sometimes while glancing through business papers simultaneously, as I had observed for myself. Both Clarissa and Aline were wearing tartan trousers, though not the same tartan. I had always been told by Cuddy that there was no Leith tartan. I have never sought further to know whether or not that is true.

As soon as we were in bed, Clarissa lay on her front, impressing the pillow with moisture from her brow, and quietly set about me; ranging far beyond the possibilities and deficiencies of Pollaporra. Any man—any modern man—would have some idea of what was said. Do the details matter? I offered no argument. At Pollaporra, I spoke as little as I could. What can argument achieve anywhere? It might have been a moment for me to establish at least temporary dominance by one means or another, but Pollaporra prevented, even if I am the man to do it at any time. I tried to remember Shulie, but of course the circumstances left her entirely unreal to me, together with everything else.

And, in the morning, things were no better. I do not know how much either of us had managed to sleep. For better or worse, we had fallen silent in the heat long ago. In the end, I heard the seabirds screaming and yelling at the dawn.

The Fetch

Clarissa put on a few garments while I lay silent on the bed and then told me that as there was nothing she could do in the house, she was departing at once.

'I should leave Aline behind, but I need her.'

'I quite understand,' I said. 'I advised you against coming in the first place. I shall go over to see Mason and try to arrange with him for a caretaker. It won't take more than a day or two.'

'You'll first need to change the place completely. You are weak and pigheaded.'

'They sometimes see things differently in Scotland. I shall come down as soon as I can.' I might have to hire a car to some station, because I did not think Mason owned one, or anyone else in his small community. That was a trifle; comparatively.

'No hurry. I shall use the time deciding what to do for the best.' She was combing her mass of hair, lovely as Ceres' sheaf. The comb, given her by the Aga Khan, was made of ebony. The air smelled of hot salt.

I suppose I should have begged her pardon for Pollaporra and myself, and gone back to London with her, or to anywhere else. I did not really think of it. Pollaporra had to be settled, if at all possible. I might never be back there.

In a few moments, Clarissa and I were together in the hall, the one high room, and I saw Aline silently standing by the outer door, as if she had stood all night; and the door was slightly open. Aline was in different trousers, and so was Clarissa.

'I can't be bothered to pack up the food. You're welcome to all of it.'

'Don't go without breakfast,' I said. 'The lumpy roads will make you sick.'

'Breakfast would make me sick,' said Clarissa.

Intrusions

Clarissa carried very few clothes about. All she had with her was in the aircraft holdall she clutched. I do not know about Aline. She must have had something. I cannot remember.

'I don't know when we'll meet again,' said Clarissa.

'In two or three days,' I said. 'Four at the most.' Since I had decided to remain, I had to seem calm.

'I may go and stay with Naomi. I want to think things out.'

She was wearing the lightest of blouses, little more than a mist. She was exquisite beyond description. Suddenly, I noticed that tears were again streaming silently down Aline's face.

'Or I may go somewhere else,' said Clarissa, and walked out, with her slight but distinctive wobble.

Instead of immediately following her, as she always did, Aline actually took two steps in my direction. She looked up at me, like a rococo cherub. Since I could not kiss Clarissa, I lightly kissed Aline's wet lips, and she kissed me.

I turned my back in order not to see the car actually depart, though nothing could prevent my hearing it. What had the row been really about? I could surmise and guess, but I did not know. I much doubted whether Clarissa knew. One could only be certain that she would explain herself, as it were to a third party, in a totally different way from me. We might just as well belong to different zoological species, as in the Ray Bradbury story. The row was probably a matter only of Clarissa being a woman and I a man. Most of all rows between the sexes have no more precise origin; and, indirectly, many other rows also.

I think I stood for some time with my back to the open door and my face to the picture of an old gillie in a tam, with dead animals almost to his knees. It had been given us by the Shepstones. It was named *Coronach* in Ruskinian letters, grimly misapplied. Ultimately, I turned and through the open door saw what Aline may have seen. The auld carlin was advancing across the drive with a view to entering.

Drive, I have to call it. It was a large area of discoloured nothingness upon which cars stood, and before them horses, but little grew, despite the lack of weeding. Needless to say, the woman was not approaching straightforwardly. Previously, I had seen her only when she had been confined to the limits of a staircase, albeit a wide one, a landing, and, later, a lift. If now she had been coming straight at me, I might have had a split second to see her face. I realised that, quite clearly, upon the instant.

I bounded forward. I slammed the door. The big key was difficult to turn in the big lock, so I shot the four rusty bolts first. Absurdly, there was a 'chain' also and, after I had coped with the stiff lock, I 'put it on'.

Then I tore round the house shooting other bolts; making sure that all other locks were secure; shutting every possible window and aperture, on that already very hot early morning.

It is amazing how much food Clarissa laid in. She was, or is, always open-handed. I am sure that I have made that clear. Nor of course does one need so much food—or at least want so much —in this intense heat. Nor as yet has the well run dry. Cuddy refused to show me the well, saying the key was lost. I have still not seen either thing.

There is little else to do but write this clear explanation of everything that has happened to me since the misfortune of birth. He that has fared better, and without deceiving himself, let him utter his jackass cry.

Not that I have surrendered. There lies the point. Pollaporra is not on the telephone, nor ever could be, pending the 'withering away of the State'; but before long someone may take note that I am not there. The marines may descend from choppers yet. Clarissa may well have second thoughts. Women commonly do, when left to themselves. She loves Pollaporra and may well devise a means of wresting my life interest away from me, and welcome. I don't know where Aline would enter into that hypothesis. Possibly I made a mistake in not writing to Mason that I was coming. But I doubt whether in such personal matters his time-scale is shorter than months.

Off and on, I see the woman at one window or another; though not peeking through, which, as will have been gathered, is far from her policy. At least twice, however, it has been at a window upstairs; on both occasions when I was about to undress for some reason, not necessarily slumber, of which I have little. At these times, her slimy-sleek head, always faceless, will tip-tap sharply against the thick glazing bars. The indelicacy, as Jack might put it (I wonder how Cuddy would put it?), set me upon a course of hard thinking.

So long as I keep myself barred up, she can achieve nothing. Mason seemed quite certain of that, and I accept it. But what does the woman aim to do to me? When she appeared to me before, my poor mother soon passed away. When she appeared to me a second time, my dear, dear Shulie vanished from my life. It is not to be taken for granted that either of these precise fates is intended for me. I am not even ill or infirm. There may be a certain room for manoeuvre, though I can foresee no details.

More often, I see the woman at corners of what used to be the lawn and garden, though never in my time. It lies at the back of the house, and far below lies the loch. Sometimes too, the creature perches on the ornaments and broken walls, like a sprite. Such levitations are said to be not uncommon in the remoter parts of Scotland. Once I thought I glimpsed her high up in a bush, like dirty rags in a gale. Not that so far there has

The Fetch

been any gale, or even any wind. The total silent stillness is one of the worst things. If I die of heat and deoxygenation, it will be one solution.

Yes, it is a battle with strong and unknown forces that I have on my hands. 'But what can ail all of them to bury the old carlin in the night time?' as Sir Walter ventures to enquire; in *The Antiquary*, if I remember rightly.

THE BREAKTHROUGH

WHATEVER MIGHT HAVE been said thereafter, I firmly testify that there was nothing unusual about the death of the previous rector, the Reverend Eliphas Jaunt D.D.

I had the most explicit assurance upon the point from Dr Chard, than whom no one was ever more dependable. Chard had been with Dr Jaunt within hours, merely, of the end; and had come to me immediately he received intelligence of the final passing.

I had already learned from experience that men often came to me or sent for me when they had something particular to say, and occasionally women too. So it was in due course with the Reverend Zebedee Stooling.

John Chard was equally adamant that there had been no parting message to the parish from Dr Jaunt. About actual last words, I do not know. The old rector spoke very little, at the best of times, to his niece, Lizzie Summerday, who was the only person to remain after the doctor had been called away. Lizzie herself never referred to the matter.

Dr Jaunt had ruled the far-flung parish with notable and proper firmness, so that he would have been a difficult man for anyone to follow. Moreover, the rector had to bear an exceptional measure of responsibility owing to the long absence of the squire, young Hugh Tathan-Mortlock. It was not that the boy was merely roving; on the contrary, he was prostrated by sickness, to lighten which balmier airs were required than any to be encountered on our wide marshes.

Of course by the time the Reverend Zebedee Stooling was inducted, the squire too could have been young no longer. It was simply that all still thought of him as young. What the squire could have done for the parish was in any case limited, because he had been raised as a Roman Catholic, and at a Roman Catholic school on the far side of the country; his father having been converted to that faith by the woman he insisted upon marrying. That the two children had been raised accordingly was inevitable.

It will at once be noted that the Reverend Zebedee Stooling was not a Doctor of Divinity. I suppose that the then churchwardens had assured themselves of such professional qualifications as he may have possessed, but I do not know what they were. The patron of our living was a Member of Parliament for some factory place; and few of us had ever seen or heard from him. I sometimes saw his name in the newspapers, however, and I noticed that in the end he was given a portfolio of some kind, though without a seat in the Cabinet, being an utter Radical. I suppose he was just the man to advance such an one as the Reverend Zebedee Stooling, who was a foundling, and from Lancashire.

It is necessary for me to be fair to the Reverend Mr Stooling, as we first encountered him. What told most against him was his appearance; and the extent to which we should judge people, men and women, by their appearance, is something that nobody agrees upon, because nobody really knows.

The Reverend Mr Stooling was smaller than almost any of us, though our locals belong to no race of giants, but noticeably the opposite; and there was also something yielding and boneless

Intrusions

about him that made one flinch at his touch. There is here an uncertainty of the same kind: to what extent should we be guided by intuitions of that kind? I thought that Stooling could be commended for kindness and gentleness (in so far as these should be male qualities), not for brilliance. What happened when the visitation lighted upon him did but confirm these impressions.

Not that the visitation was upon Stooling alone. It was upon very nearly all of us, and I have never seen that Stooling could justly have been blamed for anything very much, except perhaps for ever taking up a living for which he was so plainly too frail, even bodily. He had weakening hair, the colour of our marshland barley when it has rotted in the stem; and eyes which, though pale grey, were vague and did not seem to see very far. One could hardly find his mouth, but, on the other hand, his nose was remarkably long and prominent. On the strength of that nose, Napoleon himself might have advanced Mr Stooling. It was just such a nose as constituted Napoleon's main requirement for promotion. Above all, the poor little man moved with a very personal gait, highly delicate and noticeably sidelong.

And our parish was more than twenty-eight miles wide at the greatest extremity! That extremity took much working out upon a map, because the parish boundary wandered wonderfully, and hardly anywhere persisted in a straight line for as much as one-third of a mile. The Reverend Mr Stooling could not even ride a horse; though few would blame him for not tackling old Jaunt's horse, Fire, which had simply been left behind. He was not unfed because Lizzie went on feeding him. I knew that well. No one better. One could not properly call the structure in which the beast dwelt, a stable. We are a poor parish, and most of the parishioners would not care for their

The Breakthrough

pastor to be greatly more favoured in any way than most of them are. They are demanding people, as will be seen.

The Reverend Zebedee Stooling should, in many ways, have been just the man for them; but people are perverse. The rector's stipend was minimal, and it could soon be surmised that Stooling had very little of his own with which to augment it; possibly nothing whatever. This situation led to his being looked down upon and made it doubly difficult for him to exercise the miscellaneous duties that, as I have said, fell upon everyone of our rectors from the outset, however arbitrarily.

The hard, and only in part Christian, matter of pounds, shillings, and pence bore down upon the parish severely at that time because the church had been so completely neglected that it looked as if about to fall; so that the womenfolk, normally the prop of parochial life everywhere, were refusing to enter it. The churchwardens had been too deeply involved for too long a time with transactions at our local public house, The Magpie; and a few said that Dr Jaunt in some degree had actually connived at this. I can only confirm that one of the churchwardens in question, the rector's man, died during an incident of *delirium tremens*, with John Chard standing by. That was soon after the Reverend Zebedee Stooling had replaced him in his office by another.

The successor was a humble man named Toddy Lewis, who with his wife and daughters kept a small shop: not exactly a popular appointment. Of course, Stooling at that time hardly knew anyone in the parish, and had to accept what he could find.

None the less, he managed to eject the people's warden also, so that the man actually left the parish, perhaps also while under the power of his drink. Assuredly, he never returned. I do not know how Sailor Onslow came to take his place. I never heard

Intrusions

of a discussion or an election. Sailor Onslow was so called by everyone. I have reason to believe that he had never so much as sighted the sea, even though the sea was not all that far off, and a very wild and frisky sea too, of which we could feel the sting through much of the winter. Sailor Onslow was even more unlettered than poor Toddy Lewis, but, I fancied, greatly more devious. He was not even securely settled in matrimony. Again, everyone, including Mr Stooling, had been compelled to make the best of what could be found.

All things considered, it was amazing how much progress the three of them seemed to make. At the outset, that is. All know how things ended, though few trouble themselves with any accuracy of detail.

The Reverend Mr Stooling managed to bring an expert from near London, who reported that the women had been right all the time, and that the church was no longer safe to go near. All who had attended the Reverend Zebedee Stooling's induction must have stood in appreciable peril. I admit that I had not been among them. We understood that the expert had assured himself and us of this for no more than the bare expenses of his slow journey.

There could be no question of our affording a fashionable contractor. There were three stout men in the parish who some time before had set up together as builders, and to them, of necessity, the rector and wardens had recourse. The trio had banded together on equal terms, always a precarious arrangement; and there was not even a definite name for the enterprise. None the less, they agreed to go ahead with the work at the church as the money might come in to pay for it. In the intervals, they would continue, as thereunto, with mending cottage roofs, and reflooring the damp farms, and generally making themselves useful. The three stalwarts were known to all as

The Breakthrough

Zack, Aar, and Reba. Nomenclature from Holy Writ has always been preferred in the parish. Reba, it will be recalled, was the leader of Midian who was killed on the Plain of Moab. I myself took care to abridge and modify my name before settling. I also put my Imperial title of nobility into abeyance.

But the amazement to which I have referred was, in the nature of things, mainly a matter of how well and how fast the money seemed to flow in—and, necessarily, out. One could not divine how it was happening, but the three heroes seemed in no time to be continuously at work in the shut-up church; and one knew well that they were in no position to offer unlimited credit. The church had been founded by a blessed saint who had come in from the sea (legend declared from the seabed) and had soon converted the entire region, from gilded king to blue swineherd. Somehow the building had crept into history as dedicated to this saint, though such a dedication can only have had effect after the saint's elevation, as is obvious. It was natural for a few to think that the ceremonial reopening of the west door (a single, not a double leaf) should be the occasion for a total rededication of the entire structure. Wild expedients of that kind always find a following.

In the end, the popular amazement about where the money was coming from died down. Soon there were other matters to wonder about; and to grieve about also. But in my wish to be entirely just to the Reverend Mr Stooling, I set down what came to my ears about the money, though not to my eyes. Ah, my gaze had long been inturned; and my panorama of the fixed past!

It is true that there was a public appeal of a kind, but what could be hoped from it in such a place, and with even the squire sick and overseas? I only knew what old Slow whispered to me that evening when all my cherry trees were flickering into bloom.

Intrusions

Old Slow is worth a word from me in his own right. He was huge and grey and bald and shambling, and his garments were beyond all description for mess and makeshift, and no one could put a name to any work he did or to how, with any honesty, he survived, but he knew more than anyone else, far more, about everything that happened to each single soul in the parish, and to their beasts too. I was aware, for example, that he knew more than was needful about me, and I acknowledge that I made a point of keeping on terms with him. On the other hand, I knew that he liked talking to me, because in the nature of things I was able to understand more than the others, so much more. I do not know whether Slow was his real name. It seems doubtful; especially at this distance of time. He lived in a biggin on one of the deserted holdings far out to the north-west; in fact, on the most direct line to the sea. Old Slow claimed that he could hear the sea every night as he lay abed, but it seemed unlikely, and no one ever visited him to check. To start with, it was simply too far for most of them to go. It was true, however, that Slow had unusually keen ears. That was always obvious. Keen eyes, and a keen nose also, and keen stubby fingers, like a pig.

As I fondled the cherry buds, the talk turned, as it always did at that time, to the works at the church and to the apparent availability of specie to pay for them. How did the rector come by it?

'He digs for it,' said Slow, in his knowing way, aiming to take one by surprise. The habit could be irritating, but one had to endure it if one wished to know what was going on, let alone to be on terms with the wayward old fellow.

'Where does the rector do that?'

'In his garden. I watched him.'

'Did he see you watching him?'

'It made no difference. It was God's work, the digging.'

The Breakthrough

'Did the gold come up in single coins?'

'In pieces of all kinds. Some big. Some small. Some light and shining. Some bent and rusty.'

'I'm not sure that gold does rust, Slow,' I said, smiling.

'Every metal moulded by man goes to rust in the end, master. You know that.'

'What did Mr Stooling do next?'

'He fell upon his knees and gave thanks. That's what he did.'

'And you?'

'I offered thanks too, master. How should I not? You would have offered thanks yourself.'

'And then?'

'When I got to my feet and put back my hat and looked over the hedge, the rector had gone away. And the gold too. There was only the hole.'

'Is the hole still there?'

'No, master. It's been filled, has that hole.'

I considered for a moment or two. There was no need for haste.

'Do you suppose it's some kind of buried treasure?' I enquired. There had always been tales; though I understood that there were tales of the kind in most places.

'Buried by God,' said old Slow, touching his hat, which lacked all shape but had its own dignity. 'He provides for all of us when the need is there. You know that, master.'

It was something that, by any reasonable standard, I did not know at all, that I was the last person in the parish to know; and Slow had a better idea of this fact than most. But Slow's statement was of a kind that one seldom debates.

'A remarkably opportune find,' I observed; and we went on to other local topics.

Intrusions

Whatever my inner attitude to the nature of the universe, the idea was thus first brought home to me that the Reverend Zebedee Stooling might be a man marked out, and that his superficial shortcomings, including intellectual shortcomings, might be misleading in important respects. I fear, however, that the notion did not draw me any nearer in feeling to Mr Stooling, but rather the contrary. I had been positively avoiding all chance of coming near Stooling, and never once went to a service in the disused tithe barn, which had been deputising for our parish church since his arrival.

The only other specifically ecclesiastical structure that exists, as far as I know, in the entire parish, is in ruins. It was in ruins then, and had long been so. Once it had been the church of another parish, but the two parishes were amalgamated when the other parish found that it had no congregation left. I do not think it was a matter of disease or of anything prodigious. It was simply that in ones, twos, and threes, the people had hoped to fare better elsewhere. By the time of which I speak, their church had been virtually demolished to mend walls and provide firestones. Having been formally deconsecrated by the Lord Bishop, it was believed to harbour evil spirits, and very possibly did, as far as I am concerned. Looters were not deterred, and, after the deconsecration, no doubt the looters were within their rights. On days of holidays, one could sometimes see the village lads winging fragments of the crockets and statuary through the air at one another, and at the creatures, and at all strangers.

Through the long winters, the wind from the sea would for weeks on end blow so hard that only the very strong could stand against it, and the dykes and rhenes would flow unconstrainedly across farmland and marsh alike, often isolating the parish for unpredictable periods, yet in anything like warm weather the land would seem quickly to parch and crack and the supply

The Breakthrough

become uncertain of water fit for humans to drink. One would notice the womenfolk tramping for miles, there and back, with pails, sometimes suspended in pairs from the yokes used in the rustic dairies. Water was then offered for sale as in India, and one felt that the bearers well deserved their modicum of reward. One tended to lose one's head as the heat and airlessness increased past all bearing. It seemed to happen each year, and each year the summer seemed endless. I suppose the climate was much the same as in Madrid, where I lived for above three years: but in Madrid there were lovely ladies and the grand opera and poetry; and cockfights and bullfights to keep other men occupied.

That summer when the church was being repaired seemed the hottest ever, but as one thought the same every year, I daresay it was nothing of the kind. There was a thermometer in the rectory, but I was aiming at the time not to visit the rectory, as I have said. One wondered how the three church toilers could possibly continue in the stagnant mist. In Spain, there was at least the custom of the siesta, but English workers have always preferred to return home in good time, by eight o'clock or half-past. In fact, the heat may have contributed to the incident in the church; or at least the heat could be in part blamed for it by the freethinkers, if we had any.

'They had a great big lump of lead up there or perhaps it was iron,' explained old Slow across my garden gate. 'It was needed for their work.'

The cherry blossoms had withered now, as cherry blossoms so instantly do. They were brown and foetid on the branches. The plum and greengage flowers were beginning to come forward.

Slow paused, in his tantalising way; demanding that one contribute a question.

'And what did they do with it?' I asked.

Intrusions

'They let it fall,' said Slow. 'That's what they did. You must have heard, master.'

'I heard nothing.' It was not clear whether it was the concussion that I should have heard, or the rumour. If the latter, I heard little but from Slow himself, and Slow knew that perfectly well also.

'It was heard by one and all, master,' said Slow persuasively.

'Not by me, Slow, I promise you. What happened then?'

'It split the stones in the floor. They haven't told anyone. They daren't.'

'I can understand that,' I said. 'How long ago was this?'

'Nine days and a half, and they've not told anyone.'

'I suppose they hope to mend the floor before anyone hears about it.'

'One and all heard, master. Everyone heard.'

'Well, I didn't, Slow,' I persisted, smiling.

'The Reverend heard,' said Slow.

'Do you actually know that?'

Possibly I should not have asked such a question, but my relationship with Slow, if one may use such a word, was always rather odd and involved.

'I do know it, master,' said Slow, with great conviction; such as he displayed when giving consideration to the affairs of other people.

At that point, the whole incident seemed of small importance; so I directed the conversation, as usual, to other local procedures of no greater seeming consequence.

When, in turn, the plum and greengage blossoms were tending to over-maturity (I have always been one who prefers the flowers to the fruits), old Slow actually brought me a message. It

The Breakthrough

was the first time it had happened; and even now, the message was but verbal.

Suddenly Slow loomed at my gate; I being in the garden, as so often, the year round.

'The Reverend says he wants to see you, master.'

'Surely not, Slow? Whatever about?' One asked such questions of old Slow without a second thought.

'About the church floor, master,' said old Slow, with a what-did-I-tell-you look on his huge face, cratered as they say the moon is.

'I'm not an architect, Slow, nor yet a theologian, nor yet a stonemason.'

'I know that, master, and the Reverend knows it too. That's for certain sure.'

Slow knew well how to be perfectly accurate and highly impertinent in the same instant. He achieved it frequently. One simply had to bear with him.

I looked at him hard. 'When?' I asked. 'Did Mr Stooling suggest a time?'

'At once, master, if you ask me. Now. As soon as may be. The Reverend's in a difficulty.'

I managed to abstain from asking what the difficulty might be. It must concern more than a few cracks in the church floor, if I had been summoned: that was for sure, as Slow would have put it.

None the less, I was certainly not proposing to walk hand in hand with old Slow clean through all the locals to the rectory; or, for that matter, a step behind him or a step ahead of him.

'Tell Mr Stooling that I shall be pleased to wait upon him this evening at six o'clock.'

Slow looked doubtful; but cunning also.

Intrusions

'It's urgent, master. The Reverend needs the help of an educated man.'

I could not but hesitate. 'What exactly do you mean by that, Slow? How do you know?'

'I know, master,' said Slow. 'But the Reverend will tell you about it himself—though not all about it, perhaps. He's an educated man too, is the Reverend, though not like you, master.'

This was Slow at his most typical and his most irritating, and all too well did I know both things. Still, I was bound by my obligation as a parishioner.

'Six o'clock at the rectory, Slow. That is my last word. For the present, I have no more to say.'

I turned aside and began to fondle the plum and greengage blossoms, in corruption though they already were. I perceived perfectly well, none the less, that old Slow was taking his time in going upon his way. I refused all response, except to the faded flowers.

But in the end, the blossoms saddened me beyond bearing. I stepped into my house, with all the slowness of grief, and on the polished floor of my hall, polished at my cost by women from the foundry cottages, polished by them daily, was a single muddy footmark.

It was small, but, as far as I knew, nowhere in the district had there been soft mud for many weeks. In any case, though I might spend much of my time in the garden, I seldom left my little demesne entirely, and had certainly not done so since that morning, when equally certainly there had been no such mud on my fine floor, or I should have directed the women to it, possibly even shrilly. There could have been no flesh-and-blood intruder upon me. I admit that I recalled the tales of the Winter Folk, who in full summer leave just such evidences of their

The Breakthrough

continuing entry: much as girls notice single grey hairs on fine spring mornings.

I made no attempt to remove the mark. I had long ago succeeded in making myself a creature of routine and this mark gave no reason to depart from it.

Therefore, as was my wont, I drew out a bottle of *fino* from the bin in the cellar and withdrew to my stone seat, where I spent the rest of the afternoon musing. The habit of drinking *fino* as a *vin de table*, a bottle at a time, was something else I had learned in Spain.

It is a scattered village, as I have said, so scattered as to be hardly a village in the usual sense at all, and I required a good third of an hour for the walk to the rectory. At twenty-five minutes to six, I changed my clothes, assumed my visiting hat, and drew my stick from the stand. My visiting hat, now replacing my scarecrow garden hat, had been bought in Baden-Baden during my years of illusion. I should have been glad that torrid evening of a wider and more malleable brim, but I strode forward warily. The locals offer little in the way of greeting, in any circumstances. Why should they? In particular: what could they have possibly said to me, or I to them?

At the big gate of the rectory, I looked at my repeater and waited for it to strike the hour at my touch before I entered and sauntered up the drive. I certainly did not wish to embarrass the Reverend Mr Stooling by arriving prematurely.

The rectory had been planned in the last century as an extremely large building, but had been only about one-third completed or less, leaving an effect as curious as it was desolate. The place was amply large enough, notwithstanding, for its present diminutive and solitary tenant.

Intrusions

A burly lug had always been necessary at the bell, but there had never been any doubt about the resounding response, when the necessary exertions had been applied; nor was there now. Despite all I knew and had surmised, I was distinctly taken aback when the huge dark door was opened by the Reverend Mr Stooling himself. Dr Jaunt had always, even at the worst, kept two or three persons around the house to look after him and Lizzie and such visitors as might occasionally present themselves.

Clearly our new incumbent could see the facts of the matter for himself. 'I'm so sorry' were his first words. 'I am all alone in the house.' He smiled weakly beneath his nose, as he uttered.

But, before I could reassure him, he went on—or more or less on. 'Well, that is to say—' he said. He then tried to smile again, though less successfully; and came to a standstill.

'Say no more,' I cried out. 'No man can answer for all things at once.'

'I should hardly know what to say,' responded the Reverend Mr Stooling. He was still clinging to the edge of the door, like a puppet to its curtain, and ascending, as to the top of his head, about to the third button upwards of my checked summer waistcoat.

'Shall I enter?' I enquired. 'I understand that you have summoned me.'

'Oh, come in, come in by all means,' he said, seeming to droop still further as he let go of the knob. He spoke as if it were I that was soliciting, but the thing had to be seen through to a conclusion, and it would have been absurd to delay any longer.

'One thing those labourers of yours, Stooling, might do,' I said, 'would be to restart the church clock.'

Of course I was mainly trying to set him more at ease. The church clock had never moved since I had first beheld the

The Breakthrough

village, and it had been one of the subjects upon which I had never found Dr Jaunt helpful.

The hall within was dark, because all the roller blinds were down. I at once doubted whether they had ever been raised since Jaunt's illness. The hall was a very big room; indicative of the proportions which should have been sustained through the entire structure, but never had been.

'I am not quite sure about that,' said Stooling, finding his voice, and even venturing to argue. Then he added: 'I am not quite sure about anything at the moment.' I could see his pale grey eyes glance at me through the gloom. 'Not about anything at all.' He partly pulled himself together. 'In any case, I fancy that a professional horologist might be needed. He might have to take the clock away. There is very little remaining behind the two faces, as you possibly know. I once climbed up to see for myself.'

'It was all there the last time I saw it,' I said, speaking the firm truth. 'It only needed a large can of oil and reasonable elbow grease and perhaps a hammer.'

'That is by no means the case now,' said Stooling. 'Better go carefully here. The floor is weak.'

'I recollect,' I said.

I could hardly be expected to argue with him any more about the parish clock, but I could at least make clear that I had known the rectory, off and on, for a good many years now.

We entered a room which was not the one Dr Jaunt had used as his study and library. The room we were in had in fact been Lizzie's closet. It was quite small, and, by now, foetid in the heat.

'I'm sorry, but could we begin by letting in some air.'

'I think not,' said the Reverend Mr Stooling, and delivering himself quite firmly; wherever the firmness might come from.

Intrusions

'You will see why I hesitate when—' But again, he merely stopped speaking.

'Perhaps, then, another and larger room?' I suggested. It was to be noted that Stooling had not argued about the conditions in this one, as he had argued about the church clock. 'What about the room Dr Jaunt used to work in?'

'No,' said Stooling, turning away from me, so that I could not see his face. 'Not that room.'

'Well then, the dining room?' I persisted. It was the last of the so-called reception rooms on the ground floor—as the house had been left so far from completed. There was supposed to be a large drawing room upstairs, but Dr Jaunt had been unmarried, and Lizzie was said to have filled it with her looms.

'I have not had occasion to make use of the dining room, and you may find it dusty. But if you would really prefer. . . . Shall I take your stick?'

'No, I shall retain it, if I may.'

We returned to the hall, and Stooling forced open the dining-room door. The room inside was indeed neglected, but, in other respects, exactly the same as in Dr Jaunt's day. It had been impossible to find a buyer for any of the rectory furniture, so that Stooling had been fortunate enough to take possession of it. Again, the air needed to be changed, as was inevitable, but at least the room was spacious in its proportions.

'Please sit down,' said the Reverend Mr Stooling.

I walked round the room, behind the college chair in which Dr Jaunt used to preside, with Lizzie always at the very far end of the long table; and seated myself with my back to the windows over-looking the northern part of the lawn, now an expanse of withered hay. The house was more distinctly set east and west, than north and south. Throughout the village, one was always conscious of the compass points.

The Breakthrough

Stooling merely stood himself against the big mantel, which Dr Jaunt had had decorated with the arms of various places of learning that boasted theological faculties. Jaunt had constantly alluded in conversation and in the pulpit to theology as 'the Queen of the arts'. Stooling hardly reached to the arms of Freiburg; hardly more than half the distance up to the spacious horizontal shelf, above which had hung always, and hung still, the picture of Queen Guinevere entering her convent after her great sin; a just requital no doubt, but a hard one, and a rare one.

'Mr van Goort,' said Stooling. 'It is good of you to visit me.'

I bowed from my seated position.

'I am sorry that I have no refreshment to offer. I live humbly and soberly. Or so I had supposed.'

Ignoring the last words, of a kind so frequent and no doubt so proper on the lips of clerics, I bowed again.

Stooling went off in a new direction. 'I take it, Mr van Goort, that you are of Low Countries origin?'

This remark was an example of the Reverend Mr Stooling's simplicity of mind to which I have alluded earlier; but I merely responded with the facts.

'My father was an Englishman of the second generation, but of the second generation only, and his mother was a French lady. His wife, my mother, was half Spanish and half Greek.'

The pale grey eyes wandered in my direction once more; and this time they even lingered. The room was all dark surfaces, as rectory dining rooms tend to be, and doubtless suitably are. The embellishments attributable to Dr Jaunt did little positively to lighten the total tableau. The weather without was as usual in the village, throughout the year; more misty or steamy than lucid. The Reverend Mr Stooling, as he stood there, barely half way to the mantelshelf, looked positively elfin, shrimplike.

Intrusions

'I need to talk to what is known as an educated man.' He spoke and, without this time actually breaking off midway, paused unduly, while giving the impression of proposing to continue.

Again I thought it best, after a moment, merely to rejoin with the facts.

'I was educated by tutors, excellent tutors; and later at Louvain and Uppsala Universities; later still at the Collège des Pages.'

'I hardly need to say, Mr van Goort, that being an educated man in the sense I had in mind, is only in part a matter where the man in question went for formal learning.'

As can be imagined, I was somewhat surprised by a remark of this kind, despite what old Slow had said; but all I replied was 'Certainly', while slightly bowing yet again over the top of my stick. I tried to recognise that as a man of the cloth he had the right to go considerably further than others, and sometimes the obligation.

'Besides,' he now continued, 'I take you to be a man of wide experience? It is so reported of you. That you are what is called a man of the world?'

'I do not know about the reporting,' I said, and indeed I did not, and had no wish to; 'but it is true that in earlier years I lived for extended periods in Valparaiso, in Peking, in Smyrna, and in Madrid. I do not know whether that makes me a man of the world or not.' And, once again, it was true that I did not know. I still do not know. Who does know?

'And now you live here?' said Stooling. 'And have done so for a quite long time?'

As I said nothing to that, he paused a few seconds, and then came out with it. 'Why, Mr van Goort? Why? I should not ask if I did not need to know. Believe me, I should not.'

The Breakthrough

My reply came at once.

'I found myself disappointed alike in the affairs of the state, of the Muses and graces, of the sociabilities, even of the pocket, and, above all, of the heart: that above all, my good Stooling.'

Steadily the facts; simply the plain facts so seldom spoken. Perhaps I was addressing Stooling's office and authority, rather than the minuscule man himself.

He turned aside once more; this time right round until he faced the empty iron grate, looking down into it, and stood with his back to me.

'You know about the cavity made in the floor of the church? You undoubtedly heard the detonation that broke the floor open? You could not conceivably have missed it?'

'I cannot claim that I have not heard something—very little—of the occurrence you mention, but I did not hear the event itself. I assure you of that.'

'My God,' said Stooling still with his back to me. 'Where can you possibly have been?'

'Very probably in my garden, Stooling. None the less—' I spread my hands wide, as one does; before realising that he was not looking at them. It was in any case unexpected for a clergyman, and especially for such a comparatively young one, to resort to such an expletive.

'You are the only man who missed it,' cried Stooling, turning back to me, so that at least I could better hear what he said. 'Here—in the rectory—it was as the single discharge of thunder promised us upon the last day.'

'I am sorry I missed it,' I said. 'I am sorry too that it happened; no doubt causing further damage when there was so much already. But what follows? Is it a matter of money?'

I had, of course, borne that in mind from the first, as who would not? I was perfectly prepared to contribute fairly handsomely, as one should when one resides in a place. I spent money on little now, save on inexpensive plants, trees, wine, books, random curiosities.

'No,' said Stooling. 'It is not a matter of money. Or not immediately. I have been able to come upon some money. Enough for present purposes, though not for all that is needed. Perhaps this will surprise you, Mr van Goort?'

As I could not admit to gossiping with old Slow, and as Stooling plainly expected me to be surprised, I did my best in that direction.

'It is natural that you should express such astonishment,' said Stooling. 'You will be even more astonished to learn that I was guided.'

'It is the benison of your cloth,' I responded.

'No, Mr van Goort, it was not that. Not that at all. At least, I think not. Most people would think not.'

He had been staring at me across the long, dusty table, but now was beginning to falter once more.

'Stooling,' I cried out. 'If you wish to tell me whatever it is that you have in your mind, please do so plainly and directly. You are right in supposing that I have seen much of the world. I am a man difficult to surprise either by angel or by devil, but especially by the latter, especially by the latter, Stooling.'

He drew out one of the heavy carved chairs on his side of the table and sank down upon it; to all appearance, the size of a schoolboy, or even smaller. He gazed up at one of the college crests which Jaunt had lined out above the picture rail. He took his time before beginning.

'I knew at once, Mr van Goort, that the crash had come from within the church, and because of the works that were supposedly being carried out there, I was fearful. Very unexpected things are known sometimes to happen when churches

The Breakthrough

are under heavy repair. There are always quite particular perils. I ran out of the rectory, and I admit that I left the door open. There is little here of value to any thief. Certainly little of mine.'

As he paused, I took it for my part to help him on.

'Why describe the works at the church as being supposedly carried out? Was there any doubt about it?'

'At the start there had been very little money, and the workers had formed habits of their own, which were difficult to break. They were often absent. When I reached the church that afternoon, it was a case in point. I found the door locked. I hammered upon it, but of course there was no response.'

'But do you not, as rector, have a key? More than one key, I should have supposed?'

'There is only one key to the church, Mr van Goort. I am told that my predecessor withdrew the keys from the churchwardens because of alleged irregularities. I do not know what has become of those keys. They are said to have been cast down the well. As you know, both the churchwardens of that period ceased to serve, and neither in happy circumstances. Their successors are simple men, and, while perhaps more devout, know very little.'

'But surely another key can be cut?'

'That involves a visit to a locksmith, Mr van Goort, and is not an easy matter. I cannot ask the churchwardens to attend to it, and I myself cannot attend to it now. Least of all, now.'

'So the one key is in the possession of the workers, and they were not in the church when you heard this crash? Perhaps it was as well, or they might have suffered injury?'

'I at first thought that they had, Mr van Goort. I feared the very worst for all of them. Then of course I reflected that dead men cannot lock doors.'

Intrusions

'We take it they cannot,' I confirmed: though I was one who knew better.

'At first I was greatly relieved by that consideration,' Stooling went on, 'and, as there was no means of telling what had happened, I sped back to the rectory. I admit that I was in a confused state of mind. There have been many troubles in this parish, Mr van Goort, that only I know of, though it is right that only I should know. I have acknowledged also that I had left the front door not merely unlocked but open. I had left open as well the door into my predecessor's study. As soon as I came into the house I saw at once that there was something in that room. Something dreadful and appalling, Mr van Goort.'

As is my way, I found words at once for what had come to my mind.

'Do you mean that you saw Dr Jaunt's ghost? Or thought that you saw it?'

However much or little a man of the world I may truly be, I at least know enough to take apparitions, portents, and many kindred visitations as among the most serious and real phenomena there are. Men are but fools or cravens who do otherwise. The womenfolk never think of doing otherwise, so, under this head, they are exempt from stricture.

'No, Mr van Goort, it was not that at all. Allow me a moment to seek words. It is in the nature of things that I find it difficult to go further. Assuredly, it is in my nature to find it difficult.'

'Stooling,' I said firmly, perhaps even sternly, 'once again there is nothing you can say that will disconcert me in any degree. Now that you have summoned me from my house, I take it for your duty to tell me every detail you can recollect.'

All the time, an unhappy bee was buzzing and bumping round the stuffy room unable to find freedom because Stooling

The Breakthrough

refused to open a window. Of course I had begun to have more than an inkling of why he refused. It was not the moment to speak.

Stooling did as I had suggested to him.

'It was very tall and triangular and in very bright hues, and at the tip of it was a head—of a kind, with what seemed to be long hair, quite colourless.'

'How tall was it? Or how high? Perhaps that is the better word.'

'Six or seven feet, I should estimate. I myself am under five feet. That may make my estimate unreliable.'

'As well as the hair you speak of, could you see a face?'

'It was as if a face had been painted on.'

'On what, do you suppose?'

'On my own eyes and mind, I daresay,' said Stooling, a trifle vacantly.

'This thing—whatever it was—did it move in any manner?'

'It did not then,' said Stooling. 'Not then.'

'What made you think it was anything but a joke by the boys? A village joke. I've suffered from village jokes several times. Dr Jaunt suffered from them too until he took very strong action.'

'I did think it might be that.'

'Did you go forward and examine? Give the whole thing a pretty sharp shake or push? I accept that it might not have been easy to do.'

'I did nothing, Mr van Goort. I fled once more from the house.'

'I can understand that,' I said. 'But you must have come back?'

'Not for a long time. But I had nowhere to go. My church was inaccessible, and I have not found this a friendly parish. Not friendly in any way, Mr van Goort. I was far from sure who would take me in. And with such a story. Starting with that terrible crash, which must have agitated everybody! I admit that it passed through my mind to walk on and visit you.'

'I am habitually at home,' I said. 'You would of course have been made welcome.' There was nothing else that it would have been proper to say, or thinkable.

Stooling continued. 'I am ashamed to say it, but I was left with no other possibility than to go back, and quite soon. I could not allow myself to be observed merely loitering.'

'And then?' I asked.

'That time, upon taking to my heels, I had shut the front door. It made no sense, because I had merely shut the being in. I really believe my idea was to prevent anything else entering. You can see how disordered I myself was.'

'It is an instinct to shut the door when one leaves the house,' I rejoined. 'Or it should be.'

'When I returned the being seemed to have gone.'

'The boys had dismantled it.'

'I thought that too. But it was not so. There were no boys involved. I learned that when I saw the thing again.'

'Indeed!' I said. 'How soon after was that?' I was resolutely and authentically unshaken. My task was to be a wall of stone from which the Reverend Mr Stooling's successive waves of panic should rebound.

'When I went to bed, it was in the room before me.'

'The boys had moved it upstairs. They knew that in the end you would have to retire. Had you previously gone to your bedroom after returning to the rectory?'

'I must admit I had not. But it is beside the point. Because this time the being moved. I saw it move.'

'I can only reply that when the boys visited me, they set up things that moved too. On more than one occasion. They were

The Breakthrough

lucky I did not shoot them dead. Are you sure it was not the same with you? They would have known that you would be unlikely even to possess a gun.'

'As a matter of fact, though I do not own a gun, I can lay hands on several. And upon the bullets too. They all belonged to my predecessor.'

'I recall,' I said. 'I know well.'

I had assumed that Lizzie had taken all her uncle's weapons when she removed to her cottage. That might well have been wise when access by the boys would have been so easy.

'The whole affair was nothing whatever to do with boys, Mr van Goort. I promise you that. So much was made perfectly plain to me on the night I speak of. Was not. And is not.'

'And is not?' I duly picked up the point, as presumably I was intended to do.

The Reverend Mr Stooling simply shook his head.

For the moment, he changed the subject.

'Do you think we should kill that bee?' he said. 'Is it not distracting us?'

'I think we should expel it,' I corrected. 'But that will be difficult when we cannot open a window.'

So the poor bee continued to buzz and break itself while we did nothing but talk of other matters.

'Are you implying,' I went on to ask, 'that the thing you speak of is still within the rectory? The thing, the object, whatever we take it to be. That it is still here with us?'

'I take it,' said Stooling, 'to be neither a thing nor an object. I take it to be a person. Of a kind. Of a very singular kind, without doubt. That became clear to me on the evening of which I have spoken. And I imply that it is not merely still within the rectory, but elsewhere in the village also. In many other places, according to reports, and in many other shapes, too. I take it that you have not seen it yourself?'

'No,' I replied. 'I have not.' I was aiming neither to ridicule nor to belittle. Perhaps for that reason, I added, 'Not yet.'

'You will see why I needed to speak to an educated man,' observed Stooling. 'I sometimes suspect that many of the parishioners take the other side against me not merely in some things, but in all things. They do it because I am the man I am.'

'You will recall what I said, Stooling, about angels and devils, and there being more of the latter, according to my experience, which you rightly describe as wide.'

'That is against divine teaching,' said Stooling.

'Tell me,' I said after a moment, 'what happened about the church, and about entering it?'

'I will tell you. A certain amount of what followed falls into place. Up to a point, I can even see a certain logic.' But he stopped once more.

I tried again to encourage him. 'I suspect that point of being the point at which most of us cease to see logic,' I said.

'All the world is in the hands of its Maker, Who created it,' said Stooling. Then he went on. 'Many weeks later the three men came to me. They said they wanted to make a confession to me. They were in so forlorn a state that I admit to thinking at first of the Roman usage, prohibited to our church under its Articles.'

'There is much in favour of the Roman sacrament, Stooling. I speak as one who has lived long in lands where it is habitual.'

'That must be so, Mr van Goort, or the sacrament, as you describe it, would hardly have endured in so many places for so long. But to us it is categorically forbidden, as you are aware. My three visitors that morning had probably not even heard of

The Breakthrough

its existence. They came very early in the morning, very early indeed. As if they had come to be hanged or shot.'

'That is a striking simile, Stooling.'

'I heard them tap-tapping at the rectory front door when I was still in bed. I have never managed to repair the bell wires, which I understand were torn down. I hoped that whoever it was would go away, especially as no attempt was being made at a louder noise. Most of my parishioners seem to be far less restrained. In the end, I descended in my nightshirt. They were standing with their caps in their hands. That too is not as customary here as it should be.'

'Dr Jaunt used to strike the cap from the man's head, in cases of doubt,' I said.

'Yes,' said the Reverend Mr Stooling. 'But Dr Jaunt was, in cases of doubt, capable, as I understand, of next striking the man himself. To the ground, if necessary.'

I had, after all, to recognise a certain verbal adroitness in Stooling. Nothing could have surprised me more.

'Truly,' I said. 'Dr Jaunt had at one period entered the ring as an amateur and caused great carnage.'

Stooling wisely proceeded no further with such comparisons, but resumed his narrative.

'What the men had to confess, as they called it, was that between them they had let fall the great iron globe from a high place. I do not fully understand the normal usage of the globe. For breaking thick walls, I presume. On the present occasion, it breached the floor of the church, making the uproar we all heard—all but you, Mr van Goort. Awestruck and half deafened, the men scrambled down from their place under the roof and gazed into the pit they had created. What they saw down there filled them with much greater awe. They told me most graphically how they had behaved. The three of them actually clung to one another. Three fully grown men from this village, Mr van Goort.'

'I know by sight the three fellows in question,' I said. As a matter of fact, and as I have remarked before, the people of the village are in general of not great stature, nor were these three exceptions. The picture that Stooling had left with me was more of three conjoined gnomes, as in Sicily.

'Upon the instant, they one and all made off. Never forgetting, however, to lock the door of the church, and to retain the single key. That I understood. I fancied that I knew well how they had felt.'

'From the way you put it,' I interjected, 'I take it that what the three fellows saw in the open vault was something akin to what you saw, or thought you saw, in Dr Jaunt's study and library?'

'Not only in that one apartment, Mr van Goort, I must remind you. By no means only there. But, yes. It was the same being. They too saw it stir. All three of them saw it do so. It was that which finally drove them forth, still not forgetting to lock the being in behind them, whatever they had managed to make of it. They did not omit to do what they could in their simple way.'

'One might possibly put it that the thing stirred upon being too roughly awakened?'

'Possibly, Mr van Goort. The three men were naturally frightened to come to me with the tale of the damage they had done to the church. And the rest of the story was far more frightening to anybody. So it took the men many weeks to collect themselves and reach a decision. Whole weeks, in the lives of perfectly hale craftsmen, by no means well endowed! And when they did speak to me, they conflated the two aspects of the matter, whether by prepurpose or otherwise. I admit that I should

The Breakthrough

have been much more severe, as far as lay within my power, in the matter of the ruination to the church, had I not felt from my own experience that they had probably suffered enough already for their carelessness.'

'Is there a memorial above the vault in question?' I asked.

'There is no memorial. I have lately wondered whether a Red Indian, male or female, was once laid to rest beneath our church,' said Stooling. 'There are such cases at various spots in England, I understand.'

'Or possibly a gypsy? Or a stage player? Or a Roman cardinal?' I suggested; perhaps a trifle facetiously, and therefore no doubt improperly, owing to the man's obvious distress with the whole business.

'I do not think that what I have seen appertains to any of those categories, but most of all to that of a painted Indian,' said Stooling seriously.

We had come to something of a standstill. Even the imprisoned bee had ceased to buzz. One could but hope that through some crevice it had returned to the parched blooms of our wilderness. It had always been unlikely that Stooling had any precise plan to lay before me. It was for me to do what I could with the situation. For that I had been summoned. I tried to assemble the loose ends in Stooling's tale, and the open questions.

'The men went back to work in the church?' I enquired.

'No. They refused. But they are at work elsewhere in the community, as you may have noticed.'

'They gave you back the key?'

'Oh, yes.'

'And you have since seen this precious hole for yourself, and what lies within it?'

'Nothing now lies within it.'

Intrusions

'You have seen as much with your own eyes?'

'Yes, I have accomplished that much.'

With my fingers I began to draw shapes in the dust upon the table.

'Your plain suggestion, Stooling, is that the object or thing—'

'*Being*, Mr van Goort. *Being*, I swear to you. Even *person*.'

'I will accept that at this point. Your suggestion then is that the being, as you wish to term it, has left its place in the church and begun to haunt this house. I must tell you that I have heard of many such cases following incidents such as you have described. However inconvenient, it is not, I fear, a happening unusual in itself.'

'I am not suggesting, Mr van Goort, that this house alone is now haunted, though that term is yours, and not one that I have at any time employed. I think the word haunting implies occasional appearances only, merely intermittent activities. A more proper term in this case might be simply inhabited. But it is not this house only that is so inhabited. I have heard of many other houses in the village, though you can guess for yourself how reluctant the sufferers are to tell me. In fact, it is only in a few cases that the sufferers have told me. I hear usually from neighbours, and from the prayers and gossips who seem so plentiful in the parish. But I am satisfied that there are many houses involved. I think that soon it may be every house in the village. As you noticed, I was surprised that you yourself had encountered nothing. What is happening can be compared with a visitation that is creeping, or sweeping, through the parish.'

'Are you saying that all these people, for the most part very simple people, are seeing all the things you have described to me?'

'There are many shapes but it is really only one single thing, Mr van Goort,' said Stooling. 'One single being that is wholly

The Breakthrough

appalling. And I have always tried to make clear that it is not a matter only of seeing.'

'What you described was like something in a child's nightmare?'

'Yes, Mr van Goort. Adults for the most part do not have such frightful dreams. All children have them, and most of all the little saints, the rare children who are naturally good, and therefore first to be tempted and betrayed.'

'Then, are you telling me that all these different fully grown people are having the same nightmare, and a child's nightmare at that?'

'No. In this case it is a nightmare for none. It is a reality for all. A reality that is new to most. It is the nightmare come to life. After all, that must happen in divers times and places, because no one can dream of what no one has experienced.'

At that point, I saw that the big bee had simply been reclining in the deep dust of the table, about two feet and four inches to my right. It was unclear to me at the distance and amid the dust, whether the bee was living or dead. At least it was not lying on its back.

'Do you mind,' I asked Stooling, 'if we break off for a moment and I take that bee outside, in case it is still alive?'

'I should suppose it dead,' said Stooling. 'But do you not object to handling bees?'

'There is no risk if you know how to do it. Bees are friendly, sensible creatures. Especially wild bees, such as this one.'

'I was not thinking of the risk, but of the contact.'

'Watch!' I could not but enjoin.

I rose, and, with care, picked up the suffering bee, which managed still to vibrate slightly in my palm. I walked to the front door, and laid the bee under a large unkempt yew, in order that, reasonably concealed from predators, it might recover, if recovery were its destiny. I cannot claim that on the return journey I could pass the closed door of Dr Jaunt's study and library without a tremor within me, alike to the tremor within the bee. I had been verily infected by the Reverend Mr Stooling. I glanced at the familiar rectory thermometer. It indicated 86 degrees Fahrenheit.

Having been the one to interrupt the discussion, I bowed slightly to Stooling before I resumed my seat.

He spoke at once, as if there had been no break at all. 'The misdemeanour of those three men has released a curse upon the parish, and I must tell you, Mr van Goort, that I am at the end of my resources for meeting it.'

As far as my view went, the parish had always stood far from Paradise, but I could see that the Reverend Mr Stooling, when he spoke of a curse, had something very different in mind from common observation, or common sense. One question that fell upon me, now that I had entered the rectory, was whether or not it was my duty to direct that Stooling be examined by John Chard. I was well aware how heavily the parish had borne even upon so resolute a guardian as Dr Jaunt. Falterers and defaulters of assorted varieties had always been noticeable there and John Chard had already certified a number of them. I was under an obligation to observe Stooling from that aspect also. It might be that I alone would be in a position to do so.

'Are you suggesting,' I asked, 'that this—this appearance—this bogey—moves at its sweet will from house to house?'

'I think there are many different manifestations of a single evil,' Stooling replied. 'I have received reports of other visions and shapes, of animals, some of them quite small creatures, creeping and bounding. Some are unknown in species to those who have the misfortune to behold them. There are even reports

The Breakthrough

of big insects; not so much unknown, but, we must hope, normally impossible.'

At that I could not but remark that the late rector's warden had claimed to see such insects in his drunken dementia. Chard had given me exact details.

'I am aware of the fact,' replied Stooling. 'The insects to which I have just referred, have, however, been seen by innocent children. Principally, I suspect, by children.'

'Children often see and hear things that we do not see and hear,' I remarked.

'That fact is referred to in Scripture,' said Stooling.

'I recall as much,' I said.

'I have heard,' went on Stooling, 'about wet straw suddenly being found, and of its manifesting a life of its own. Also about forms of whom people see only the backs and never the faces. Also about rooms turned inside out or upside down: rooms moving from the ground floor to the floor upstairs, or substituting what had been a window for what had been a door.'

'I should be interested to inspect an example of that last,' I observed.

'The sufferers will admit no one. Alas, they refuse access even to their rector! But I admit that I myself will give no access to my predecessor's apartment, where the being first settled and went to work.'

I was not altogether regretful. It was absurd to suppose that there was really anything to be viewed by an eye such as mine. I should merely have become unduly involved with the locals, which I had always avoided.

'Finally, there are reports of actual people. New people who have appeared in the various households, and will not be expelled.'

'Do they enter with muddy feet?'

Intrusions

I had slightly clutched my stick, as one does by instinct, before asking such a question.

'In certain cases, yes,' said Stooling.

Again I could not refuse inner acknowledgement to the sangfroid with which he had replied.

Then he said: 'You have received a visitation yourself. I always supposed it.'

'I have lighted upon a single mark upon the polished floor of my house which should have been cleared up by the women,' I rejoined. 'No more than that. But, I admit, no less.'

'It is enough,' said Stooling. 'There may be no more, or very little more. You perhaps have more resistance than many. I earnestly hope that proves to be so. Pray that it may.'

'It was the mark of a foot, Stooling, not of a boot or shoe. I acknowledge that.'

Stooling bowed his head slightly and said nothing.

'It can be scrubbed away, and it will be. I am sure that the same applies to many of the other occurrences. Popular gossip is mainly a matter of exaggeration.'

'Very reluctantly, they come to me and tell their tale. It is usually a tale of what has happened to someone else. They do not trust me enough to speak of the terrors at their own hearts. And I am powerless. So powerless that the common opinion of me is confirmed.'

'There must,' I said, 'be provision made in the liturgy. The liturgy is expressly designed to meet every contingency possible under Heaven.'

'I should have to seek leave of the Bishop, and the Bishop is at present incapacitated, as I daresay you know. It would be quite irresponsible to raise such a matter just now, though we all hope and pray for better things in God's good time. Instead, I have turned to you, Mr van Goort, to one who may be regarded

The Breakthrough

as my leading parishioner, at least in worldly terms. A minister of the Established Church has a right to do that. And, on occasion, a duty. Pray advise me, Mr van Goort. I beg of you.'

I reflected, taking my time, such time as I could take. After such an appeal, Stooling could but wait until the oracle spoke.

'I'm not at all sure that I believe a single word of it,' I said in the end. 'After all, I'm the man who never heard the original disaster. But let us put it to the test. Are you claiming that the thing you spoke of, the thing you say began it all, is still in this house?'

'It is in my room upstairs, Mr van Goort. It has succeeded in driving me out, and it has settled there itself. By now, I am relieved that it seems content to stay there. Others have been less fortunate.'

'I take it that the door of the room is locked?'

'It is locked, Mr van Goort.'

'Pray lend me the key. I propose to mount and to see for myself.'

'You misunderstand. It is on the inside that the door is locked.'

I certainly had misunderstood. Who would have not?

'Then I shall have to rap,' I said brusquely.

'No, Mr van Goort. Remember that it is I who would bear the consequences, suffer the retribution that others have suffered. If I felt that to be my duty, of course I should humbly submit. But it is not a thing to enter upon frivolously. If you seek proof, I shall vouchsafe it nearer to your own person. Look in that corner, Mr van Goort.'

Stooling toddled a few steps away from the mantel and stood pointing. I rose to my feet, leaning upon my stick, and I gazed. The strong sunlight in the room left the corner in question very dark. I advanced round the table towards it.

Intrusions

'See for yourself, Mr van Goort!' said Stooling.

Suddenly I saw. Lying massed in the dark corner between the floor and the two walls was what appeared to be a substantial reptile, though I could see neither head nor tail, and, emphatically, no eye or pair of eyes.

'It was not there when we entered the room,' I cried. I exclaimed in this simple-minded way without thinking. But on three occasions that afternoon, I had myself passed round the big table at that very corner.

'I daresay,' said Stooling, not for the first time, having recourse to discourteous dryness. 'They tell me that the great heat brings the snakes out when at other times one seldom sees them.'

'But that is no British grass snake or much abused adder,' I said.

'I do not think it is,' responded Stooling, 'though, to my knowledge, my own poor eyes have never seen a grass snake, still less an adder. So, Mr van Goort, you have proof. Now will you please apply your great knowledge and wide experience to thinking how best to lift the evil from your parish! Do it, in God's name, Mr van Goort.'

'You are sure,' I asked, 'that I should not see and hear whatever I may be able to see and hear upstairs?'

'I am sure,' said Stooling. 'I am sorry, but I am sure.'

While striding homewards, forcing my stick firmly into the baked ground at every step, I realised that fear had entered into me and that I was glad to evade further investigation and to be on my own.

None the less, it was difficult to see what I could possibly do to help Stooling. His reliance upon my greater knowledge and wider experience was merely the exaggerated conviction of

The Breakthrough

one who had come within sight of goals he had then proved unequal to, or been inhibited from himself reaching. I of all men, and not only of all men in Stooling's sparse parish, knew best how little knowledge and experience helped towards anything that the human heart truly seeks. Stooling knew just enough not to know how unavailing are men like me; as my whole life had proved.

I struck into the dry earth of the lane more fiercely than ever as I thought the matter out. I could have felt sorry for Stooling, but I doubted whether it was the proper sentiment. There was even a sense in which Stooling himself had released the murrain of which he spoke, and of which he had offered a proof that was perhaps unnecessary. The three toilers might have been the immediate actors, but, in all good law, the master is held responsible for the misdemeanours of those he employs; and to the bitter end, if necessary. I was sure that with Dr Jaunt things would have worked out differently.

The unseasonable mark was still upon my polished floor as I entered, and I examined it. There were indeed certain odd features which I do not dilate because I realise that my power of observation was impaired. Undeterred, I placed my stick in the stand. I then ascended to doff my visiting clothes. I should have changed them in any case, but now I felt they were infected with the pestilence that Stooling himself had said was within the rectory, within the whole parish, and which he purported to have shown to me. It is usual even for a man, even for a man long and resolutely solitary, to keep his garments in his sleeping chamber. That cannot be gainsaid. It is perfectly normal.

The door of the room in question stood open by day for greater aeration in that repellent heat and stillness, and what I saw I saw first from the landing at the top of the stairs, as I stood foursquare upon the dark green carpeting thereof.

Intrusions

There was a figure kneeling at my bedstead. The arms were upon the made bedding and the face sunk down upon the supposed hands and the hair long and pale, as in Stooling's narrative, and what was more and worse, the dress brighter than anything seen by me on this earth, of which earth I have seen so much. I could understand why Stooling had spoken of Mohawks and Iroquois, but then he had never beheld for himself, nor I for that matter. Well I knew, notwithstanding, even if Stooling had not known, or wished he had not, that bright as this the Mohawks could not be; or the White Men would never have prevailed against them, never this side of Doomsday. From the back, from outside the room, one might almost have said that the kneeling shape was of a girl or woman, but, after only one short step more, one perceived that it was far too tall, or perhaps long, or, as I had myself suggested, high.

I should perhaps observe here that my bedstead by then was of plain black iron, as strait as the bed of the Great Duke or of the Pope; whatever had been the case in Iberia or Cathay, in my days of illusion. The women set it tightly and neatly for me each morning. The figure, or shape, or form, kneeling beside it was not acceptably human at all; or, perhaps I should say, not acceptably human any more. It had been stretched upon the rack. It had been pleached and bleached. It had been cruelly bedizened. It had been confronted with near-ultimates.

I remembered too what Stooling had said about entities of which or whom the parishioners sighted only the backs. I had apprehended as he spoke that, for more than that, the parishioners in question had almost certainly been unprepared; and emphatically unprepared by the Reverend Mr Stooling.

However my own case might have been, the matter was taken out of my hands. As I gazed and trembled, the strip of carpet upon which I stood slipped away under my feet, so that I

The Breakthrough

stumbled. It had often happened before, as I have always been a person of heavy build, and as I refused to have any of my polished floors impaired by cottager's nails or tacks being hammered into it. The clatter had the effect of confirming Stooling's assertion that before him, and now before me, was no mere simulacrum or construction but a thing of sense.

I suppose it was the clatter though plainly there are other possibilities. Beyond doubt the kneeling form twisted upwards and round like a python, however little else about it was like a python, and half directed itself towards me, as I stood gasping on my own landing, by now in horrid terror.

I have referred to the dolours that had been inflicted upon what I must still call the body of it. The face, such face as it was, reflected things most dreadfully worse. It has often been said, and sometimes rightly, that the eyes are the windows of the soul. This being (yes, Stooling's word was the right one) had eyes no longer, not even the roughly painted eyes that Stooling had implied; and from places on its macerated left cheek (which was the cheek turned towards me) a horrifying greenish ichor exuded, the farthest extremity, as I knew instinctively, in desperation, torment, and woe.

Stooling can only have imagined full features. He had, indeed, admitted to the possibility. More probably, he had not been wholly sincere in what he had said to me. The truth was so greatly worse than he had suggested, and so greatly different from it, and so greatly greater in all ways.

I wondered whether Stooling had even discerned that truth; to me so clear and fearful.

If the being before me had until lately been the occupant of the vault which Stooling's men had broken into, then that occupant was straight from the endurances of Hell; or perhaps from those of Purgatory, for the Roman Catholic, and more hopeful, alternative must always be allowed for. I recalled Christopher Marlowe's line: 'Why this is Hell, nor am I out of it.'

All that had happened in the parish was now perfectly plain to me. It was no longer even conceivable that my questionable stock of knowledge and experience could have the very least bearing upon the matter. There had been what is known as a chain of events, and the chain would continue to be paid out till it came to its end and the parish settled to its anchor upon new seas and possibly under a new commander.

Perhaps it was true that I was the man best trained and equipped to perceive at least this; though little more. There was no limit to what might be necessary. I had been averting my eyes from the room, and when I looked again into it, the room was empty.

I descended shakily and re-entered my garden. The parching of the soil and impurity of the air had diminished the fragrance of the growths, but something was still for a moment or two to be enjoyed as the earlier dusk promised the advance of autumn. There are few full sunsets in that region, where the sun in summer is felt rather than seen, and in winter is merely the distant clown in a hemispherical circus.

I saw that old Slow was in attendance again; this time actually leaning across my gate, and waiting for me.

'I knew you were back,' were his first words.

'As you see,' I responded evenly.

'All safe and sound,' insinuated Slow.

'Perfectly, as far as I know,' I replied, smiling.

'And the Reverend?'

'I heard what he had to say, Slow. I promised him to think it over.'

The Breakthrough

'There's not much time for thinking, master. I tried to tell you that.'

'I'm not sure that time is the essence, Slow,' I said, smiling again, or at least trying to smile.

'I dunno about essence, master. I dunno what essence rightly is. I know that everyone is talking of finding a new rector. A rector more like Dr Jaunt. Or Dr Liverwright.'

Slow's memory was always as old as history. I knew from past conversation that he really did appear to have known Dr Liverwright, and intimately, despite all the years that Jaunt had been in the place. In the parish, one had as strong a sense of the past as of compass orientation.

'Or even Dr Blunderstone that was,' said Slow, groping back further still. I had heard tales before this of Dr Blunderstone's doings, but it was no moment to refer to them, or in any degree to diminish faith, as the phrase runs.

'You must be more patient,' I said. 'Mr Stooling will prevail yet.' I did all I could to suggest that I believed it.

'It's not me, master, not me at all. I'm quite ready to pay out rope, master. You know that well. It's not me. It's the others. It's them.' Here his central metaphor had been particularly disconcerting.

'You must calm them, Slow. Everyone must let things ride for a little. You will tell them that. I know that you have great influence.' I did not really know, one way or the other; but it was plainly the point to make at such a moment.

'They're restless,' said Slow. 'You'll understand that, master. Weeks are passing. They want a proper reckoning.'

'What form do you see that taking, Slow?' I expect I sounded ironical, but I really wanted to know; conceivably even needed to know. I suspected some confused link between reckoning and rector.

Intrusions

'That's not for us to say,' was all old Slow had to reply. 'Except that it will be a bad form. I think we can count on that. The working out is in God's hands, master. We all know so much. And it's just about all that any of us do know. Except that it will be bad when it comes. That's for certain sure, master. We can count on that, one and all.'

'All right, Slow,' I rejoined, in my firmest manner. 'I have given you my advice. My very strong and most earnest advice. And I gave it after talking at his request with Mr Stooling. I am an educated man, and I am sure that what I say will be heeded.'

It was difficult for me to expect Slow to look anything but rustically cynical. It was his normal stance at all times.

'If it's what you say, master,' was his only response, as he replaced his shapeless hat upon his exceedingly bald head.

Slow never essayed Good Mornings and Good Evenings, and no one expected them.

To begin with at least, I was glad that the exchange with old Slow had been so brief; but I was now aware of a stir in the air that was new to me. I even walked to the gate and looked over the bars. Slow was still in sight as he walked at his leisure down the lane towards the comparatively populous part of the parish; but he did not turn his head. I was in little doubt that he had come as an official, though self-appointed, messenger, and was returning to report.

I do not claim that courage was not needed to re-enter my house, which could now be regarded as in the same ill state as the rectory; but I am the man I am, and I merely resolved to search the place, room by room. This I did, without moving a muscle other than the muscles needed for the task in hand.

I found nothing new that was noticeably out of the way. To the misconceived muddy footprint I had become all but indifferent. Even when confronted by mystery and torment, we have

The Breakthrough

none to depend upon but ourselves. If it is God Who inflicts, then no lesser being can remove, or even palliate.

When I had completed my search, and satisfied myself for the moment, I descended to my cellar for another bottle of *fino*, and then sat on my garden seat as darkness drew near.

I was still aware of the stir to which I have referred, and there seemed to be a faint glow above and around the more distant cots and cabins, which was also unusual. I did not care for either phenomenon, but was well prepared for life to be harder than usual for a spell: a prospect for which the vision I had received gave every warranty; there was no course better than steady habituality. Before I was halfway through the bottle, I heard afar off the tinkling tune of a hymn, as on a small cottage piano. The hymn was familiar enough:

> Day of Wrath! O day of mourning!
> See fulfilled the Prophet's warning!
> Heav'n and earth in ashes burning!

I was only surprised that any of the locals could have afforded a musical instrument beyond the simple hand-cut pipe and home-made drum. Possibly a group had formed themselves into a primitive club. It was well known that the organ in our church was rusted away through failure of an organist. And to think of all the Netherlands churches in which as a child I had played the great organs!

Now the bats were flying thickly; fluttering, darting, and changing course almost every moment. I am one who had been granted the favour of hearing the cry of bats, as I hear so many other cries in nature. I hear, and, though I cannot claim fully to understand, I seem to sympathise, where I sympathise so seldom with the utterances of my own fell race, be the tongue spoken what it may, or almost what it may. What else is in the mouth of man or woman but boasting and sneaking? None the less, I acknowledge that I love to hear the voice of a fair woman speaking Spanish; or of a pure girl speaking any language. All in all, my favourite hour was late dusk, with the bats thickening and crying in and around my house and garden; and the local humans creeping at late last to their precarious habitations.

The cottage piano played on, and played the same tune yet again. Later verses in the hymn came back to me:

> Death is struck, and nature quaking,
> All creation is awaking,
> To its Judge an answer making.

> When the Judge his seat attaineth
> And each hidden deed arraigneth,
> Nothing unavenged remaineth.

Though proper pride has always reinforced Holy Writ in keeping me from the vulgarity of personal revenge, I was glad to brood upon the intrinsic character of the universe in that important particular, as manifested by the hymnologist. 'Only be patient,' proclaim the infidels, 'and you shall see the body of your enemy carried before your door.' Again and again I heard that said during the years I dwelt among the Ottomans, and I am convinced that there is nothing in it but the truth. It is always too late when it occurs, but the infidels do not say otherwise. It is revenge of any kind that most makes real to all of us the nature of time. Revenge is an aspect of time. That evening before I had finished the bottle, I had reflected long and deeply.

I passed the night in my shell room, with the murmur of far oceans slowly rising and falling around me as I sank, louder and more real than the local billows that Slow claimed to hear; and soon submerging all menace. I lay upon the folding bed which

The Breakthrough

had accompanied me across the Cordilleras and amid the peaks of Ararat; and through the single glass panel in the roof of the shell room, I could see a solitary star. In the parish, stars are faint, owing to the conditions of the atmosphere. The appearance of a star as bright as this would be taken by many as an augury; as of course it was.

When the women came the next morning, they began at once to complain, and to say that they would come no more. They asserted that the state of things in the parish at large made it impossible for them to leave their homes for so long as to reach and work at my comparative outpost. They also remarked that the feel of my own house had changed, and said that they did not like the change.

'If there is a change,' I said, 'it is the same that has come upon all of you.'

The women nodded silently, but seemed unappeased.

'Yesterday I visited Mr Stooling, your rector, at his request, and we had a long talk.'

'Talk's not much,' said one of the women, and the others sibilated in agreement, though still softly.

'Have patience,' I cried, 'and all will be well in God's good time. It will advantage you not at all to abandon your obligations.'

'When the time is right,' said another of the women, 'we might return.'

'When the time is right,' said the woman who had spoken first.

'When,' said the woman who had not previously spoken at all. And she confined herself to the monosyllable.

'Just now we're needed at home,' said the second woman; she whom I had always found the most pliable.

Intrusions

'We have things to do of our own,' said the first woman.

'Our own things,' said the third woman.

'Things that must be done,' said the second woman.

Nothing short of American slavery procedures would have availed with the women at that moment, and, though I had often witnessed such procedures in their native land, I could hardly contemplate them under present circumstances, and when the locality was already under particular siege.

The women refused even to scrape up the mud from my polished floor.

Nor did there seem any sensible prospect at the moment of replacing these women by others. I might be forced to consider decamping totally to some other spot in the land.

For such as me there are advantages in moving house intermittently. None the less, I remembered with sorrow others who had served me, and in particular the pretty people who had attended me so tactfully during my sojourn in the Celestial Empire. I spent the whole of that day cursing and fuming; and, I suppose, fumbling also. When I am in the High Places, I can do anything whatever for myself, and most things for others also, but I am not the man to engage in personal domestic labour within my own homeland and house.

By the evening of that grotesque day, airless as ever, a solution offered of a kind.

No less a person walked in unannounced than Lizzie Summerday, she who had said she would never come again. It was the first time I had set eyes upon her, let alone spoken to her, since our final tourney more than three years before her uncle's death. Among the reasons why I left my house and garden so seldom was my extreme disinclination once more to encounter Lizzie. It was not my strongest reason, but it was a reason potent in itself.

The Breakthrough

'I hear you're in difficulty,' were her first words now. It had been she who had recruited at the foundry cottages all the succession of women who had worked for me. In those days, every woman in the parish was in fear of her, as the men of her uncle.

'I am,' I replied, stating the truth without shame, as always. 'But I cannot accept help from you.'

'Further help,' said Lizzie sarcastically.

I bowed. What she implied was perfectly just. I had accepted things from her only because of her powerful position in the place, and then because of the common needs of man; even of a man fortified as I was. But they had been many things, and varied.

'Partly for that very reason, I can accept no more,' I said.

'It is my own services that I am offering now, you must understand,' said Lizzie.

'No,' I said, refusing any offer.

'No one else will work for you now.'

'Now? Why now?'

'Not after your visit to Stooling.'

'It was upon Stooling's invitation.'

'You shouldn't have accepted Stooling's invitation.'

Lizzie's clothes were more farouche than ever, if that were possible; made from grey material closely woven on her own machines; the bodice and the skirts hanging freely about and around her. Her hair was left to stream over her shoulders and bosom. There was nothing new about that, but now the hair was greying too. Her feet were bare and dirty, and harder than hooves, as I knew well. Her dark eyes were large, limpid, and vatic. Little had changed in four years, except age and time, of which women, like revenge, are aspects. But I had not known Lizzie as a young girl, and I had always doubted whether she

Intrusions

had ever truly been one, when Dr Jaunt had been her preceptor since infancy. I had not treated Lizzie well, nor she me. No doubt I had known too many women: she not enough men.

'Old Slow brought the invitation by word of mouth and said it was urgent. I accept my obligations in the parish alike to your uncle and to his successor, however insufficient.'

'How can you even speak to old Slow in the light of what he knows and we know?'

'It is he who speaks first to me, and perhaps it is as well. You may think so yourself upon reflection.'

'No one at all will speak to Stooling that can help it, and no one now will speak to you.'

'It is I who have no wish to address any of them.'

Lizzie stamped at that, as she so often did.

'I am willing to work for you, Walmen. Daily with my own hands.'

I realised that she might well have apparelled herself for the task; or considered that she had. Not that her clothes were ever other than finely fashioned in their own plain and free way.

'I cannot accept that. I can accept nothing.'

'Then what will you do? No one will come near you.'

'I shall leave the parish.'

Lizzie looked at me hard. 'It will be better after Stooling has gone. It will be as it was. Things will slowly return to what they were.'

'Stooling,' I retorted, 'has no intention of going. Perhaps not even the wish. Nor, indeed, the choice. He too has obligations.'

'Stooling will go,' said Lizzie. 'In one way or another. And in a very short time. He has brought a bugbear upon us. A bane.'

The Breakthrough

'He is also the man who was chosen,' I pointed out drily. 'He has been inducted, and, before that, presumably also consecrated. He cannot go. He must not. He will not.'

'The parish will not submit to him,' said Lizzie. 'They do not hold him in reverence.'

I said nothing.

Lizzie simply reflected. 'He will go. And it will not be long. Until then, Walmen, accept my offer. If I can sink my pride, you can sink yours.' And when perhaps I hesitated for a moment, Lizzie added, 'Look at that dead animal on your floor! It's been lying there for days.'

We were, in fact, standing one on either side of the thing I had taken for a muddy mark. Earlier, I had examined it closely. But, within the context, it was not a matter to argue.

Thus I remained silent, and Lizzie went on, 'I offer nothing else. Be sure of that. Only the work of my hands, Walmen.'

'No,' I said. 'I shall leave the parish.'

She stretched her hands out to me at the end of the loose grey sleeves. Lizzie's hands had always been unlike those of other women I had known. There was an extraordinary pause between us, of who knows how long duration? Then, without another word, I walked into my garden.

Lizzie followed me. I sat on my stone seat, and Lizzie sank upon the earth.

'Lizzie,' I said. 'Do you still ride Fire?'

Latterly she had ridden him almost more than her uncle had done, and even harder than he, and in fantastic garb. None the less, and with all the regard there is everywhere for appearances, she had still managed to keep the parish in subjection. Not even her visits to me, not even what old Slow had bustled to report, had ever shaken that subjection while her uncle lived.

'Fire is old,' replied Lizzie. 'Soon he will be dead.'

Intrusions

I had taken little account of that, as I had from time to time heard the great horse continuing to thunder and stamp in the poor byre that was all that could be afforded him.

'Lizzie,' I said. 'Do you still play Field and Alkan?'

It had been in order to play out of her uncle's earshot that Lizzie had first entered into possession of the tiny hovel where now she dwelt entirely. A handsome woman playing a once very fine piano alone in her own house for hours on end was a procedure unlikely to commend itself to the diligent parishioners, and at the beginning some stones had been thrown, but not for long. Those locals who had broken panes of glass had soon replaced them at their own labour and at the cost of their own pockets. They had also been given opportunities to contribute other works of improvement in the little abode; and all inside a week or two.

'I play only psalms,' Lizzie replied. 'The piano is past being tuned, but with psalms it matters less. Their power is not only musical.'

'Lizzie,' I said. 'Do you still swim in the rhene to the dam?'

She had swum two or three evenings each week, and virtually unclothed. No doubt it could have been expected to give more offence in the parish than almost anything else, especially as Lizzie was a fine and fortunate woman in her shapeliness; especially as the distance was upwards of two miles each way; especially as no one (and certainly not I) knew what business took her to the dam, as business there certainly was, such as to hold Lizzie sometimes for an hour or more. One young lad, acting perchance for all, as old Slow spoke and acted for all, set upon Lizzie from the bank at nightfall, or attempted to set upon her. I can only add that the idle fool was never again seen; or, for that matter, spoken of; or probably even thought about.

The Breakthrough

'The rhene is silted,' replied Lizzie, 'and the dam is broken. You have been within doors a long age, Walmen.'

A hare sped across the path behind Lizzie, almost touching her. I could hear its croon as it fleeted. The hares in my garden were many, as were other creatures of the field, the swamp, and the air; the less habituated the better, as far as my wish went.

'Tell me,' I said. 'Have you seen many of these appearances they speak of? These beings? These bugbears?'

'I have seen enough,' said Lizzie, but without surprise at my enquiry. 'We are at all times beset, as my uncle never ceased to warn. They are never more than inches away. They never cease from the endeavour to encroach. Strength is needed all the time to hold them off. Our own strength or that of another. As faith directs.'

'They are as various as the terrors in the dreams of children,' I observed. Of course I was in part citing the Reverend Mr Stooling and without much acknowledgement.

'They are shaped accordingly,' said Lizzie, 'and their shapes change continually, and the places where they have lingered are changed too, and always to the peril of the proper householder.'

'Do they take direct action against us?' I asked. 'Are there reports that they do?' After all, Lizzie, even now, saw far more of the parish than I did, and heard much of the talk and the gossip. I was fairly sure that there were still people who came at night and confided in her.

'The action that they take is seldom or never direct, Walmen. There is nothing direct or indirect that you yourself need to apprehend.'

I smiled at her, though by now it was deep dusk. 'Nor you, Lizzie,' I said.

Intrusions

 Despite everything, I even touched her thick hair with my left hand. Random gestures of sentiment are difficult to extirpate, nor need we necessarily make the attempt.
 'Lizzie,' I said, 'I have not returned to my room since I saw a figure within it. Indeed, I saw the figure only from outside, through the open door. I refer to my bedroom.'
 Lizzie merely said, 'Yes. In your bedroom.'
 'I suspect that it may have been the figure that Stooling said he saw. Exactly the same figure.'
 'They are all the same figure,' said Lizzie. 'Only the shapes change.'
 'I saw no reason to suppose it wished me ill. On the contrary. It seemed to be in agony.'
 'They are all in agony,' said Lizzie.
 'It was kneeling and I felt like kneeling myself. But in the end, I came out here. Into the garden. That seemed best.'
 'Yes,' said Lizzie. 'It was always best in the garden.'
 'Old Slow was at the gate again.'
 'You shouldn't speak to him. You should have killed him that first time. No one would have protested.'
 'It is forbidden to us,' I rejoined, as I had rejoined so often before to Lizzie, who knew better than I in any case, after Dr Jaunt's incessant hammerings.
 'It is hardly a good moment to return to *that* theme,' I added, smiling again in the thick twilight, devoid of air, and this evening, devoid of sound and sight also, at least as yet.
 'I shall always return to it,' said Lizzie. 'You failed as a man. I should have done it myself.'
 Now the hares were beginning their nocturnal dance, to their own small music. I could half-hear them, as Lizzie could too.
 'Lizzie,' I said. 'I went back into the house. After a very short time I went everywhere. I examined everything. There were no

The Breakthrough

one and nothing there, and there was nothing changed. But I slept in the shell room and I have not looked through the house again today. Will you return to the house with me and look with me again? We can take a candle. We can take a candle each.'

'We shan't need candles or lamps as yet,' said Lizzie, and rose to her feet.

It is true that I am more favoured to see in the dark or near-dark than most, and Lizzie could see anything anywhere, even under deep water. It is also true that when darkness is incomplete, a light can conceal more than it discloses.

'I acknowledge that I am glad to have company for the task,' I said. 'I am less than the man I was, Lizzie.'

'All men are less than they suppose,' said Lizzie.

'I am neither less nor more than I suppose. As always, I know exactly what I am. And that is less than it was.'

So Lizzie and I soon came to converse always; when once we had managed to start conversing at all, ceased to eye one another as duellists and wrestlers do.

We passed through the front door and saw that the mess on my polished floor, whether mud or small corpse, was there no longer.

'We've made a start,' I cried, pointing to the spot with my right hand.

'It has changed shape,' said Lizzie calmly. 'They change shape all the time.'

We ascended directly to my bedroom, my proper sleeping apartment. To both of us, without a further word spoken, it seemed best to tackle things at their supposed centre.

At once I saw that the door of the room was shut. It was not how I had left it and last seen it. We did not at once open the door, but stood there on the landing listening. There were sounds within and they were loud and they were harrowing.

Intrusions

'Lizzie,' I said, 'you have seen more than I of these appearances. And presumably you have heard more also. Have you ever heard cries such as those?'

'No,' she replied. 'But I know what they are.'

I said nothing, and she continued.

'The Scriptures call them weeping and gnashing of teeth. Open the door, Walmen.'

I still hesitated.

Lizzie then opened the door herself, remarking, 'I too have wept in this room. I too have cried out in pain.'

We entered together. As we crossed the threshold, the sounds ceased. Or perhaps they were no longer to be heard when one was so near to them and amongst them. Perhaps the visible bugbears vanished too, or, as Lizzie put it, changed shape, when approached with full resolution. That was taken for granted in the Philippine Islands, as I knew well.

Lizzie called out, 'There are scratches on the wall that were not here formerly.'

'I advise you to look away,' I said.

'There's so much light upon them,' she replied.

But after a moment, she crossed to where I stood at one of the windows. Light there was indeed. On the evening before, it had been a faint glow, though febrile. Now it was a blaze; and all in the minute or two since the pair of us had left my garden.

I threw up the bottom window sash. Last night's low mutter had become a grumbling, though still distant, roar. The heat of the fire crept in like water.

'I knew it would happen,' said Lizzie, who was standing a little behind me. 'You didn't really think, Walmen, that I had come here to work with my hands? You didn't believe that?'

'I remind you, Lizzie,' I said, 'that I most firmly refused any offer from first to last.'

The Breakthrough

'So you did, Walmen.'

'Your hands are for the reins and for the keyboard, Lizzie; and no doubt for the looms.'

'I needed an excuse.'

'Do you mean that it was you who led the women into leaving?'

'No. That would have been unnecessary. This house will be attacked.'

Having lived in divers places, I was scarcely surprised by what she said. Most men and many women clutch at all pretexts to diminish those they envy and to despoil their property, especially when it is beautiful. The recent events in the parish could find resolution only in carnage and havoc. I could see that for myself and that I was plainly a probable sacrifice; the most likely but one.

'What about Stooling?' I enquired.

'I trust that he's fled,' replied Lizzie.

'I doubt if he *has* fled. What then?'

'He should have seen that he is not the man for this parish. Let him find another where God is more safely distant.'

'I do not see Stooling leaving his post. He's been under fire already, from all he told me.'

'He'll be under fire again now,' said Lizzie. 'You can see the flames. We must hope the little man is hiding in a dyke. Fortunately there is not much of him to hide and our dykes lie low and broad. He could scramble through them for leagues.'

'I must go down,' I said quietly, 'and exercise some proper authority.'

'Do not stir,' said Lizzie. 'When they've burnt the rectory, they will come this way.'

Intrusions

'I shall unlock the arms chest. But it should not be needful to do any more. Your uncle never once found it necessary, if I remember aright.'

'My uncle never allowed things to become as bad as they are now,' observed Lizzie. 'Pray God it may not be required to burn down every homestead in the parish!'

'We cannot know,' I rejoined. 'It is not for us to surmise.'

'See the shapes moving about in the light of the fire!' said Lizzie.

And so, though only after she had spoken, I distinctly could.

The heat of the burning buildings through the opened sash brought back to me the great legation fire in Caracas which we had been entirely unable to stem, sweat as we might, until it had destroyed virtually the whole quarter. I knew well the stench and swelter of rebel wildfire.

But every moment the number of ill-defined shapes was increasing, though I could see them only as shadows and masses against the pink and flickering light, and for a necessarily very short distance around my house. About their dance of death was something insectile, as Stooling had implied. The great variations in their bulk and proportions suggested all the species in the world, vastly enlarged, and there were species also that were not in the ordinarily visible world at all. Many of the forms were monstrous and utterly defiling.

'They are going,' said Lizzie. 'Yes, they are going.'

She spoke as if she had seen such spectacles on previous occasions, but I said nothing as to that.

'Which is to say,' observed Lizzie, 'that they are ceasing to be discernible by the outer eye. They do not really go at all. They do not go anywhere.'

The Breakthrough

To me, acute as my vision is, the number seemed still to be rising. But Lizzie's next remark was 'We must think what to do for ourselves. The arsonists are coming.'

My answer was clear. 'I shall go out and meet them, armed,' I said. 'The impulsion to rapine seldom lasts long in England, I think. A quick parley should bring them to heel. You will wait here, armed too. It is fortunate that you are trained in arms, because you will not then use them unnecessarily.'

'No,' said Lizzie, 'you must not leave the house now, or you will be lost. Forces are massed without which are not to be cheated by arms.'

'If those forces are a menace to me,' I pointed out, 'then they will be an equal menace to any marauders.'

'Not equal,' said Lizzie. 'Not by any means equal.'

I could but gaze before me.

'Wait, Walmen,' bade Lizzie. 'The ferment will soon die down and pass from normal human sight, dull as human sight must be.'

'And the fire too, Lizzie, from what I discern. It is fading already.'

'The work is all but done,' said Lizzie. 'But now they will turn on us.'

'I shall employ the period of waiting in preparing our weapons,' I said. 'At last my house is now clear of intruders. Or so I suppose.'

I turned on my heel from the open window, but Lizzie clutched my left arm in her hard grip.

'Look!' she said, and pointed outwards. 'Look!'

Outside the house, and before our gaze, the manifold apparitions were carrying through a final transmutation before their presumed passage across their special threshold, always within an inch or two of us, as Lizzie had said, and as many have witnessed, including, I believe, the speculator, Swedenborg. They were coalescing, one and all, into a vast, faintly luminous head or skull; neither entirely one, nor entirely the other; neither fully alive, nor, one could be most assured, wholly dead. There were, and are, no standards for measuring the dimensions of any such phenomenon, and there was no time either; but at one point, for seconds, the shape seemed to me huge enough to fill most of the space that could be filled. As I have said, it was dimly refulgent, yellowly so, like a person lost in fever; and its jaws were lantern, though perhaps smiling too, and set at a very odd angle.

Lizzie, I saw, had covered her eyes.

But she had recovered in a moment.

'Now,' she said. 'Now, Walmen, is the call to arms.' She was almost chuckling; transformed in an instant, as had always been her way, changed more instantaneously and pervasively than any other changeable woman I had known; her undying gift, as I must admit.

The *danse macabre* surrounding us had withdrawn into final indistinctness. I could see only the far-off falling flames of the burning rectory, and no doubt of other structures burning also, by accident or intention. In my immediate area, the flames illumined and silhouetted only the familiar walls and trees; hollyhocks and mast poppies.

We sped downstairs, almost as children released, to the small gun room and strongroom. Few of the guns had even been loaded for many years, though I had insisted upon the women thoroughly cleaning all of them each week in my presence and, naturally, under my close supervision. In addition, there were divers sabres, cutlasses, and glaves to be polished; and polished to brilliance all of them regularly were. Recourse to such hand-to-hand armaments was beneath all dignity in present circum-

The Breakthrough

stances, but the gleam and glitter gave ardour, none the less. Lizzie and I took each a military piece of reasonably recent manufacture, and one each of my glittering Ottoman pistols, set with malachite, and, it was said, with infidel hair and bone also. We took each a lighted lantern; Venetian lanterns at that, though small ones only.

Now that all was quiet outside, indeed excessively and unpleasantly quiet, Lizzie and I sallied from the house together. I should of course have greatly preferred to go alone, but Lizzie was not to be denied unless by personal force and locking up, which did not seem to suit the particular occasion. My fundamental policy was to intercept any possible troublemakers before they had reached the house, as the landlord of The Spaniards did with another group of sanctified enthusiasts, the Gordon Rioters.

I was not wholly successful in this aim, since the whole mob of them was streaming through my gate in the darkness before Lizzie and I confronted them. Where lately my property had been polluted by evil simulacra, it was now to be polluted by half-crazed insurrectionists.

And here I approach the sad and awful climax of the apocalyptic occurrences that I have endeavoured to narrate. Let me describe it quickly and clearly.

There was a group of seven or eight men ahead of the rest, one or two with primitive lamps of some kind, providing little in the way of illumination. It was therefore hard to see how far even the seven or eight were armed, let alone the rest of the mob; but of course there could be no reasonable doubt that evil intent was backed by shotguns and bill hooks at the least. I had been perfectly accustomed to like situations in many different places; and with more savagely makeshift weapons than were likely here.

Intrusions

Holding my Venetian light high above my head and at the full stretch of my left arm, I called out 'Stop', and strode towards the intruders, with pistol hidden and military piece unobtruding. The party of seven or eight stopped at once, and the mass behind them even began slightly to retreat.

'How can I serve you?' I cried out, and at the fullest *fortissimo* of my not inconsiderable delivery.

'We've come to burn your house, master,' said one of the men, with a leer. I knew him by sight and name. His name was Joshua Gorm.

If I had judged by experience elsewhere, I should have expected a cowardly but affirmative bellow from the supporting mob at these words. But, in fact, only silence followed.

'You're late,' I cried back. 'The plague's over. They're all gone. I promise you that. I promise. Come in and have a beaker of barleycorn instead. At least the leaders among you. I fear I lack supplies for all. I'm sorry, men,' I called to the rear ranks even more loudly, as they crowded, invisible, in the darkness.

'Stooling *promised*,' said the man, Gorm. 'Stooling promised everything.'

That did produce a response: a low mean growl of spite and rage, from every throat, or so it seemed.

'I am not Mr Stooling,' I proclaimed, and gave the Venetian lantern a good flourish. 'But I am a man of education, and what I say is true. I promise you all that we are our own masters once more.'

'How can we know?' called out someone.

'I shall tell you. Go back to your homes, each one of you, ask your wives and your mothers and your sisters, and find out the truth for yourselves. If I have spoken falsely, return here at once, and with brands burning, if you see fit. I can and shall say

The Breakthrough

nothing more.' With that, I lowered the Venetian lantern to shoulder height, and pleasantly rested my left arm.

It was at this point that among the insurrectionists emerged the familiar and critical defect of all democracy, to use the cant word. The defect, needless to say, is dispersed leadership or leadership only by hypocracy and from the rear, which latter is the more common arrangement, as men in society cannot survive more than a few hours without leadership of some kind, even dissimulated leadership.

In the nature of things, the mob at large was incapable of responding to my reassurances unless vouchsafed a cheery word of guidance from its own spokesmen. I daresay that a few individualists in the darkness had quietly departed at once, but the number of individualists is always small, and perhaps usefully so. It was pitifully plain to all that the seven or eight supposed ringleaders were managing to disagree among themselves; and providing no leadership at all, nor yet any good prospect of leadership emerging.

All this time, Lizzie had been standing well behind me, not from fear, I need hardly say, for she knew none, but from wisdom and instinctive strategy. Her lantern had been dangling from her right hand. Now she raised it, much as I had done, in order to command and concentrate attention; and she stepped forward beside me. As I have made plain, she was one well accustomed to exerting authority both on her late uncle's behalf and on her own.

'There's nothing to fear,' she said to the invaders, quite quietly, and in a perfectly female manner. 'Go now to your homes and see for yourselves.'

Such acquaintanceship as I had formerly experienced with Lizzie Summerday had been, at the same time, tempestuous and of strictly secondary significance in my life as a whole, but I should proclaim that at the moment I now describe she looked little less than magnificent: masterful and confident, but dignified; with no ostentation and with no excessive self-assertion. I had observed her in that light on past occasions. She looked her best when in command; which cannot be said of all women, according to my rich experience of the sex.

Very possibly that was where she offended the hirsute and homely throng confronting us. When in the presence of a master, men do not like seemingly to accept direction by a mistress. Moreover, despite old Slow's impure tales, Lizzie and I had never before been publicly seen to collaborate in anything. What was she doing in my house, at such a time in the life of the parish, and at such an hour?

The consummation was utterly appalling.

Upon Lizzie's last word, two shots were heard, and Lizzie fell dead at my side. She must have been killed at once, because her clothing caught fire from the dropped Venetian lantern and she made no stir.

'Joshua Gorm,' I cried, 'and Elkanah Tuttle. You shall surely hang for this. You shall hang very high. That is another of my promises. My voice is one that will be heard.'

There was no more shooting, no more interjecting. There was only a universal scrambling and scuffling and scattering.

Yes, universal. I had to stamp upon and otherwise quell the flames unaided; without aid from one single man amongst them.

It was neither a difficult nor a dangerous task, as the flames had by no means taken full hold.

With the remaining lighted lantern in my hand, I carried Lizzie into my house, and upstairs, and into my own room, where I laid her upon my strait iron bed. I passed the night with her, disposing her, and keeping watch. I found myself wondering what else could have happened to her, if this had not. I was

The Breakthrough

glad that almost her last words had been 'There is nothing to fear'. I remembered one of the great poet's remarks in my hearing, so many years before: 'Hope and fear are the two great enemies of mankind.' I have regularly found it to be so.

As for the vile miscreants, Gorm and Tuttle, I saw the matter through to the end, as I had promised them. I discharged everything I could in person. At the end, I had no relish for their hanging, and had never before attended an event of that precise kind, but it was a duty to poor Lizzie to be there. The others asserted that Tuttle, the supernumary, made a good end, but that Gorm, leering no longer, failed to do so. I did not care for the proceedings, and offered no view of my own.

Remarkably early in the morning after Lizzie's foul murder, I found myself waited upon by Toddy Lewis and Sailor Onslow, our two brave but comparatively green churchwardens. Their caps were in their hands and their gaze was earthwards. I myself might well have seemed dishevelled and unkempt. It is important never to offer oneself in that manner, but I then made a certain exception, and admitted the pair to my business room.

'Sit down,' I said to the two of them, and offered them a glass of cordial, which each accepted. I made it a large glass, and the cordial was strong. *In vino veritas*. I then took a seat myself.

'And what, gentlemen, can I do for you first?' I enjoined.

They started speaking simultaneously, but it was Sailor Onslow who held to his course.

'We need a letter written, sir. Properly, it's the squire should do it, or his sister should do it, with the squire telling her what to say. But they've both gone away, as you know, sir, and we hope you'll do it instead. If you don't mind us asking, sir.'

Of course it was true about the squire and his sister, and, indeed, it was true also that there was no schoolmaster or even

Intrusions

schoolmistress in the parish, to whom otherwise the wardens would presumably have had recourse. There had been no schoolmaster or schoolmistress for the last seven or eight years. Instead, Lizzie had provided classes of her own, and I daresay the pupils learned more in that way than they would have done from any average pedagogue, and how much more rapidly!

'Do you mean a letter to the police authorities?' I enquired. 'If so, you need not trouble. I've written a letter of my own. I wrote it with much care and grief during the hours of darkness.'

I observed that whereas Lewis flushed, Onslow slightly paled, despite his always somewhat unconvincing tan or rubicundity.

'No, sir,' said Lewis. 'It's not that. We all know that's in good hands.'

I bowed slightly towards the pair of them. 'What then?' I asked.

'It's a letter to Mr Ridgeway,' said Lewis.

'As patron of the living,' said Onslow.

'Indeed,' I said, and paused, while they waited motionlessly, not even for the instant supping their long cordials.

'Tell me,' I resumed, after a due interval. 'Is all quiet again in the parish? I take it that you were not among the persons that visited me uninvited last night, and to whom I gave certain assurances?'

'Not us, sir,' said Sailor Onslow. 'We weren't there.'

'Certainly not, sir,' said Lewis, cringing none the less.

Of course one could not believe a word that either might say on such a topic, and especially not Onslow, who could not be believed on any topic.

'Then favour me with your opinion, none the less. To a certain degree, you are both temporarily responsible for the community. Is all quiet in the parish once more? I ask you that.'

'All quiet, sir,' said Onslow, in his deceptively bluff way.

The Breakthrough

'All quiet, sir,' said Lewis. 'Everything is quiet. But we need a new rector, and speedily.'

I fixed the two of them with my gaze.

'What, then, of Mr Stooling? How is he? And where?'

Naturally, they had made particular preparations for an answer to those questions.

'He's gone away,' said Toddy Lewis. 'To Furness in Lancashire.'

'He won't be back,' said Onslow, with excessive boldness.

It was true that the Reverend Mr Stooling had come in the first place from Lancashire; from a small orphan and foundling asylum there, as I understood. I had been told as much at the time of his arrival amongst us. The particularisation of the Furness area was new. Lancashire and Yorkshire were, and are, notoriously replete with institutions of the kind now in question; the little inmates being drawn from the whole of England. It in no way followed that Stooling was a North Countryman by blood, nor perhaps did it greatly matter. He was an ordained Clerk in Holy Orders, and such are by definition citizens of the wide world or of no world.

'Have you his address there?' I enquired. 'An address that a letter would in due course reach?'

'No address,' said Onslow, a little too hastily. 'He didn't leave one.'

'We didn't exactly see him go,' said Lewis, with a certain sly irony, hardly called for.

'But he told us he didn't like it here,' said Onslow, with the obtrusive eagerness that he had displayed before.

'He wanted to minister among mountains,' said Lewis, plainly catching hold of some casual remark, and improvising boldly upon it. 'He needed that.'

'Like when he was little, I suppose, sir,' said Onslow, obviously supposing nothing of the kind, but palpably having just thought of the words.

'It is unfortunate that you have no precise address,' I remarked. 'I cannot apply to the patron of the living for a new rector unless I have it in writing that the former one wishes to resign or retire. That, I fear, has to be the end of the matter, at least for the present.'

'He *told* us, sir,' said Onslow, now with an air of conscious patience and forbearance. 'He told us he didn't like it here and that he wasn't coming back.'

One could indeed, as Onslow described the supposed scene, visualise the unhappy man as speaking in just that childlike way. None the less, I naturally believed not a word of it.

'We can't leave the parish on its own, sir,' said Lewis. 'The squire went away, and now the rector's gone. There's no one left with position.'

'And certain other things have gone, too,' I put in, by way of antidote to Lewis's importunity.

'Things that should never have been permitted to come,' said Lewis, in his pert, churchwarden tone, albeit newly acquired. 'You know that, sir, as well as we do.'

'Well, perhaps I do, Lewis,' I said. 'But I still cannot write to the patron of the living until I hear from Mr Stooling in his own voice or by his own hand. I might almost say that it is the law of the land.'

With fairly simple people, matters are often most specially clarified by a reference to the fundamental aspect, the common law.

But Sailor Onslow responded somewhat cheekily. 'As for the law, you saw for yourself what happened last night, sir. The

The Breakthrough

parish needs a new rector badly, and some say a new squire too, with him a Roman Catholic.'

'I understand better than most, Onslow,' I said. 'But I have defined the position and I cannot change it. You are plainly aware from what you said that there was a terrible occurrence here last night. Could one or both of you bear a message from me to Dr Chard?'

The difficulty was that John Chard lived as far out on the directly opposite side of the parish as I did on my side of it. Lacking a horse by reason of my determinedly eremitical existence, I could not practically or safely have reached him through the darkness; nor should I have cared to leave the mortal remains of poor Lizzie unguarded in my house, and at such a disturbed period in the parish life. It would be just the opportunity that the boys would be waiting to seize.

Toddy Lewis and Sailor Onslow looked at one another before replying. I knew perfectly well that visiting Dr Chard was never a light matter.

In the end, Onslow said, 'I'm not sure that we rightly can, sir. We have both of us our allotted tasks, and we've spent time already in coming out here.' Of course it was hard to know what tasks had been allotted to Sailor Onslow, and better not to enquire, far better.

Lewis said, 'They'll be waiting for me already. At a time like this, they'll keep me busy every moment of the day. And my poor wife too. And my daughters. I'm very sorry, sir.' Both the Lewis girls were more than a little weak in the head, it being hard to say which was the weaker, and hard to believe that either could help more than she hindered. But such are families, and such is life. Chard had desisted from certifying either girl, out of consideration for their father.

Intrusions

Onslow, having had time to think, added, 'It's like you not being able to help *us*, sir.' I might have known that he would be resourceful, albeit but craftily.

Lewis had a suggestion to contribute: 'Suppose, sir, we were both to watch out for old Slow? He'd take a message.'

I had heard enough. I rose to my feet and turned on them fiercely. 'Do you clearly realise that there is a dead person lying in this house? I think you do. And I think you also know what person it is. It is necessary for Dr Chard to issue a certificate. Legally necessary. I ask both of you for your help to that end.'

There was another pause while they looked at one another and then carefully looked away from one another.

Lewis emerged this time as the spokesman. 'We'll see what we can do,' he mumbled, and with no conviction or true helpfulness at all. They had remained seated. Possibly that was attributable in part to my cordial.

I had seen for some time that both their large glasses were empty. It could not be said that my strong liquor had helped very much to the reaching of an understanding. But now I saw something else. Through the business room window my outer gate was visible, and I noticed at that moment that old Slow was leaning upon and across it in his familiar way, further in than ever.

It was not at all my intention that Slow should be the man to take my message to John Chard, as my response to Lewis's words had made clear. Still, Slow would have to be dealt with. That was regularly necessary.

As always, I stated the situation fully and exactly. 'Gentlemen,' I said, 'I have to pass the time of day with old Slow, who is now at my gate, but I do not propose to entrust to him the urgent message I have referred to; he being too far sunk in years for the distance and responsibility involved. Pray remain seated,

The Breakthrough

and decide what you can do for me yourselves, and for the dead woman too.' I was aware that my words included an ingredient that was complimentary to Lewis and even to Onslow, and I had intended it to be so.

I then strode out to tackle Slow, having small idea of what he might feel himself called upon to say.

'I fancy you had visitors last night, master,' were his first words.

He never troubled himself with formal greetings, but now he had not even removed his shapeless hat.

'Yes,' I replied. 'Were you among them?'

'Not me, master. You saw that for yourself.'

'The night was dark. I should not have enquired if I had seen.'

It was unworthy, schoolboyish repartee on my part, and I was immediately ashamed of it, as I still am. It is proper to face shame, when it comes one's way; to confront it and remain with it, as with everything else that slights or mortifies.

But Slow merely said, 'You wasn't the only one to have visitors, master. You know that.'

'I supposed it,' I replied cautiously.

'You're seemingly still alive, master.'

I took it that he was hinting, in his usual manner, at what had happened to Lizzie, which must by now have been gossip throughout the parish.

'I am alive,' I said, 'and I shall see to it that the law takes its full course.'

'That might be difficult, master. He was up a tree. The lawyers will have to prove how he found his way there.'

I had been quick in jumping to a conclusion and slow in perceiving what the conclusion was. Now I seemed to discern all things instantly.

Intrusions

'If Mr Stooling has been murdered too,' I cried, 'justice will be done against those responsible there also. Mr Stooling has the same claims upon the law as everyone else. This is not matter of a village joke.'

'The law will have to prove it, as I say, master. The Reverend was simply *found dead*, as the coroner puts it.' Again and again, old Slow came out with such odd scraps of knowledge.

'Who found him?' I enquired; in full suspicion of what the answer would be.

'I did, master. I found him.'

Possibly this was the circumstance that predominantly explained Slow's attendance upon me at so early an hour. Considering where Slow resided, and also what he had just said, I deduced that he had been up all night. There would be nothing unusual in that. Old Slow only slept when he meant to.

Having this time expected Slow's answer, I lost nothing of my self-possession. 'Where is the body now?' I asked.

'Still up there, master. Where should it be? It's too high for *me* to fetch. It's for the wardens to get him down.'

It was my cue, as they say in the theatre, or used to say. 'I'll speak to the churchwardens myself,' I replied. 'They're with me at this moment.'

Of course Slow knew that as well as I did, but he accepted his *congé*.

'If they come to me,' he said, making to move off, 'I'll show them where the Reverend is hanging. I'll do that much for them, master.'

'Hanging?' I cried, with the vision of Joshua Gorm and Elkanah Tuttle, and the fate ahead of them fully before my eyes, as it inevitably was every moment at that time.

'Oh, don't mistake me, master,' Slow responded very coolly. 'He's hanging quite naturally. I didn't mean any offence.

The Breakthrough

Simply found dead, master. You mightn't even call it hanging. You might use a different word altogether.'

He was shambling away, still without even touching his patched hat.

I strode back to my house and confronted the two churchwardens. Their heads were as close as two chestnuts in one husk.

'I have dealt with you frankly and openly,' I proclaimed. 'Why do you not behave likewise? Why did you not tell me outright that Mr Stooling had been found dead?'

'How should we have known that, sir? You did not know it yourself until now.' I need hardly say it was Sailor Onslow speaking.

'How did it happen, sir?' asked Toddy Lewis.

They scarcely troubled even to effect surprise.

'I think you both know all about it already and that there is no need for me to enter into distasteful details. You will find that specific responsibilities lie before you in the matter. I have only this to repeat: that if anything has happened that is contrary to the law, you can depend upon me to make sure that those responsible make answer to the law.'

'The rectors here die in strange ways, sir,' remarked Onslow, as if musing. 'It was the same with Dr Jaunt, and the same with Dr Liverwright, if tales be true. No one knows about Dr Blunderstone.'

'It was *not* the same with Dr Jaunt,' I replied with all possible firmness. 'The circumstances of Dr Jaunt's death were perfectly natural, and were so certified by a man of medicine, Dr Chard, than whom no one was ever more dependable.'

'Dr Chard will certify this time too,' said Onslow, with the ghost of an impudent smile. 'If he can be reached quick enough.'

Intrusions

Toddy Lewis was shifting about, plainly deprecating this line of discussion, as well he might. He insinuated his pressing thought between Onslow and me.

'*Now* will you write to Mr Ridgeway, sir?' he asked.

'I can promise you one thing, Lewis,' I said. 'If I do so, I shall lay great stress upon the parish being provided with a man who knows his own mind and his own power and powers.'

'That is as it should be, sir,' responded Lewis.

'We have no squire, sir,' said Onslow superfluously. 'No squire who lives amongst us and orders our ways and holds our faith, that is.'

'I shall write to Miss Tatham-Mortlock,' I said, 'informing her, on her brother's behalf, of all that has occurred. Mr and Miss Tatham-Mortlock are at Bodighera in Italy. For them I have an address.'

I then struck out on a line of my own.

'I take it that work will now resume at the church? And that the fissure in the floor will be covered as a first task? I should suggest that the opportunity be taken of filling in the entire vault, if vault it is. We none of us want a repetition of what has been happening. The duty to act in these matters now rests firmly upon you two gentlemen.'

'If Mr Stooling is really dead,' said Lewis, 'then he might be put down the vault before it is filled. That would seem safest.'

'I think it would require a faculty.'

'Perhaps you would be so good as to apply for one, sir, on behalf of the parish? You would be sure to get one and we, being so new to the wardenship, might not.'

'I promise to think about that too, Lewis. I shall bear all things in mind.'

As often, Sailor Onslow attempted the last word.

'I don't think there's any other answer, sir.'

The Breakthrough

I had of course remained standing, and at length the two of them rose to go.

'See that neither of you treads on that stoat,' I enjoined sternly. 'Or the last word may be his.'

THE NEXT GLADE

'I AM COMING to see you,' said the man. 'Tomorrow. Tomorrow afternoon.'

He looked into her eyes quite steadily, but he certainly didn't smile.

Noelle did smile. 'You don't know where I live,' she said.

'I know very well,' said the man.

Obviously, it would have been easy enough for him to have found out from Simon and Mut, whose party it was, but it seemed strange that he should have done so before even meeting Noelle, before setting eyes on her, almost certainly before being told about her. Not until that moment had he implied that he already knew anything at all about her. It would have been absurd for Noelle to ask him how he knew.

'We can't just leave it at this,' said the man, with some urgency. 'We can't.'

'Perhaps we can,' said Noelle.

'I know the district round Woking pretty well,' said the man. 'I'll call for you about three tomorrow and we'll go for a walk in the woods.'

True enough, where Noelle lived, there were woods of a kind in almost every direction; but that applied to so much of residential Surrey. Specifically, there was a wood on the other side of the road, opposite her gate.

The Next Glade

'I don't promise to be there,' said Noelle. 'I can't.'

'Then I shall have to take a chance,' said the man. 'We mustn't just leave it, and we'll get no further here.'

'What's your name, anyway?' asked Noelle.

That tone was advancing upon her with the passing years. She deplored it, but one cannot expect to find people *en masse* who speak one's private language. It is bound to suffer erosion by the *lingua franca*.

But, as if to confirm the man's point that further communication was impossible, Mut at that instant turned up the record-player and Simon turned on the new strip lighting. Simon and Mut went through a party as if it were a dress rehearsal. As little as possible was left to chance. Noelle always wondered what would happen if there were ever to be an actual performance.

Still without a smile, the man had dissolved into the glare and the din. Noelle wondered if he were making an assignation with someone else; perhaps proposing the North Downs as background. Alternatively, he might well be going home. For him, the party might have fulfilled its purpose.

Only when Melvin, her husband, was on his travels, did Noelle herself go to these parties where almost everyone was younger than she. But that was quite frequently, so she realised how lucky she was that people like Simon and Mut could still be bothered with her. Not that Mut in particular was so enormously younger. Noelle and Mut had aforetime shared an apartment. The then infant Simon had already been Mut's lover, been it for years, but Noelle had not yet met Melvin. Indeed, when Mut had been out of the room, Simon could be depended upon for a small-scale agitation, or quick pass. It was a tradition that still lingered.

As it happened, a surprising number of men seemed still to fall fractionally in love with Noelle, and to prefer dulcet and

191

tender talk with her to such other things as might be on offer elsewhere. Noelle could never decide whether it was merely her appearance or something less primary that drew them. She often reflected upon how little she had to complain of.

Noelle had been perfectly truthful in saying that she couldn't, as well as wouldn't, make a promise. Melvin did sometimes return before his time. As far as she could tell, there was nothing unpleasant or ulterior about this. It seemed natural that Melvin should be blown hither and thither by the trade winds, because everyone else was. Gone are the days of predictable grind in the high-stooled counting house; settled for a lifetime. Business has changed completely, as businessmen always point out.

Besides, Judith or Agnew might be sent home from school early. That often occurred. And if she was in the house when one or the other of them arrived, she had to give much time either to listening to a tale of grievance and storm, or to anxious effort in trying to discover what this time could ever have happened.

But, when the moment came, the clock she had inherited from her father (he had been given it by his firm less than a year before his death) struck three, and the doorbell was shimmering before the last dull echo had faded.

The man was politely extending his hand. 'My name is John Morley-Wingfield. With a hyphen, I fear I must admit. Let's get that over to start with.'

His expression was serious, but not sad. His brown hair curled pleasantly, but not unduly, and was at perhaps its most impressive moment, fading in places, but not yet too seriously grey. His brown eyes were sympathetic without being sentimental. His garb was relaxed without being perfunctory.

For Noelle, hesitation would have served no purpose.

The Next Glade

'Do come in for a little,' she said. 'My children return from school in an hour.'

'Are they doing well?'

'Not very.'

She led him into the room which Melvin called the lounge and she called nothing in particular.

'If you'll sit down, I'll bring us a cup a tea.'

'We must keep enough time for our walk.'

She looked at him. 'The wood's not all that big. None of them are round here.'

He sat on the leathery, cushiony settee, and gazed at his brightly polished brown shoes. 'I always think a wood is much the same, however big or small it is. Within reason, of course. The impact is the same. At least upon me.'

'You don't actually get lost in these particular woods,' said Noelle. 'You can't.'

He glanced up at her. It was plain that he took all this for delay, wanted them to make a start.

'I'll hurry with the tea,' said Noelle. 'Will you be all right? Perhaps you'd care to look at this?'

She gave him the latest *Statist*. She did not remark that it was her husband who subscribed to it. The man, who had known her address, probably knew about her husband also.

'Or this might be more cheerful.'

She held out a back number of the *National Geographical* magazine. It was Melvin too who subscribed to that, though he complained that he never had time to read it, so that the numbers always lay about unsorted until Noelle gave the children an armful for use as reinforcement in and around the sandpit.

Noelle went to the kitchen.

When she came back with the tray, the man was on his feet again, and looking restlessly at the books. They were, yet again,

Melvin's books. Noelle's were upstairs, not all of them even unpacked, owing to shelf shortage.

'Milk and sugar?'

'A very little milk, please. No sugar.'

'I know we *shouldn't*,' said Noelle.

He stooped over her so that she could hand him his cup. He had a faint but striking aroma, the smell of a pretty good club.

'Careful,' said Noelle.

He drifted, sipping, round the room, as if it had been full of people, or perhaps trees, and every settling place occupied, or, alternatively, gnarled and jagged.

He spoke. 'You have the most wonderful hair.' He was on the far side of the big television.

Noelle sat up a little, but said nothing.

'And eyes.'

Noelle could not prevent herself dimpling almost perceptibly.

'And figure. It would not be possible to imagine a shape more beautiful.'

One trouble was that Noelle simply did not know how true or untrue any of these statements were. She had always found it impossible to make up her mind. More precisely, she sometimes felt one thing, and sometimes almost the complete opposite. One had, if one could, to strike an average among the views expressed or implied by others; and others seemed to spend so much of their time dissimulating.

'Have a chocolate finger?' she said, extending the plate towards him at the full length of her arm. She was wearing a dress with delicate short sleeves. After all, it was August. Melvin particularly hated August in Pittsburgh, where now he was supposed to be.

'Nothing to eat, thank you.'

The Next Glade

The man was ranging between the Astronaut's Globe and the pile of skiing journals.

'I like your dress.'

'It's very simple.'

'You have wonderful taste.'

'Stop being so civil, please.'

'You seem to me quite perfect.'

'Well, I'm not.' But she made no further reference to any specific defect.

'Have some more tea? Bring me your cup.'

He traversed the Eskimo-style carpet with measured, springy tread.

'Then we must go,' he said. 'We really must. I want to see you in your proper element.'

She handed up the refilled cup without looking at him. 'You're right about one thing,' she said. 'I do love our woods. I only wish they were larger.'

'You love all music too,' said the man, standing over her.

'Yes.'

'And the last moments before sunset in the countryside?'

'Yes.'

'And being alone in a quiet spot at noon?'

'I usually have the children's meal to prepare.'

'And wearing real silk next to your skin?'

'I am not sure that I ever have.'

He dashed the cup back on the tray quite sharply. Noelle could see that it was far from empty.

'Let's go. Let's go now.'

She walked out with him just as she was. He followed her down the crazy concrete path, mildly multicoloured. The reason why the gate groaned was that the children liked the noise. They swung backwards and forwards on it for hours, and threw fits at the idea of the hinges being oiled.

She crossed the road with the man, surprised that there was no whizzing traffic. All life had eased off for a moment. They ascended the worn, earth slope into the wood.

'You be guide,' said the man.

'I keep telling you it's not the New Forest.'

'It's far more attractive.'

As it happened, Noelle almost agreed with that; or at least knew what the man might have meant. Melvin and she took the children to the New Forest each year, camping at one of the official sites; and each year she found the New Forest a disappointment.

'You fill the wood with wonder,' said the man.

'We just go straight ahead, you know,' said Noelle. 'Really there's not much else. All the other paths come to nothing. They're simply beaten down by the kids.'

'And by the wild things,' said the man.

'I don't think so.'

They were walking side by side now, among the silver birches, and it was true that the voice of the world was becoming much drowsier, the voice of nature more express. It was, of course, a Tuesday: probably the best day for such an enterprise.

'Will you permit me to put my arm round your waist?' asked the man.

'I suppose so,' said Noelle.

He did it perfectly; neither limply, nor with adolescent tenacity. Noelle began to fall into sympathetic dissolution. She had a clear thirty-five minutes before her.

'The beeches begin here,' she said. 'Some of them are supposed to be very old. Nothing will grow around their roots.'

'That clears the way for us,' said the man.

The Next Glade

Hitherto, the path had gone gently upwards, but now it had reached the small ridge and begun to descend. Noelle knew that here the wood widened out. None the less, the broad and beaten track led nowhere, because at the far end of the wood lay private property, heavily farmed, and with the right of way long closed and lost, doubtless through insufficient public resistance at the time. Noelle, if asked, would have been very unsure who owned the wood. It seemed to exist in its own right.

'Glorious trees,' said the man. 'And you are the spirit of them.'

He was looking up into the high and heavy branches. His grasp of Noelle was growing neither tighter nor looser: admirable. They walked slowly on.

'That's the end,' said Noelle, pointing ahead with her free arm.

Two or three hundred yards before them, the wood ended in a moderate-sized dell or clearing; probably no more than the work of all the people who at this point had rotated and gone back on their tracks, returned up the slope.

'I keep telling you how small the wood is,' said Noelle. 'Not much bigger than a tent.'

'Never mind,' said the man, gently. 'It doesn't matter. Nothing like that matters.'

All the way there had, of course, been strewn rubbish, but at the terminal clearing there was considerably more of it.

'How disgusting!' said Noelle. 'What a degradation!'

'Don't look at it,' said the man, as before. 'Look upwards. Look at the trees. Let's sit down for a moment.'

It could not be said that the sections of beech trunk lying about had been hollowed out by the authorities into picnic couches, but the said sections had undoubtedly been sliced and trimmed for public use, and arranged like scatter cushions in a television room. It must have taken weeks to do it, but Noelle was of course accustomed to the scene, and had long ago resolved not to let it upset her. She realised that the vast population of the world had everywhere to be accommodated. It was as if there were a war on always.

Seated, the man began to cuddle her, and she to sink into it for the time available to her. They were sitting with their backs to the wood end and the farmland beyond. But, after a few moments—precious moments, perhaps—he unexpectedly took away his arm and rose to his feet.

'Forgive me,' he said. 'I should like to explore for a little. You wait here. I'll soon be back.'

'How far are you going?'

'Just into the next glade.'

Naturally, she knew that it would be perfectly silly and embarrassing for her to say any more. Melvin often wandered off in that way for a few minutes, and had done it even when they were merely engaged. All men did it. Still, there was one thing she simply could not help pointing out.

'I must go back in six minutes at the very most now.' The constant care of children makes for exactitude in situations of that kind.

He had taken several steps away before she had finished speaking. Now he stopped and half turned back towards her. He gazed at her for a perceptible period of time; then turned again, and resumed his course without speaking. Noelle had later to admit to herself that she had been aware at once of some difference between the man's deportment and the deportment of men in general. It was almost as if the man slid or glided, so tutored was his gait.

The man strode elegantly and effectively off into the woodland to her right. Here there was fairly dense brush and scrub,

The Next Glade

so that the man disappeared quite rapidly. Noelle could hear his brown shoes crushing the twigs and mast, no doubt scuffing the high polish.

Presumably he was shoving through brushwood, but he seemed to advance very steadily, and soon there was no further sound from him.

Noelle gave him four uneasy minutes, then rose in her turn. She called out: 'I shall have to be going. I must go.'

There was no response. There was no sign or sound of him.

'Where are you?'

Not even a woodpecker signalled.

Noelle called out much more loudly. 'John! John, I have to go.'

That was the limit of possible action. She could not be expected to shout for the rest of the afternoon, to mount a one-woman search party. There could be no possible question of the man being lost, as she herself had already remarked.

So there was only one thing for her to do. She walked quickly home, much confused in mind and feeling.

When she had arrived, only a single aspiration was definable: that the man, having emerged from the wood in one way or another, would not reappear at her home when the children were having their tea.

He did not reappear. But Noelle remained in a state of jitters until she retired to her single bed.

The next morning she telephoned Mut. She had not cared to do so while the children were in the house.

'That man at your party. John Morley-Wingfield. Tell me about him.'

'John Morley was a nineteenth-century politico, darling. He wrote the life of Gladstone. It's a good book in its own way.'

'I'm sure it is. But it's a different man.'

'It always is a different man, darling.'

'I'm speaking of John Morley-Wingfield who was at your party.'

'Never heard of him, darling. I don't know half the people by name. Do you want me to ask Simon when he gets back?'

'I think I do. Something rather funny has happened. I'll tell you when I see you.'

'What's he look like?'

'Suave and competent. Like a diplomat.'

'At *our* party?'

'I got on rather well with him.'

'The trouble with you is you don't know your own strength. Never mind. I've written down the name. I'll ask Simon. But don't expect much joy. Any news of Melvin?'

In the event, there was no joy at all, because for some time nothing more was heard from Mut on the subject, and Noelle swiftly passed beyond the stage of wanting to know. She realised that one is often half picked up by men who soon think better of the idea, and for one or more of many different reasons, not all of them necessarily detrimental to oneself. Nothing in the least unusual had happened.

Indeed, the only discernible upshot was that Noelle ceased to walk in the woods: not only in the particular wood opposite her front gate, but all the other woods in the district. Some of them in any case were mere struggling strips of scrubland and thorn bush: hardly worth visiting unless one was utterly desperate.

But one Sunday, four or five months later, Melvin suggested that they go for a stroll with the children. It was because one car had been lent to a business friend, whose own had apparently been stolen; and Noelle had forgotten to licence the other. Melvin had been very forgiving, as he always was, always.

'Just give me a minute or two to get kitted out,' said Melvin.

Noelle knew what that meant, and herself changed into tan trousers and a lumber jacket. The least she could do was co-operate in those supposedly secondary matters that so often proved to be primary. The children were dressed as pioneers already.

Melvin, when he reappeared, eclipsed them all, as was natural. A casual looker-on could hardly have distinguished him from Wild Bill Hickok, especially as Melvin purchased most of his fun gear in the States or in Toronto.

There could be no question of going anywhere but into the wood, because for anything else a motor would have been needed. The children were permitted to walk to and from school, because Noelle had put her foot down and refused to tie herself to driving them so short a distance four times a day, whatever the other mothers might do and say. Melvin in turn put his foot down when the possibility arose of the mites straggling along the highway at any other time.

'Don't forget it may rain,' now said Melvin.

Of course, Noelle had felt certain qualms from the outset, and as soon as they were among the silver birches, she rejoiced that at least she was so differently arrayed, all but in disguise. Moreover, the woods always felt quite different when one entered them with one's entire family. The things that happened when one was with one's family were amazingly unlike the things that happened when one was not. It was this fact that made the transition between the one state and the other always so upsetting.

'Just wait till we meet a buffalo,' said Melvin to the children.

Intrusions

Agnew screamed with delight, but Judith hitched at her belt and looked cynical.

'Got your lasso ready, son?' asked Melvin.

Agnew twirled it round his head and started leaping about among the tangled tree roots. Judith also began to run about, holding her arms in front of her above her head, and bringing them together at short intervals, as if she were catching butterflies, which she was not.

There were no butterflies. There never were many.

'I'm dead to the world,' said Melvin softly to Noelle, when the children were at what could be regarded as a safe distance, short though that distance really was. 'I'm fagged out.' In the home circle, Melvin expressed himself conservatively, domestically. He never used the words he used at work.

'You look a bit pale,' said Noelle, without turning to him. She had noticed it ever since his return from Johannesburg the day before yesterday. Pallor of any kind would be quite incompatible with his ranch-hand rig.

'I don't know what I'm going to do, Noelle,' he went on. She had always disallowed any contraction or distortion of her Christian name, or any nickname. 'My head feels as if it will burst. I've felt sicker and sicker ever since that February bust-up in Edmonton.'

To Noelle it seemed that Melvin went to Edmonton more often than to anywhere else, and that always it led to trouble, though that last time had doubtless been the worst of all, because Melvin had spoken of it ever since, shaking with rage and bafflement. Edmonton in Alberta, of course; not John Gilpin's homely Edmonton.

'You'd better lay up,' said Noelle. 'I expect we can afford it.'

The Next Glade

'No such thing,' said Melvin, with what Noelle deemed an unreasonable darkness in his tone. He had never permitted Noelle to look for even a part-time job. It was one of those various things about which she was never sure whether she was glad or sorry. She knew that she somewhat lacked any very specific qualifications.

'I can't let up for a single day,' said Melvin. 'I'd be shot out if I did. Make no mistake about that.'

She supposed that there he must probably be right. Many of her local acquaintances already had husbands who had been declared redundant, as the usage now was.

The matter was settled for the moment by Agnew falling over, his feet and legs entangled in his lariat, as if he'd been a steer.

Noelle hoicked him up. She had the readiness of experience, as with an acrobat or exhibition wrestler.

'No bones broken,' she said, stroking Agnew's stylishly unbarbered locks. 'No blood spilt. No nasty bruise.' One could not really know about the last, but it was the thing one said, and very possibly the utterance terminated the danger.

Judith was still running about catching phantom moths. She was a lissom, leggy little girl, but already deep, much as Noelle herself was deep.

'You was riding the range,' said Melvin, stubbing Agnew between the shoulders with mock manliness. 'You've had a spill, but you're up again, and riding high.'

'It was the silly rope,' said Agnew.

'Ride on, cowboy,' directed Melvin, patriarchal, example-setting.

'Why should he?' enquired Judith at some distance and to no one in particular, no one short of the universe.

'Get going,' called out Melvin. 'Show 'em. Prove it.'

Intrusions

Agnew looked doubtful, but began once more to plunge about. Fortunately, they had now reached the beeches, where the roots, though thicker, were for that reason more noticeable. Agnew had begun to use his lasso as if it were a fishing line. All the pockets in the roots were full of fish. Some of them actually did contain a little water. It had been raining on and off for many weeks. Noelle had been going everywhere in a stylish mackintosh.

'I'm nearing the end of the line,' said Melvin to Noelle. 'Something will just have to give, or I shall break.'

The two children began running down the slope to the cleared space at the end, where everyone turned and went back up again. The relatively long-limbed Judith, relatively unencumbered with miniature ranch gear, arrived easily first. She started an Ashanti dance she had seen on colour television at school.

Noelle's heart began to sink further and to beat faster with every descending step. She had, as usual, forgotten how all courage leaves one when the peril, whatever it be, is really close in time or space or both.

'I've thought of applying for a transfer,' said Melvin. 'I haven't told you, because I didn't want to worry you.' He was trying to struggle out of his trapper's jerkin, though the weather was no warmer than it had been, and Noelle felt chillier every minute.

They were all assembled in the clearing. The circumambient litter was now sodden, much of it eaten away by enormous, conjectural rats. There was no other human being visible, or even audible; doubtless owing to the unsettled forecast.

'Well, there's nothing else to do but go back,' said Noelle almost immediately.

The Next Glade

'No!!!' At school the children had learned the trick of negating loudly in unison.

'Let's sit down for a moment,' said Melvin.

'It's all too soggy,' protested Noelle.

'I've got *The Frontiersman* from last time,' proclaimed Melvin, producing it from the rustler's pocket in his cast-off jerkin. 'I'll rip it up and we can take half each. I never have time to read it anyway.'

'We can't sit among so much litter. It's disgusting. It's degrading.'

But Melvin was settled on one of the adapted tree trunks and was chivalrously holding out the bigger portion of the bisected journal.

'Just for a moment, Noelle,' he said wistfully, all but smiling at her. 'I need to get back some part of my sanity.'

So she slumped on the trunk beside him. She tried hard to keep her bottom on the small, thin package. 'Don't go too far away,' she said to the children. 'We're only stopping here for a minute.'

Melvin had drawn his lumberjack's knife, and was running his finger along the blade. His gaze was at once concentrated and absent-minded. Fortunately, the blade was unlikely to be very sharp.

'I often dream of what it *should* have been like,' said Melvin. 'On some island. Our island. You in a grass skirt, me in a leopard skin, perhaps a snow leopard skin, sun all the time, and breadfruit to chew, and mangoes, and coconuts, and flying fish. All day and all night the throbbing of the surf on the reef, and every now and then a distant schooner to wave to. Birds of paradise sweeping from palm tree to palm tree. Monkeys chattering and swinging. Loving you on the warm sand in the darkness beneath the Southern Cross.'

Intrusions

'Beautiful,' said Noelle, gently taking his hand. 'I'd like that.'

Melvin looked at her doubtfully. Agnew often had just that same look, inherited or acquired.

'I mean it. Truly,' said Noelle softly. 'I'd like it too. But we have to be practical.' She could not help squirming a little on the tiny, extemporised cushion.

'Do we? Must we?' He was drawing the lumber knife across the back of his hand.

'Of course we must, darling. I'm sure we can work something out together. Something practical.'

She always said that, and she would have been sincerely pleased if it had ever proved possible. What happened every time in actuality was that she had nearly expired of combined boredom and nausea before Melvin had made any real progress in describing the full details of the particular crisis. She never doubted that Melvin's business life was truly terrible. One trouble was that a terrible life is less fulfilling to others than a happy life.

He squeezed her hand. 'If the men in white coats don't come for me first,' he said.

'I'll keep them away,' she replied softly. 'I'll distract their attention.'

Inevitably, the children, forbidden to go far, were enjoying themselves among the litter. They were investigating discarded food and drink cans, deciphering sodden letterpress, speculating about indelicate proprietary utilities. Really they were only a few feet away. All along, surreptitiousness had been enforced upon the parental intimacies.

'You'd distract anyone's attention, Noelle,' said Melvin, almost whispering.

The Next Glade

Noelle looked away from his fatigued face and glanced for a moment towards the thicker foliage to the right of the clearing.

'I'd like you to distract mine this very moment,' said Melvin, *sotto voce*.

'We must be *practical*,' said Noelle.

Melvin threw the knife into the ground, though it failed to enter, and merely lay horizontally, adding to the litter.

'Children!' he called out. 'Run away and play for a bit.'

Noelle rose. 'No, don't,' she called to them.

Confused, the children came to a standstill before reaching the thicket towards which they had started charging. They began to play triangles on the rough ground. It was a game that everyone was playing and involved much darting about in a small area. Preferably, there should of course have been more players, but Agnew and Judith were still young enough to improvise. The game was something like rounders, an elementary version of it.

'We can't possibly,' said Noelle to Melvin. She sat down again beside him. 'We'll stay just a few more minutes, so that the children can have a run about, and I'll see if I can get them to bed a little earlier than usual.'

'I want you *now*,' said Melvin.

Noelle smiled at him, but said nothing. Though she rather fancied herself as a backwoods girl, she really preferred Melvin in one of his executive suits. At the time of Watteau and Fragonard, people played in the woods wearing wigs, panniers, and flowered silk from Lyon. They carried ribboned crooks.

'*Now*,' said Melvin. He picked up the knife and reattached it to its thong. 'Let's get lost in the forest. The kids won't even notice for a long time.'

Intrusions

Melvin often had whims of that kind. Noelle supposed them to be outlets for the pressure under which so much of his life was passed.

He rose to his feet and pulled Noelle to hers. 'Let's see how lost we can get.'

She had found it best at such moments to go along with him as far as was practicable. At the moment, it was quite true that the children seemed absorbed in their running and tumbling. Triangles is a far more physically demanding game than, say, ring-a-ring-a-roses. The children seemed not even to notice their gaucho parents departing across the worn clearing; exactly as Melvin had said. And, after all, there was no real reason why Noelle should not enter those bushes.

'I don't think we shall get *lost,*' she said. 'It's just into the next glade.'

'Have you been there?'

'Not really.'

'Then how do you know? When we stray from the warpath, we enter the impenetrable rain forest.'

All the same, Noelle did know. She had a precise mental picture of what it was like on the other side of the bushes. She always had had. She must have been there some time, though she could not remember the circumstances.

'It's impossible to get lost in these woods,' she said. 'Or in any of the other woods round here.'

Melvin had produced the knife once more, with a view to hacking and slashing a path for them.

'Truly, it's not as dense as that,' said Noelle. 'A very little pushing will do it. You could almost get through in evening dress.'

So, though the whole idea was Melvin's, it was she who went ahead, while he made a more proper job of it.

The Next Glade

Duly, she was through the thicket in about ninety seconds, and in the next glade. As she expected, it was quiet there, reassuring; unlittered, because untracked. The trees were taller and more dignified. There was an element of natural architecture, an element of mystery. Foliage hid the sky, moss the ground.

The moss was so deep and so apparently virgin as, in the exact present circumstances, to be suggestive. Noelle paddled through it across the width of the glade. The children might be temporarily out of touch with their parents, and she was fleetingly out of touch with Melvin, left further behind than mere yards would account for. She could not even hear his woodsmanship exercises; perhaps because she was not particularly listening for them.

She entered the trees on the far side of the glade; not in the least overwhelming, all conforming to perfectly acceptable proportions. Beyond this, however, she was sure she had never penetrated; and she was very aware of it. She had no idea of what she might find, though she knew perfectly well how small was the scope. She was in momentary and diplomatic flight.

She stopped. She had reached the end of the world already; even sooner than she had expected. It was marked by a tangle of wire: several different varieties and brands of wire; stretching between rotten leaning posts, with wood lice at their feet.

There was a house, timbered but not thatched. The rather large windows were one and all filled with diamond panes. There was a squinting figure in artificial stone above the garden door. Much of the detail was monastic in style. There was a very neat, big-leafed hedge all round the rectangular garden, every item in which was perfect. The hedge was low enough for Noelle to see across it where it ran parallel with the world's tangled boundary.

Intrusions

A man was digging a hole in one of the garden beds. For the purpose, a quantity of blooms had been displaced, which now lay forlorn on the grass. Indeed, one might well define the new artifact not as a hole but as a trench. The man was in his braces and wore a shirt and tie, as if he were acting upon impulse. They seemed to be an elegant silk shirt, and a handsome moiré tie. His was the only figure in sight, except for a mammal of some kind which scuffled ceaselessly up and down in a small cage near the house. The man was concentrating on his work and a minute or two passed before there was any question of his looking up.

As far as Noelle was concerned, it was unnecessary of him to look up. She knew quite well who he was. If the wires in front of her had been taut instead of tangled, she would have clutched at and clung to them.

It had at no time so much as occurred to her that John Morley-Wingfield was so near a permanent neighbour. At least it explained whither he had so casually disappeared. Furthermore, if he possessed a house of the type before her, he almost certainly possessed a wife and family also. Everything seemed unbelievably normal and familiar. There was even the pet in its cage.

But still she could not move or look away. This it was to be turned into a pillar of salt, even if only provisionally, and even though Melvin must surely be coming up behind her, with a knife in one hand, a miniature axe in the other. Necessarily, the man before her, almost certainly unaccustomed to steady manual effort, would soon be taking a short breather.

In an instant, he looked straight into Noelle's eyes.

Though his hair was hardly disarranged, his face was a confused mask, surrounding eyes filled with horror, eyes so large as to suggest that they would never again be their former size.

Noelle turned and ran. She managed, as everyone does at such times, to avoid all the roots and briars and potholes. Within seconds, she was tripping back across the tranquil and unvisited glade. Within a minute, she was making a disturbance. She was calling 'Melvin! Melvin!'

Melvin answered. 'Here, curse it.'

Before she could find him, she was out on the other side of the thicket. The children had at that very moment stopped playing and were strolling towards her. 'What's the matter, mummy? Has something happened?'

'I'm *here*,' roared out Melvin, from among the bushes. 'Blast it.'

'I think your father may have hurt himself,' said Noelle. 'Let's go and see if we can help, shall we?'

Melvin's left hand was streaming with blood. It had always been one of the most individual things about them that he had less than the usual differentiation between right-handedness and left-handedness. In most matters he seemed able to use both left and right with equal results. Noelle had never before met anyone else like that.

'We must just get you home as soon as possible and tie you up. You must lie down and rest, and Agnew and Judith will go to bed as quietly as mice.'

'*Why* must we?' asked Judith.

But Agnew was good and helpful all the way back.

This time Noelle remained in a state of jitters for considerably longer than on the previous occasion; and her nerviness was exacerbated by the unexpected complications that followed Melvin's mishap. He was required to remain at home and most of the time in bed, while his depleted system struggled with the toxins; and, all the time, but more and more vividly, he saw his position with the firm diminishing, receding, vanishing. The vision was so transparent to him that for much of the time Noelle could all too lucidly see it too.

'But they can't just get rid of you. It wouldn't even be legal.'

'They have ways and means. Make no mistake about that. We're going to starve, Noelle. But do come over here first. Take that dress off.'

In the end, Mut telephoned. Melvin was in bed with a particularly demanding group of complications. In the strict and immediate context, his absence from the scene downstairs was merciful.

'How's Melvin going on?'

'Not too good. He thinks the infection is poisoning his brain.'

'What do *you* think?'

'I've simply no idea. It's impossible to tell. It's just one thing after another.'

'You know that man you asked about? The one you said you met at our party?'

'I certainly do,' said Noelle. 'Has Simon anything to say about him?'

'Simon had never heard of him, but that doesn't matter. The point is that I think you just got his name out of the paper. I think you were dreaming.'

'Perhaps I really was,' said Noelle. 'But what makes you think so at this moment?'

'There was a criminal of that name, and apparently his case keeps turning up. I've come across him in the cornflakes crime book. You know, you get a copy in exchange for the backs of the boxes. Simon collected them and sent them in. It's the sort of thing you do if you're a barrister. William Morley-Westall. He lived in Kensington Square.'

'What name?' asked Noelle faintly.

'William Morley-Westall. The name you gave me.'

'It wasn't the name I gave you. It's you who are in a state of muddle, Mut.'

'I'm sure it was.'

'Well, it wasn't. What happened in the end to your man, anyway?'

'He was sent to Broadmoor. I expect he's out by this time. Ages ago, in fact. They only keep them for a matter of months nowadays. Simon says it's all wrong. But people are still arguing about the case. It's in the news the whole time. I'm sure that's where you saw it.'

'I expect so, Mut. I haven't much time to think about such things at the moment.'

But of course it was difficult to think much about anything else. Men and their dreams! One man driven to crime, obviously horrifying. The other prostrate with complications, and almost certainly dragging himself and his family to ruin.

That disaster was not immediate, because there were scattered savings that could be drawn upon, but in the end Melvin had to be taken to hospital. Probably he would have been taken sooner, had there been room for him.

Noelle began to read the jobs advertisements in the local paper, buying odd copies for the purpose, but not yet very systematically. She even found herself glancing at the offers and miniature proclamations in the window of the shop.

Intrusions

Week followed week, and as it became more and more necessary to be sensible, it became more and more difficult. Noelle suspected that the doctors were baffled, though of course they never said so. Certainly she herself had begun to find life as a whole baffling as never before. It was all but impossible to decide how big a step it was appropriate to take.

Judith had begun to ail in various different ways, two or three of them at a time; and had no difficulty in making plain that fundamentally the trouble lay in her anxieties about her daddy, and her doubts about her mummy. Agnew, on the other hand, had quietened down and become a quite nice little boy. It was as when a running bull calf ceases to be chivvied and goaded. Noelle began in small ways to confide in him; in trifles, positively to rely upon him. Previously she had never been able to speak to him, to endear herself, to trust him.

One night the telephone rang. It was well after eleven.

'Get up please, darling,' said Noelle to Agnew, whose unkempt head lay in her lap. 'Just for a second.'

Agnew responded quite obligingly.

'Hullo. Oh it's you, Mut.'

'Come to a party on Friday. Sorry to be so late in asking you. It'll be the usual people and the usual things.'

'I don't think I'd better, Mut.'

'It'll take you out of yourself.'

'No, not really.'

Agnew was gazing at her with big eyes, though less big than those other eyes, which she saw for so much of the time.

'Thank you very much, none the less,' said Noelle. 'It's sweet of you.'

'How *is* Melvin, anyway?'

'Worse, as far as I can tell. The doctors seem to be baffled.'

The Next Glade

'Quite seriously, Noelle, I suggest the time has come to fetch him back home. Where he is, it's the blind leading the blind.'

Agnew had crept up to her on the floor, and was nuzzling into her thigh.

'I daresay you're right, Mut. But you know how bad I am as a nurse. You'll remember for yourself how hopeless I always was.'

'I remember,' said Mut. 'In that case, I suggest you come to the party. At least, it will take your mind off.'

'I'm not sure it will. It didn't the last time.'

Agnew took away his nose and cheek. He had very nearly suffocated himself.

'You mean the mystery man. Simon's got a new idea about *him*. From your description, he thinks he can only have been a man called John Martingale, who lives quite near you. He's supposed to have a lovely garden.'

'I don't want to talk about it,' said Noelle. 'There's been far too much of one thing leading to another from it. I'll try to tell you one day.'

'I'm sure the whole thing's a fantasy, as I said before.'

'It is, and yet it isn't,' said Noelle.

'Oh, it's like that!' said Mut. 'Then come to our party and take your mind off two things. I think you need a big change.'

'Thank you, Mut, but no. Really no. Please ask me next time.'

'Well, of course I shall. The best possible about Melvin. And from Simon.'

The impression made upon Noelle, as she put back the receiver, was that Agnew had drawn himself tightly together in the manner of a small soapstone idol, though a brightly coloured one. He was squatting there like a holy pussycat. Never once in previous years had she noticed anything so peculiar about him, not even when he had been a baby; so equivocal also.

'Well, darling?' she said to him, a little cautiously.

He looked at her, and then crawled back to her. She caught him up, set him on her knee, and hugged him.

Almost at once, the telephone rang again. Noelle clung on to Agnew, and managed to stretch out her arm, supposing it to be renewed supplications from her best friend, Mut.

'Yes, it's me,' she said, in Mut-like tones, and giving Agnew a squeeze.

But it wasn't Mut.

'Is that Mrs Corcoran?'

'It is.'

'Mrs Melvin Corcoran?'

'Yes.'

'Then you'll remember me at the hospital. I'm sorry to say I have some bad news.'

There was a woman who lived about half a mile away named Kay Steiner. When Noelle had gone to parties in Melvin's absence, Kay Steiner had almost always taken in the children for the night. They had seemed almost to like going to her. They managed, both of them, to praise the food and they both appeared to respond to her way with them. Mrs Steiner had no children of her own, but she was not a widow, as might for much of the time have been supposed. It was merely that her husband, Franklin Steiner, was often away from home for long periods. Noelle fancied she had never been told what he did at these times, or at any other time, but he seemed nice enough in his own way when occasionally encountered. About Kay Steiner, there could be no doubt of any kind. Kay was a brick.

The Next Glade

After the funeral, attended by several people who had not been expected, and otherwise by hardly anyone whom the bereaved knew at all, Noelle had a quiet talk with the solicitor, who had remarked that it might be useful if the position of things were roughly indicated by him as soon as possible.

He asked if their talk could be attended also by Mr Mullings, who was an executor. Noelle had several times entertained Melvin's friend, Ted Mullings, to dinner or supper, and put him up subsequently for the night, and she knew that the other executor, who was rather elderly, had been included simply for form. Ted Mullings had already played a prominent part at the funeral, to which he had driven all the way in his Jaguar from his home near Sandgate.

At the end of the discussion, which was quite short, the future stretching before Noelle and the two children seemed just about as open as it could possibly be. She would have to create an entirely new world for the three of them. Noelle looked white. What Americans call challenge never brought out the best in her.

They had all had a first tea after the funeral itself, but, during the little talk with the legal people, Kay Steiner had been quietly preparing a small second one, for consumption before the men went their ways.

Trying to lap down her fifth or sixth cup of tea, Noelle reflected that in less than three weeks she would be thirty-eight. Kay Steiner did not know this, though of course Mut did, who, however, would never tell, or never tell the truth. The two children knew the date, and celebrated it, naturally, but had not been told the full facts. Now, perhaps, they need not know for a long time. Noelle also reflected how strange it was to be dressed quite ordinarily for her husband's requiem.

Intrusions

Anyone could see that she was worn out. Kind Kay suggested that she take in Judith and Agnew for a few days, so that Noelle would have time to find her feet. The children were not in the room at the time, and Noelle accepted with hardly a demur. Judith had been weeping excessively, and was now lying down. Agnew had been looking paler and more mature every moment.

There was resistance at the time of departure, but Kay dealt with it skilfully, and Ted Mullings offered a ride to Kay's house in his gamboge Jaguar. Agnew stepped in ahead of everyone, but Judith declined furiously to go at all, and had to be dragged all the way on foot by Kay, while Agnew waited on her doorstep, as Ted Mullings had to be on his way back to his wife in Kent.

The solicitor had a quantity of work to take home, especially as he had been away from the office for so much of the day; and thereafter Noelle was alone in the house. She had declined Kay's offer to take her in also for that one night at least. She had much thinking to do, and solitude might help the process, though she was far from sure whether or not it would.

It was autumn and she threw the remains of the funeral baked meats into the fire. Melvin had always insisted upon as many open grates as possible, and today one of them had been put into use. Noelle regularly had to stand over the daily woman, Clarice, while it was done. Noelle disliked such sustained exercises in authority exceedingly.

Her father's clock struck six. Noelle felt like midnight, but at least there was a reasonable amount of time for all the thinking she would have to do; all the bricks she would have to make without straw, without the right kind of experience, or the proper temperament.

She could scarcely make herself another cup of tea; scarcely just yet even want another cup. She picked up a boomerang with which Melvin had returned from Darwin. Melvin had admitted

The Next Glade

that he had only bought it in a shop, but it had been a special shop. The boomerang was not a commercially produced plaything, he had said, but a real weapon. Ever since, it had lain on his desk. Noelle handled it wistfully. The house was of course packed with all kinds of things that would have to be disposed of somehow; and profitably, if at all possible. Not even Melvin's life assurance had proved to be of a kind best suited to the circumstances as they had turned out. Noelle realised that she really must start thinking at once. Her situation was considerably better than that in which many widows found themselves. She knew that well.

But the bell rang.

Noelle looked at her father's clock. It was not yet ten minutes past six. Doubtless someone had left something behind. Instantly, it occurred to Noelle that she herself had been left behind. She flushed for a second and managed to open the door.

The man from the house on the other side of the wood was standing there. Naturally, he showed no sign of the disarray in which Noelle had last seen him. His eyes were quite unstaring. This time he even wore a hat, though he swept it off as the door opened. He spoke at once.

'I was so sorry to hear of your great loss. I did not think it right to intrude upon the funeral, but I wish to say how much I should like to do anything I can which might help you. It seems to me the sort of thing that should be said as soon as possible. So here I am to say it, and to say that I really mean it. Perhaps you would permit me to think for you about the many matters that must arise?'

'There are indeed many matters,' said Noelle. She felt that she was being watched from the houses on the other side of the road, beyond the worn entrance to the wood.

Intrusions

'Possibly it would help if we ourselves could define our position in the light of the changed circumstances?'

Noelle glanced at him for the first time. 'All right,' she said. 'If you think so. Please come in for a few minutes.'

He followed her in. She felt that she should take his hat, but in a modern house there was nowhere in particular to put it.

'I have sent the children away,' she said.

He sat on the same sofa; the sofa on which she herself had just been scrying the opaque future.

'This is a boomerang,' he said, as if most people would not know.

'It was my husband's.'

'Yours is a terrible loss for anyone.'

Noelle nodded.

'Most of all for a woman as sensitive and highly strung as you. Your cheeks are wan and your lovely eyes are shadowed.'

'I was very fond of my husband.'

'Of course. You have a warm heart and a tender soul.'

'In some ways he was not very grown up. I think he needed me.'

'Who would not need *you*?'

Noelle hesitated. 'Would you care for a glass of sherry?'

'If you will join me.'

'Yes, I'll join you. It may be the last sherry I shall see for some time.' She filled the two glasses. 'I admit that I have been left in a difficult position, Mr Morley-Wingfield. All this will have to be sold. Everything.'

He seemed to smile. 'You do not really suppose that I can agree to be addressed by so absurd a name?' He raised his glass. 'To the best possible future!' he said very seriously.

The Next Glade

'You told me it was your name,' said Noelle, not responding to his toast. 'Actually, you volunteered the information. What, in fact, *is* your name?'

'My name is John,' he said, now undoubtedly smiling, but smiling at her.

'Mut and Simon seem to know nothing about you.' She was sitting on one of the leather-padded brass ends to the fender.

'I can return the compliment. I know little about *them*. All I know is that I met you in their company. That matters very much. I hope to both of us. I greatly hope it.'

'I think I should tell you,' said Noelle, 'that I saw you digging in your garden. I was with my husband.'

'You are mistaken,' he replied. 'Never willingly have I held a spade in my hands since I left Harrow.'

'Do you know how my husband's illness began? His last illness?'

'I must acknowledge ashamedly that I do not.'

'We went for a walk in the wood with our children. My husband insisted on breaking through the next glade, while we left the children playing. He slashed himself quite badly, and he never really got over it. Some kind of blood poisoning, I suppose, but the doctors were baffled. In the end, he died of it.'

'It is a sad moment to say such a thing, but I admit to being baffled also. I cannot follow the story. I think there is an element of fantasy somewhere, my sweet Noelle. It is because you are so upset by everything that's happened.'

She thought it was the first time he had addressed her by her name. Indeed, she knew very well that it was.

'That is just what Mut said to me on the telephone. But it's not true. It was when we were in the next glade that we saw you digging. We saw you quite clearly.'

'So your husband saw me too?'

Intrusions

'No,' said Noelle, after a second. 'I don't really think he did. He was preoccupied. But I know perfectly well that *I* did.'

'How was I dressed?' asked the man. 'Seeing that I was digging. How then was I got up?' His tone was perfectly friendly, perhaps quizzical, though he was gazing straight at her.

'You had taken off your jacket.'

'My dear girl! Whatever next? Was I digging in my braces?'

'As a matter of fact, you were.'

The man looked away from her and down at the Eskimo-style carpet. He had drained his glass, as, for the matter of that, had Noelle.

'It all seems rather unlikely,' said the man, though only in a tone of mild remonstrance.

'The sincerity of your belief,' he added, 'makes you look more charming and delightful than ever. What suggestions had our mutual friend, Mut, to offer? Another delightful woman, by the way, though a daisy in a spring field, where you are the lovely lily of the world, body and soul and spirit.'

He had ceased to fondle the boomerang and was letting it lie beside him on the leathery cushion. Noelle crossed to the sofa and picked it up. She continued holding on to it.

'Would you like another glass of sherry?'

'If you would.'

She filled the two glasses and went back to the fender seat.

'Previously,' she said, 'I had no idea at all that you actually lived in the neighbourhood. You should have told me.'

'But I don't!' he cried. 'I merely came to know it from the time I was at Sandhurst. What days those were! The laughing and the grieving!' Then he raised his glass. 'I propose another toast. To a bright future erupting from the troubled past!'

Again Noelle did not respond.

The Next Glade

'We must expect that it will take a little time,' said the man, soberly, 'It will be the crown of my life to see the task accomplished.'

Noelle almost emptied her glass at a swig.

'You push through into the next glade,' she said. 'You go straight across it, and beyond the trees and bushes on the far side is a half-timbered house with lots of big windows, and you live there.'

'Half-timbered houses do not usually have big windows, or they should not have them. I would not live in such a house.'

Noelle was twisting the boomerang round and round. There was nothing left of her second glass of sherry.

'I saw you,' she said.

Then she threw the boomerang down. Against the Eskimo carpet it looked like every modern painting.

'What does it matter,' cried Noelle, half to herself, hardly at all to the man.

All the same, it did matter: the house was only ten to fifteen minutes away, even when one was walking at the pace of one's children, and then struggling through the bushes and undergrowth in a quite sedate manner.

'I came in the hope of helping with any difficulties there might be,' said the man, 'and plainly this is the first of them. The distance is very short. I suggest we go and look for this house. We both know the way quite well. Besides, the fresh air will do you good.'

'I think it is going to rain again,' said Noelle. 'We shall be back before it falls.'

The moist surface mud on the woodland path could not but remind Noelle of the funeral. She had been surprised that Melvin had not stipulated for cremation, but the Will had proved to be immaterial at almost all points.

At the funeral it had drizzled persistently, but now it was merely a matter of a penetrating moisture in the air. Noelle was wearing her stylish mackintosh, but the man was seemingly unprotected. Noelle feared that his trousers would lose their crease, even that the entire fine fabric of his suit might lose texture and buoyancy. Already his shoes were streaked and smeared. Noelle was wearing boots.

'Are you sure you want to go through with this?' she asked him.

'I mean to drive out some of the megrims,' he said.

They descended the slope to the clearing. The recurrent raininess had left nothing but a mush. One could no longer distinguish plastic bag from squashed balloon, cigarette pack from snapcorn box. Natural forces were mounting a liquidation of their own.

'And now for the next glade!' admonished the man jovially.

'We can't possibly,' cried Noelle. 'The bushes are soaking. You'll utterly wreck your suit. I hadn't realised.'

She made no reference to his hat, which was even more inappropriate.

'I haven't been noticing the weather very much lately,' said Noelle.

'We'll be through in an instant,' said the man. 'If you've done it already, you'll know that.'

She surmised that Melvin's fate could not but be in his mind, though of course he would never speak of it, perhaps never again.

'It's just your suit,' said Noelle. 'I know it's not very difficult.' She must not permit him the slightest doubt that she had at least once been through, had seen his house. 'You really need to dress up for a thing of this kind in weather like this.' Melvin had always overdone it, as he overdid so many things, but of course he had been basically right. She had always seen that.

'I'll take off my hat,' said the man, 'and then you'll feel better.'

And, under his lead, they were through in no time. On the other side, Noelle had to admit that she could detect no particular damage to his clothes, apart from his shoes; and that even her own elegantly flowing mackintosh seemed unscathed.

The man had been laughing for a moment, but now the two of them stood silently in the next glade. The tree structures, the pendant greens and browns, seemed to Noelle more mysteriously architectural than ever. They too brought back the funeral to her, but she realised that many things would do that for some time to come, possibly for the rest of her life, which in any case might not be a long one, as Melvin's had proved not to be.

'It has an atmosphere,' said Noelle, in the end. 'I'll admit that.'

'Yes,' said the man. 'But you are almost the only being who would feel it. You are a wonderful person.'

All the time there was a faint tinking and tapping which Noelle had certainly not been aware of on the previous occasion. She realised that in the then circumstances she might well not have noticed it. She said nothing about it. It reminded her of a visit she had paid with a German business party to *Das Rheingold* in English at the Coliseum. She had not understood a word or appreciated a note of it, though at the end the Germans had been very courteous and affable about it.

'They all kissed my hand,' said Noelle out loud. 'Every single one of them.' The man looked at her.

'I *am* so sorry,' said Noelle. 'I was uttering my thoughts. I must be very tired.'

Intrusions

'Of course you are tired, dear, sweet Noelle,' said the man. 'You hardly know whether you are on your charming head or your pretty feet.' He looked at Noelle's boots. 'But we shall change all that. Slowly but surely.'

It would have been uncouth of Noelle not to smile, though noncommittally.

'The house you mentioned stands at the other side of the glade?' enquired the man, not too obviously humouring her. He had resumed his hat.

'Through there,' said Noelle, pointing.

'More bushes!' cried the man, in mock irony.

'Not such dense ones. Then you come to a barbed-wire fence. All of which you know perfectly well. I'm afraid your shoes will suffer in all this wet moss. But it's entirely your own fault.'

'But of course,' cried the man, as before. 'Please go ahead.'

Noelle wallowed across the river of moss without looking back. She wondered if there were small snakes and horrid insects concealed in it, which the dampness might bring out, perhaps for feeding purposes.

At the far side, the tapping and tonking were distinctly clearer. Noelle looked quickly back. She saw that the man's shoes were submerged at every pace, and that water streamed from them each time he took a new step. She knew from her own experience how wringing wet the bottoms of one's trousers become at such moments.

'Are you all right?' she enquired weakly.

'Go on, go on,' the man said. 'Go on as though I were not here.'

Noelle considered for a moment.

'All right,' she decided. 'I shall.'

The Next Glade

But through the second belt of trees and bushes, and short though this part of the journey was, she advanced far more slowly.

The staid truth was that now there was no other sound at all but that of the tapping, the hammering, the clanking—perhaps even clanging. It seemed to Noelle that the din was rising in a degree entirely out of proportion with the distance she was covering, as, presumably, she advanced towards it. It was continuing to be much as in the opera, when hurricanes of sound had at times risen almost on an instant from a seemingly peaceful and even flow. She realised perfectly well, however, that the present turmoil of noise was as nothing to that on a reasonably large modern building site; or not yet. There was always something for which to be grateful when one made the effort to see life in that way.

Furthermore, all the disfiguring barbed wire seemed to have vanished or been taken away; at least for the limited distance in either direction that Noelle could find time to take in.

The hedge round the garden was still there, low and thin, but now sadly shredded, selectively shrivelled.

The costly-looking half timbered house seemed not to be there. Alas for so many human certainties!

Noelle compelled herself to advance in her mackintosh and boots across the line which once the barbed wire had marked. At that moment, she realised that though barbed wire had a bad name among her friends, yet those having recourse to it might often so do for largely benevolent reasons. Melvin's friends would take that for granted. What was happening to her now was like going over the top.

She peered downwards over the tattered hedge.

There was the most enormous hole or cavity; excessively diametered, far deeper than Noelle could discern.

Intrusions

All down the hole men were working constructionally—or so she assumed. Hundreds of men—thousands, she might have been forgiven for thinking. Men were doing pretty well everything the mind could think of—and not only Noelle's quiet and reasonable mind.

Sooner rather than later, she realised that women too were working down there: to start with, at typewriters, at comptometers, at computers. Noelle knew these things from the days when she had herself worked in offices, as Mut still did.

There was noise enough in all conscience, for any auditor who was fully human; but Noelle soon realised that probably the noise was nothing like enough for everything that was being actually done. The comparison with the fully modern building site of average scale recurred to her. Properly, there should have been far, far *more* noise. She was sure of it. Perhaps that was the most alarming thought of all on that day of her husband's obsequies.

Noelle turned herself right round and stood with her entire back squarely against the garden hedge. She looked in every direction for the man who had challenged her to this strange experience on such a day of threnody.

John Morley-Wingfield, like the once-tangled wire, was no longer visible. His apparition was no more finite than his name.

Of course, notwithstanding his talk, he might have failed at the last thicket; might have decided upon some care, after all, for his suit; might even have retreated before the full moss crossing, and be composedly awaiting Noelle on her own fully domestic side of the edificial glade.

His case would in some degree have been made. Noelle had seen for herself that, in the strictest construction of words, there was no half-timbered house with overlarge windows. Possibly, indeed, Mr Morley-Wingfield was a property speculator who

The Next Glade

had demolished his dwelling to set up a factory more or less on the site, or an office block. Few of Melvin's friends would have seen much to criticise in that, and some would have pointed out that the transformation would give employment at many different levels, and thus contribute to progress.

The moisture in the air had begun to precipitate heavily and also to darken the sky. Right through the experience, Noelle had realised, at the back of her mind, how late in the day it was. Possibly the second most alarming thing of all was that at such an hour all these entities were still at work.

One could call this nothing but heavy rain. Noelle wondered if there was a way out of the wood by turning rightwards up the glade: a short-cut. She had no wish ever again in her life, short or long, to meet those furbelows of parched or sodden trash at the point where people turned; to behold those deftly shaped official seats, fouled with inscriptions, nicked in or encrusted.

But turning rightwards up the unknown, moss-bottomed glade would be far too much of a further new experience at this of all moments. The glade might appear comparatively indifferent to her, but, even in a suburban wood, the coming of darkness could bring unexpected risks, as poor Melvin had so often emphasised. Noelle was sure that Melvin had often been right in matters of that kind.

Indeed, while hurriedly reflecting in this way, Noelle had almost recrossed the spongy moss, which this time seemed less likely to harbour leeches and freshwater scorpions than to be in itself vaguely bottomless. Had John Morley-Wingfield simply sunk through a particularly soft spot?'

She pushed into the by now almost familiar bushes. At this point the noise of the rain had become loud enough to drown the faint thumping and tip-tapping of the overtime workers.

Intrusions

Noelle could not hold back a cry. The briar immediately before her was still splashed and flushed with blood; exactly as when she had last seen it. The weeks and months of rain had made no difference at all.

Up the slope from where the rubbish rotted, down the gentler slope through the silver birches, Noelle, encumbered by her boots, ran for home, with half-shut eyes. She was quite surprised to find her home still there.

But she did not enter the house: partly because the man might soon be there too; partly because, after all, Melvin might still be there (it was supposed to take forty days for the dead to clear); partly, perhaps mainly, for wider reasons still.

Instead she walked to Kay Steiner's house. Though winded by her up-hill and down-dale run, she still walked briskly and unobtrusively. But surely it was by now too dark for the neighbours to continue watching her, abstaining the while from the television?

'I've changed my mind. Can I please stay the night too?'

'Of course you can, dear. I always thought it would be the best thing. I hated leaving you in that gloomy house.'

'Yes, it *was* a gloomy house, wasn't it?'

Kay Steiner looked at Noelle. 'Well,' she ventured, 'in all the circumstances—'

'No. It was not that only.'

'Really? In that case you'd better all move in here until Franklin gets back.'

'Kay. Are you in love with Franklin?'

'Of course I'm in love with Franklin. Don't ask such silly questions. Now take off your boots and your wet clothes. These smart macs never keep out the rain, do they? I'll lend you some clothes, if you like. We're exactly the same size. Perhaps I ought to tell you that Judith is a little feverish. I think it's because she

The Next Glade

fought so hard on the way here. She's been refusing anything to eat or drink, and she's been screaming. It's nothing to worry about, of course. I'll lend you a thermometer so that you can take her temperature yourself during the night.'

Noelle entered the dining room in Kay's clothes, less sophisticated than her own, but not necessarily less expensive, or less fashionable.

Kay had laid the table beautifully, and with pink lighted candles; all as if it had been a special occasion. She was hard at work in the kitchen. The many surfaces were strewn with comestibles and accessories. Kay wore an apron publicising British Airways. The *British Leyland Cook Book* lay open.

'I see no reason why we shouldn't make the best of things,' said kind Kay. 'I'm glad you like that sweater. It's my favourite. It was given me in rather romantic circumstances.'

They consumed several glasses of sherry and a whole bottle of wine. Franklin Steiner belonged to a wine club connected with a well-known firm, which made the selections: neither costly top table nor cheap plonk.

'Let's have coffee in the lounge,' said Kay ultimately.

'Tell me,' said Noelle, while Kay was filling the two cups. 'Have you ever taken a lover? Since you married Franklin, I mean.'

'Yes,' said Kay. 'I've taken, as you call it, several. But you don't take milk, do you?'

'No milk,' said Noelle. 'But you might stick in a spoonful of sugar.'

'You shouldn't, you know,' said Kay, but affectionately, understandingly.

'I know I shouldn't,' said Noelle.

Intrusions

Kay passed across the cup. All the things belonged to a set which Franklin had bought somewhere upon impulse at an auction.

'Does it make any difference?' asked Noelle.

'To what, dear?'

'To your feelings for Franklin. To the nature of your marriage.'

'Most certainly not. How serious you are!'

'Yes,' said Noelle. 'I think I am serious.'

'It takes all sorts,' said Kay.

Noelle began to stir her coffee. 'Did you ever know a man calling himself John Morley-Wingfield?'

'If you mean was he one of them, the answer is No. Mine didn't have names like that.'

'He may be a neighbour,' said Noelle. 'But you never heard of him?'

'Never,' said Kay. 'And I don't believe you did either. You've just dreamed him up.'

Wearing Kay's solidly pink nightdress, Noelle lay unsleeping in one of Kay's beds. As Kay had no children, there were no fewer than four spare rooms in the house; and as Kay was Kay, all four were always available. It was just as well at such times as this.

The door opened quietly. In the stream of light from the passage, Noelle could see Agnew's wild head.

'Mummy.'

'What is it, darling?'

'Who was that man you were walking with after I came here? Was it Daddy?'

Certainly the almost total darkness was something of an immediate relief to Noelle.

The Next Glade

'Of course it wasn't Daddy, Agnew. It was someone quite different. But how did you see him?'

'Mrs Steiner was making a fuss about Judith, so I was bored, and just ran home. What man was he, Mummy?'

'He was a friend of Daddy's, who couldn't come earlier. There are always people like that in life. You must never let them upset you.'

'Mummy, are you going to marry him?'

'I don't think so, Agnew. I'm not proposing to marry anyone for some time yet. No one but you.'

'Really not, Mummy? Why did you go for a walk with him if he was only Daddy's friend?'

'He wanted to take me out of myself. It was kind of him. You know it's been a difficult day for me, Agnew.'

'Are you *sure* that's all, Mummy?'

'Quite sure, Agnew. Now get into bed with me for a little while, and we'll say no more about it, if you please, not even think about it.'

Agnew put his arms round her, squeezing himself tightly against her breasts; and all was at peace until the morrow.

LETTERS TO THE POSTMAN

THE SITUATION AT home had left Robin Breeze entirely free to choose what he did with his life.

His father, the doctor, had never been particularly successful in his vocation, and had from the first taken care not to influence Robin even to think of following in his footsteps. Indeed, he always referred to medicine in disrespectful terms, even though he himself seemed noticeably adroit with cases that he took seriously, as Robin surmised. Dr Breeze's main public complaint appeared to be the usual one that so little was now left to the individual practitioner, or given to the individual patient. Robin's mother had been simply a summer visitor, with whom the lonely young doctor had scraped up a flirtation. There were few summer visitors at Brusingham, which was six or seven miles from the coast. At that time, Robin's father had been the youngest partner in the practice. Now more and more of the patients were going a little further afield.

None the less, money had been found to send both Robin and his elder sister, Nelly, to non-coeducational private schools within the county. Little had been offered there in the way of 'vocational guidance'. Options continued to be left fully open. Nelly had soon found a niche in helping her mother, as the problems of running the house intensified year by year. Nelly could see for herself that she was invaluable, probably indispensable; and her mother was generous and sensible enough to confirm this daily. The family way of life would have collapsed in a moment, had it not been for Nelly. Nelly, therefore, had little ambition to type all day in a congested Midlands office, or to spend her life cauterising farm animals, as assistant to a boozy young vet: to name two other options that offered. Robin remained less decided. One day he noticed an advertisement in the local weekly, which the doctor took in for professional reasons, though it was perennially in danger of folding finally or being taken over by a national syndicate and neutralised.

The advertisement stated that Lastingham was in need of a provisional postman. It was slightly more than a temporary postman. The exact background to the announcement was not stated, doubtless in order to economise on the number of words; but Robin divined that it might be something slightly special and unusual.

Lastingham was the community on the coast; hardly a village any more, owing to the erosion of the low cliffs. Even the church had gone, except for the very west end. Dr Breeze sometimes spoke of coffins and bones projecting from the cliff face as the churchyard fell away, but Robin and Nelly had never seen anything, often though they had been on their bicycles to look. The living had been merged with those of Hobstone and Mall. What had happened of late was that the fisherman's cottages and the little shops of Lastingham had been replaced by holiday shacks and inexpensive bungalows for retired persons; scattered at random over the landscape, and challenging permanence. None the less, the one filling station that had been attempted had failed almost immediately, perhaps from insufficient working capital. There remained a cabin for selling ice cream, meat loaf, and crisps, though it was usually closed and padlocked. Robin and everyone else knew that the post office had been at last designated unsafe; so that all business was being transacted from the former lifeboat station.

Intrusions

Robin laid down the local weekly on a glass case of his father's specimens, mounted his bicycle, and rode off without a word to anyone.

As so many who undertake the job have discovered, the postal round was far more interesting than laymen would ever suppose. The overhanging threat, which made Robin's position permanently provisional, was that technological advance might at a moment's notice lead to delivery by impersonal van direct from Corby or Nuneaton or some place even more remote. Dispatch from such spots would alter all the postmarks into names entirely misleading. The availability of Robin's own bicycle might help, though perhaps it was too much to hope. At the outset, Robin was told that a retired postman would go round with him and show him the ropes. Robin could only wheel his bicycle, as the old man was past riding anything. The retired postman proved also to be a retired fisherman, and was always talking of the sea and the village market; the latter long closed.

They were in a region of unadopted roads, underdefined boundaries, random structures at uncoordinated angles.

Robin pointed to a small house at the very far corner, where the ground fell away. The road thither had been made but once and for all; doubtless in the chicken-farming period after the First World War.

'What about that one, Mr Burnsall?'

'There's no post there,' said the old postman and old fisherman. He was rubbing his left knee with his right hand. He had to stoop a quite long way to do this.

'You mean the house is empty?'

'Not empty, but there's no post.'

'Who is it lives there exactly?'

Letters to the Postman

'Miss Fearon lives there. She's said to be pretty like. Lovely as a linnet. But she gets no post.'

'Have you ever seen her, Mr Burnsall?'

'No I never have properly seen her, Robin.'

'How do people know she exists?'

'Take a good look!' said the old postman, patiently, though he was not in a position to point.

Robin, as trainee, looked much harder than before. A wisp of smoke was rising from the distant house's chimney. Robin fancied that he would not have seen it, had not this been a pale and windless day.

'Likes to keep warm, does Miss Fearon. It's always the same, winter and summer.'

'Women are like that,' Robin said, smiling.

'*Some* women, Robin,' responded the old postman, at last upright once more.

'I shall hope to set eyes upon Miss Fearon. Perhaps I could go after her for a Christmas Box when the time comes.'

'We don't do that with people like Miss Fearon. They receive no post, so there's nothing due from them.'

'Has the house a name?' asked Robin.

'No name,' replied the old postman. 'Why should it have?'

'To deliver the coal,' suggested Robin, still idly more or less.

'If she burns coal. Maybe she walks out at night and helps herself to the peat.'

'I didn't know there *was* peat,' said Robin, though all his life he had dwelt only six or seven miles away.

But the old postman had said enough on random topics for that morning and was already a few yards homeward, while Robin had been continuing to stare. If Robin really wished to glimpse pretty Miss Fearon, the old man had at least propounded a possible hour. As, pushing his bicycle, he followed the sturdy old figure, he felt manhood almost surging within himself. It could be a difficult sensation to cope with, as educationists are agreed.

Difficult in particular was the decision as to whether the nocturnal project would be seriously worthwhile. Six or seven solitary miles each way through the mist on the bicycle; a long, cold wait; the obvious unreliability of the old man's tale—put forward, moreover, even by the old man, merely as a surmise; above all, the extreme unlikelihood of picking the right night or nights. So far Robin had not even set up the scene with his father about the key.

In some ways, it would be far more sensible, at least as a start, to move in closer to the small house by full daylight; but Robin was deterred by his official prominence. Comment would almost certainly be made if at broad noon the postman were to ride so noticeably far from his paper round. People could complain quite justly that thereby the delivery of their own letters and parcels had been frivolously delayed; and that might be only the start of it. In the second place, Robin did not wish to be suspected by the house's occupant of mere snooping and spying. In the third place, Robin, if he were to be honest with himself, had no inclination to be suddenly sprung upon from within. What defence could he make? What excuse?

Problems, if meant to be solved, solve themselves more effectively than we can solve them. After Robin had been in the job for only seven and a half weeks, a packet appeared plainly addressed to 'Miss Rosetta Fearon'. It was a questionnaire from the rating authority, and all the world would be receiving one sooner or later. The old man, who had accompanied Robin everywhere for the whole of this first week, had thus been proved right about three important matters: the name, the sex, and, it would appear, the unmarried status. There was reason, therefore, to suppose that he might probably be right about the fourth and most important thing. A wave of new confidence bubbled through Robin. On the other hand, the precise name, 'Rosetta', strongly suggested an older person. Dr Breeze had once taken his children to view the Rosetta Stone, clue to so many matters. It had been quite near the museum at the Royal College of Surgeons in Lincoln's Inn Fields, which had been the primary object of the expedition. They had seen the bust of Julius Caesar at the same time; since removed.

'She never gets anything,' confirmed young Mrs Truslove, who ran the temporary post office on a part-time basis.

It was quite true that the official envelope bore no address more precise than 'Lastingham'. The old man seemed to have been right too about the house being unnamed. But the Rating Authority knew that the detective department of the post office was one that could be relied upon. Everybody knows.

When he reached the place, Robin saw at once that the name of the house had simply fallen off. Very possibly the single letters could still be found among the long grass. Patterned curtains were drawn together in all the windows that Robin could see, downstairs and upstairs. He hesitated to prowl through the weeds to the rear of the structure, where the living room overlooked the sea. The familiar trail of smoke from the familiar chimney was rising, faintly green or greenish yellow, against the azure, and soon losing itself. Robin could see that this could hardly be coal smoke, trusty and dependable. He did not know in what hue peat burned. There was no other sign at all of the little property being tenanted. Robin had laid his bicycle carefully against the rough hedge, before giving the gate a stout push. Now he was clasping the packet.

Intrusions

The letter box was not in but alongside the front door. It appeared to be a box indeed, a distinguishable capacious object built into the brickwork and removable *en bloc* with a hacksaw. The flap was unusually wide. Postmen suffer everywhere from the smallness of orifices, and so does the correspondence they handle.

As it was an almost ceremonial occasion, comparable, perhaps, to the service of a writ, Robin pushed back the flap with his left hand, proposing to insert the communiqué with his right. But as soon as he touched the flap, something white erupted from it and fell at Robin's feet.

It was a letter, folded tightly in upon itself, and quite skilfully. It was boldly superscribed 'To the Postman'. Robin pushed the effusion from the Rating Authority back into his satchel, and proceeded to read. He might be receiving special instructions concerning delivery. The handwriting continued large and legible:

> Something strange has happened to me. I find that I am married to someone I do not know. A man, I mean. His name is Paul. He is kind to me, and in a way I am happy, but I feel I should keep in touch. Just occasional little messages. Do you mind? Nothing more, for God's sake. That you must promise me. Write to me that you promise.
> ROSETTA. ROSETTA FEARON

Robin examined, as best he could, the mechanism by which the missive had been expelled. The flap of the letter box proved not to be attached to the top, but to swing upon a lower axis which made it just possible for a letter to be placed in position so that, with good fortune, it would fall outwards as soon as the flap was touched. Miss Fearon had been in luck that the house had been built in that way. Or perhaps she had made a personal alteration.

Robin drew a Packet Undeliverable form from his pocket. He took his official pencil from inside his cap and wrote: 'I promise. Back next week. POSTMAN.' He had been told always to sign 'Postman'; never to give an actual name. He thrust the form into the house. He realised that he could be standing at the gateway to romance. Even though, as might now appear, a romance with a married woman.

His heart joined the larks everywhere overhead. He began to hum 'Nearer, my God, to Thee', his mother's special hymn tune. The waves were crumbling against the low cliffs with a new impulsion.

Not until he had mounted and departed did he realise that Miss Fearon's rating questionnaire was still in his haversack. Properly, he ought to ride back, but that would attract more comment than anything he had so far contemplated. He shoved the questionnaire into his jacket pocket among the various forms. After all, he thought, he was still an apprentice.

'You're smiling,' said Mrs Truslove, when he arrived back at the temporary post office. It was half a cry of surprise, half an accusation.

That night in his room, Robin read Rosetta Fearon's odd letter again and again, and even deposited it under his pillow. In the morning, he realised from the state of the paper that this could not be done with the same letter every night. No matter. There would be further letters. They were as good as guaranteed.

Robin made no attempt to press. He had a long and treacherous road before him, but he saw that to rush things might be to lose all. He said nothing to anyone; not to Mrs Truslove, not to his

Intrusions

father or mother, not to Nelly, who was his mother's second voice, and her first voice more and more noticeably. The old postman and fisherman was rigid with lumbago. Bob Stuff, Robin's best friend, had gone to Stockport as a door-to-door insurance salesman. Not that Robin would have told Bob a thing like this, or Bob, Robin.

The seven days passed sooner or later, and Robin was leaning his bicycle against the rough hedge once more, but: this time the bell was jingling and tingling as the rider trembled. The trouble was the cold rain of late April. It soaked and chilled everything. Robin was wearing official oilskins that had either survived from earlier postmen or been found in the disused lifeboat station. Mrs Truslove never seemed to know which it was.

Robin picked up the second letter and stood holding it. The house offered no protection: not a veranda; not a porch; not an outhouse even. All the larks were holed that day. The waves moaned and clawed.

> He is never unkind, not at all, but I cannot be at ease with him. He is a total stranger. Often I do not follow what he says, and it seems to make him sad. But I am not unhappy. There is goodness everywhere, and many compensations. Thank you for writing. Please keep in contact. No more than that, under any circumstances. It seems that I am not free. Give me your solemn undertaking. Your
>
> ROSETTA

The words blurred as Robin read, keeping the water out of his eyes with an old handkerchief. The letter had virtually pulped in his hands before he had finished it. Also, the act of reading takes, at the best, two or three times longer when even light rain is falling.

Letters to the Postman

Equally, Robin had no shelter in which to indite his reply, let alone to meditate. Rain was dripping from the circumference of his sou'wester. He grubbed out another form, dashed down, 'I undertake. Back as usual. POSTMAN', and plunged the damp paper into the box.

In other circumstances, he might have essayed more warmth of expression; though, even then, 'Your Postman' would surely have stuck the wrong, improperly Yuletide, note, against which he had been indirectly cautioned? At that point, Robin realised that so far there had duly been no second communication for delivery to the remote little abode.

For that matter, the first communication was yet to be delivered. Robin supposed it to be lost. He had to acknowledge that he seemed to think of it only at the wrong moments. But, probably, non-delivery of a questionnaire made little difference to Miss Fearon or to her obscure feelings.

The third letter, discharged the due week later, read:

> I cannot deny that sometimes it is pleasant. If only I knew more about him! I should wish to trust myself to him without reserve, but it is impossible. Do you understand what I am saying to you, Postman? Often I see him wrestling with himself. I do not understand how he came into my life. Accept these confidences, but expect no more. Surely I am committed to him? You have sworn. Your
>
> R.

Now it was zephyrous weather again, and Robin gave way to impulse. 'I am your true friend,' he wrote, and that alone; and he signed with the bare initial, 'P'.

The larks were chiming to the pulses in his body; the waves whispering. Everything set up a temptation to poke and pry, but Robin had his round to resume. Neither this week nor last had

Intrusions

he any working business to be here at all, unless belatedly to deliver the original communication, which was probably gone for ever.

Before mounting his bicycle, Robin looked at the other side of the letter. Last week, it had been impossible to look as the letter had melted in reading. Now Robin saw that there was no superscription. Whether or not this was proof of advancing intimacy was hard to say; but it is permissible always to hope while breath is with us, and breath was much with Robin that morning as he pedalled away.

Soon the days were opening out wonderfully, and Lastingham was filling with summer visitors, as Brusingham could never hope to do. There were lengthening queues outside the small public lavatory block, outside the picturesque little snack bar, beneath the LOST CHILDREN sign, all round the miniature bus station. Cars were parked right to the cliff edge, regardless of the Parish Council's warning notice, regardless of the witness offered by the ruined church and deserted post office. Men were arguing on all sides as to which filling station was nearest; which was cheapest; which could still supply. Women were beginning to suffer and to long for home. Children raged and rampaged. The larks flew higher than ever. The waves lapped erotically.

Robin might possibly have forgotten Rosetta Fearon. He could have taken his pick, it may be supposed, from the girls and women flat on the shingle; first, of course, discarding his uniform. He and Nelly had paid odd visits to Lastingham during bygone summers, but that was very different from seeing the sights daily. One trouble was that too many visitors were themselves there for the day only, as the Parish Council ceaselessly lamented. If a romantic relationship was to be sustained, Robin might have had constantly to travel to Stroud Green or

Smethwick or Chorlton-on-Medlock. That he simply could not afford. Nor at the moment was it practicable to migrate for the rest of his life to one of those places, however ardent he might find himself. Rosetta Fearon was on the spot; even, up to a point, on his round.

Among the loitering throng Robin began to notice a woman always in a summer dress, different each day, that made her look more beautiful, still more beautiful. Sometimes she wore a loose summer coat; often a tilted summer hat. Her hair was perfect. Her complexion was perfect, perhaps because the hat kept off the worst of the sun. Her step was swift and sparkling. Her shoes and ankles were such as Robin had never dreamed of. For example, these were not among his own mother's assets, and it was doubtful whether they ever had been. Nelly had bicyclist's limbs.

No such woman as this would come to Lastingham as a visitor; not even by the week. Robin could never have supposed it. Robin thought that she was Rosetta Fearon immediately he spotted her.

That was two days after he had received Miss Fearon's third letter. There had always been one last claim made by the old postman and fisherman that needed to be confirmed. And now? Good old postman and fisherman! Salt of two elements in equal parts! It was sad that according to Mrs Truslove, the poor old chap was now suffering from urticaria as well. She wondered what would happen to him, all alone.

Robin made no attempt to draw close. That would have been to challenge fate, to upset made arrangements. Furthermore, he would have had to be quick, even though the crowd might well have made a passage for the postman. But he was able to see that the woman, often or always, was carrying what might have been an elegant, foreign bag in which, presumably,

Intrusions

to place purchases. Like any other woman, she was shopping, forever shopping. No further explanation of what she was doing was really needed. Sometimes he glimpsed the lovely vision at least twice in a single day—and not within ten or twenty minutes, but at wide intervals, sometimes when he was still delivering, sometimes during an approved rest period. The woman wore long gloves, stretching up casually over her wrists, or over the sleeves of her slim dress, different every day. Always she seemed about to smile.

Bicycling round the unadopted roads was hot work as the sun began to burst itself; and the trouble was that no winter satchel would contain the rigmarole demanded by the weekly visitors: cans of babyfood, flasks of anti-diuretic, grandma's Botticelli wig in tissue paper, picture postcards by the bushel each day of identical places in interchangeable weather. If all the daily visitors had become weekly visitors as the Parish Council wished, then acting supplementary postmen or postwomen would have been unavoidable, and perhaps a motor scooter. More likely would have been the dreaded transfer of delivery and dispatch to that unpredictable distance. Frequently removing his cap for a moment or two, Robin toiled on, staving off the inevitable.

When for the fourth time he leaned his machine against Miss Fearon's boundary, he saw that all the buds were proclaiming and all the thorns mobilised. He ventured to lay his cap on the hedge top, and the pencil within it.

He mopped at his face and his neck with one hand, and held Miss Fearon's letter in the other.

> He is behaving more and more weirdly. Though it may not be weird at all for those who have the key, which I have not. I feel that he would like to confine me here. Even when I

wash my hair, there is challenge. And yet he is always so kind, so gentle to me. I may have to make an appeal. Ask no more of me at this moment. Your own

R.

And the initial was followed by what Robin could only take to be a kiss; a single kiss; a very tiny St Andrew's Cross. By then, Robin was almost fainting from the heat.

Certainly he was staggering as he stumped back up the cracked path to the sinking gate. Certainly he sank upon his back as if the stony road outside had been the shingly beach below. Certainly he lost all count of time, all sense of eyes peeping through bargain binoculars from the middle distance, all recollection of hearts that hated him for having received an actual paper kiss from gorgeous Miss Fearon.

Strenuously, Robin tried to integrate himself and his thoughts. He swallowed a couple of the quick-revival pills with which his father kept his family always supplied, and constantly had recourse to himself. Robin put the big summer postage sack, fabricated by reluctant convicts, under his burning head. It seemed to him that the main definable development or advance in the correspondence had been in the expression of regard for him, the postman. What development could be more to the point? In the end, Robin managed to extract one of the usual forms from his overheated pocket. For the burning of boats this was precisely the weather. Robin rose to get his official pencil. Then he sat again in the bad thoroughfare and simply wrote: 'I shall answer your appeal. I ask nothing more. POSTMAN.' It was a moment for the word in full.

He thought for a long time, back and forth; sometimes even sucking the official pencil. Then he subscribed not one St Andrew's kiss, but two. He might as well be hanged not for

Intrusions

filching a single postal order but for seizing the entire General Post Office, as in Ireland. Robin almost ran to deliver the note. Now that the decision was made, his step would be light for a whole hour or two hours. He would hardly notice the heat. He would breathe like a young boy.

The larks had ascended so high that they were inaudible. The sea was so unnaturally flat that no wave broke anywhere. Holidays were to dream of; in retrospect as in advance. The one chimney still emitted faintly viridian smoke.

Two days later, with the lovely woman floating about everywhere, like a blue bird, a parcel turned up at the temporary post office addressed to 'Miss Rosetta Fearon, Lastingham', and no more.

'If it's too heavy, wait till tomorrow, dear,' suggested kindly Mrs Truslove.

'I'll manage,' responded Robin, as if he had been the postman in a publicity film.

He had spoken before lifting the parcel.

'What do you think's in it?'

'Something on appro. You're lucky it's not C.O.D.'

Robin toiled out into the heat with the heavy summer bag and the heavy parcel, the heaviest parcel he had yet struggled with. In more advanced places, there was of course a different postman for the parcels. Robin found it difficult to keep his burdened bicycle on course. The heat had been doing something to the tyres.

In order to unload the parcel as swiftly as possible, Robin rode past a number of structures at which he should have stopped. So to proceed might be in the interests of good and imaginative personal organisation, but he left a series of disappointed and weeping children; at least temporarily.

Letters to the Postman

If there had ever been a bell at or in Miss Fearon's front door, it had been taken out or boarded up. The letter-box flap was so hung that it would not rattle properly, though Robin tried several different methods. He was reduced to thumping on the door itself, like the police in a film. He still hesitated to thump loudly. The nearest neighbour was not more than a third of a mile away.

Fortunately, there was no need. Robin could hear steps.

He tore off his cap. Postmen were not supposed to do this, but not every postman had to confront lovely Miss Fearon for the first time, or for the first time acknowledged; and in so remote a place. Robin just had time to pick the pencil off the ground and hide it in his shirt.

The door opened, and it was no Miss Fearon who stood there, but a man in old checked shirt and dirty trousers, like any other Englishman.

'Parcel,' said Robin.

He got the word out, as the regulation prescribes, but was so taken aback that he omitted to lift the package from the step.

The man was under no obligation to lift it for him. 'What's in it?' he asked, with extraordinary suspicion. He was a suspicious-looking man, at best: brown-whiskered, small-eyed, unfeatured.

'It's on appro.,' said Robin.

'Don't know about that,' said the man.

'It's very heavy,' said Robin, volunteering a trifle more, though under no requirement to do so. Correspondents must accept or refuse items as they are delivered. The right of refusal may soon be withdrawn. It goes back to the days before the penny post.

'So what?' enquired the man suspiciously.

Things were approaching a deadlock. Robin had learned by now that this sometimes happens, but in the present case he

Intrusions

could have cried from disappointment. However, a lifeline was thrown to him; whether frail or stout was difficult to say.

A woman's voice spoke from within the abode: a most musical voice, Robin thought, though he really knew little about music, and though the voice uttered merely a monosyllable.

'Paul!'

'All *right*,' said the man irritably, and without turning towards the loveliness within, or ceasing to glare at poor Robin.

'I don't want it,' said the man, and gave the parcel a heavy kick. It came to Robin at once that this might be a dangerous thing to do, when neither of them apparently knew what the parcel contained; dangerous and silly.

'It's not addressed to you,' Robin pointed out; whether or not so required.

'Paul!' cried the musical voice from within. Robin was almost certain that it came from nearer. In seconds, something most unexpected might happen.

Robin put his hand on the door. Now might be his moment; possibly his finest hour as yet.

'You can keep the—thing,' bawled the brown-whiskered man.

Robin could see that both the man's eyes were bloodshot. Living in the country he had never before seen such eyes. He continued to lean his slightly extended arm against the open door, though as unobtrusively as possible.

'Paul!' cried the musical voice; nearer still, as Robin would have sworn.

'— you, postman,' bellowed the man. At the same time, he struck down Robin's right arm with a blow as from a crossbar, and stamped on his left foot with a heavy boot that might very well have been soled in iron. It was as if Robin had 'put his foot in the door' like a travelling salesman; which postmen are bade never to do in any circumstances whatever. The door was shut with a slam that should have torn a door like that from its hinges, and must certainly have travelled that third of a mile on such a still day as every day now was.

Robin, injured in two places, was left with the heavy and enigmatic parcel. He half hoped, half feared that the door would open again, but it did not. There was the total silence within the house that by now he could almost describe as usual. Vulnerable though his position was, he was too upset to move for what seemed to him a long time.

Then, something really strange happened. Robin, without thinking, put his hand into one of his jacket pockets, and, from among all the official forms and other documents, drew forth the communication from the Rating Authority that he should have delivered to this very house weeks ago! He reflected that he must have been looking unconsciously for his pencil.

It was time for Robin to pull himself together. He rose to his knees, and, in the kneeling position, but the questionnaire timidly into the box.

As he did so, the usual letter fluttered out, though nothing like a week had passed since the last one.

This time, Robin was seated on the actual step as he read.

> I lie crushed beneath his weight, and I ask Who is he? Nothing he does for me reconciles me. Postman, I have this to say: there is no lasting happiness anywhere. Your true
>
> R.

And Robin's two kisses had been exchanged for two others. He noted particularly that for the first time no assurance had been sought from him. None at all. Either his word had been accepted, or, by implication, his past promises were now waived.

Intrusions

As in the matter of his career, he was left free himself to decide for the best.

How had the man, Paul, not seen the replies that the postman had already made, and had delivered unsealed? How had such a man left unslain the musical-voiced woman, if he had seen them? How, living with such a man, and, as she claimed, knowing almost nothing about him, had the musical-voiced woman the courage to continue such a correspondence with a postman she could only have examined, if at all, through some crevice? The most likely explanation came to Robin even as he stood there. It was simply that such a man might not be able to read; and probably not.

Robin managed to drag another of the familiar forms from his pocket, together with the familiar pencil. 'Live with me instead,' he wrote. At the moment, his injured arm hardly permitted him to write more. He mused about the signature. He returned to 'P.' That seemed best; and with a single, almost austere, little cross. The completed form followed the municiple missive into the house.

Robin resumed his cap and limped to the gate. He left the parcel on the step. That was often done, in the absence of an alternative. Robin might bicycle back later in order to see if anything had happened to it.

Where were the larks now? What the waves?

On his way home that evening, Robin diverged (a fair distance, too) in order to look. As far as he could see, certainly as far as his duty went, the parcel had been 'taken in'. He fancied that the normal thieving hypothesis hardly arose here. The little house might be kept under observation from afar, let alone the fabulous occupant; but there were no callers other than the postman, no visitors. That simple probability explained in itself several aspects of what had happened. However, the greenish smoke could this evening hardly be seen. Swarming gnats would have tinged the air more noticeably.

Very soon, Rosetta Fearon might be emerging, quite differently arrayed, to gather peat.

Robin decided that it would be both unwise and impracticable to take a chance on it.

Robin had been keeping the three surviving letters in a red betel nut box which his Uncle Alexander had brought back from the East as a young man and had given to Robin on Robin's thirteenth birthday.

Uncle Alexander lived in retirement at Trimingham. His continuing contribution to life was a ceaseless lament for Trimingham railway station, and for the entire M. and G.N. network that once served the region so sparklingly. He spoke always of the bright yellow rolling stock, immaculate time-keeping, and totally painless fares. Uncle Alexander had hardly left the house since the line closed, but cronies of his own generation came to see him almost every evening for negus and talk about the past. Two of them had worked in the M. and G.N. yard at Melton Constable; two others in the timetable department; one old fellow on the track itself, in and around the Aylsham area.

Until now, Robin had been unable to find any particular use for the box. Never had he dared to surmise a use so ideal as this one. The box was now a casket. Robin covered Miss Fearon's last letter with kisses; every moment kissing the woman he had seen amid the listless throngs of Lastingham. The promise in the different letters was indeed by implication only, perhaps even remote implication; but Robin knew that this was how attractive women proceeded. For a woman to speak plainly was an admission. Robin hid away the casket amid the worn-out pyjamas and

Intrusions

running gear in his tuckbox and turned the key twice. He then changed out of his uniform.

All the time he could hear his mother singing. She was cooking his supper, as best she could without Nelly. Nelly was holidaying for a week or two on the shores of The Wash with a girlfriend who was slightly crippled.

> 'Say . . . Goodbye . . . to Daddee.
> He's . . . gwine away to . . . the War.'

The heavily accentuated dance tune was her favourite air. She came back to it always. She seemed to have been singing it since Robin had been in his cradle, which had once been her cradle also, and of course Nelly's, in between the two of them.

Robin's father was out that night, professionally or merely by way of a change.

As the two of them ate together, Robin's mother talked about the different men who had admired her before she married. It was her invariable topic when she was alone with Robin; which, after all, was not very often. In those days, she had worked in a pharmaceuticals factory near the Thames, and had been promoted several times. Pharmaceuticals had been a common interest with Robin's father when they had first found one another. If Robin's father were present, Robin's mother seldom said anything in particular, and neither did he. It is acknowledged officially that medical practitioners are greatly given to gloom. More of them actually kill themselves than anyone else. Nelly could be depended upon nowadays to do most of the talking at meals, and at other times.

Robin had been through a particularly hard day, physically and emotionally. He might well have been unable to eat very much, especially as it was still so hot, and as his mother hated an open window. But, surprisingly, he devoured all that was set before him, and then requested a further helping. His mother beamed nostalgically as he ladled it forth.

'Rex had such soft hands,' she said.

Robin nodded. His mouth was once more too full for words.

'And the most lovely arms.'

'Good for him,' responded Robin, with articulation still impaired.

'Right up to the shoulders.'

'Not like my arms,' said Robin, now able to grin.

'You have lovely arms, Robin boy. You too,' affirmed Robin's mother. 'I often wonder about them. I wonder. I wonder.'

'They carried a very heavy parcel today, Mum.'

'It's a shame you have to work so hard.'

'I see the world, Mum.'

'It's time you had a nice girl and a home of your own. I must think what I can do. I've had experience, you see.'

In the end, Robin rubbed wedge after wedge of sliced bread round the heavy gravy which nothing else would remove from the plate.

'Hungry hunter!' exclaimed his mother affectionately.

'I've got responsibilities, Mum.' He felt quite differently about his mother when, occasionally, they were allowed to be alone together.

Without a word to anyone, Robin, in plain clothes, set out the next afternoon to look for a room to let in Jimpingham. It was one of his rest periods, and Mrs Truslove had let him change in her toilet. She had also undertaken to look after his uniform until the evening. She had even winked at him.

Intrusions

Jimpingham was a village much like Brusingham, though a little further from the sea: possibly nine or ten miles away. Between Brusingham and Jimpingham was Horsenail, much like both of them. Robin thought, or rather hoped, that in Jimpingham no one would have a very precise idea who he was. His father's understanding with the partnership excluded him from ministering in that direction. With the other partners, much older men, a chance would have to be taken. From Miss Fearon's house, one could reach Jimpingham with hardly an inhabited structure *en route*, though the rotate was not very direct.

As will be seen, Robin had considered long and carefully. If Rosetta were to cast herself upon him, he could not bring her home to his parents and Nelly. A room in Lastingham would hardly avail: he himself was known by now to everyone, and marked out by his uniform; Rosetta seemed to flit about there almost all the time; the rent would be based upon holiday values. Least of all did he see himself trying conclusions with Paul for possession of the existing hearth. Moreover, the need might arise upon an instant. If there were no place reasonably near for Rosetta to lay her head, she might fly at once to London or somewhere.

Possession of the little house might of course come about later, supposing that Robin was really prepared to live with Rosetta where Paul had lived with her; but in the interim somewhere entirely unobtrusive was required, and not too demanding, in that the harbouring of a beautiful wounded blue bird was the primary intention. Fortunately, there had been talk all the time among the boys at Robin's non-coeducational school about love nests in the different villages: over one kind of honest habitat; under another; behind a third; within a fourth, though with no proper window. It is probable that little of the talk derived from first-hand experience, but Robin was confident that he knew the basic ropes. Shyness was not precisely his problem, in any case; but something less definable.

Robin looked around Jimpingham for some time before making a first plunge. There was plenty for visitors to look at without their being called upon to explain themselves: the remains of an ornamental pump and a pale green pond, upon which perhaps the pump had once drawn; a milestone said to be linked with King Charles II; a blacksmith's forge now selling comb honey and souvenirs; the fair maid's grave in the old part of the churchyard; Dr Borrow's grave in the new. Dr Borrow had been a prominent local mathematician and preacher; descended collaterally, it was claimed, from Lavengro himself. Not all of these things had Robin previously inspected with any care.

Robin's first choice of a possible tenancy led almost at once to an embarrassing conversation of a character he had not allowed for, though he realised that he should have done. He had been warned often enough. He brought the conversation to an end by affecting to be simple; a device that still has its uses in the less sophisticated parts of the countryside.

True courage was required to try again; within minutes; within only a certain number of yards. But Robin would not have said that courage was what he lacked, and this time his choice was better, for he lighted upon the helpful Mrs Gradey, a refugee from Dublin itself, with no proper man behind her and her living to make. There were seven children, away just then at school, but Mrs Gradey said that they would make no sound of a noise. Mrs Gradey was most accommodating about the rent and about every other matter that Robin could think to raise, such as the whereabouts of a bathroom. She even promised to cook steaks and french fried potatoes for the poor blue bird, if the need arose, and if the costs and so forth could be settled in advance.

Robin stated that at this point he would like to rent the furnished room by the month only, as he did not quite know when the blue bird would be free to move in. He implied that only a little later, he and she might well book a suite, a penthouse, the entire grand edifice.

After his last experience at Rosetta's house, Robin saw no reason why he should visit her only once a week, or when there was a heavy parcel in need of delivery. There might never be another parcel. On the morning after he had driven his bargain with Mrs Gradey, he sat writing to Rosetta while his mother repeatedly summoned him to piping hot breakfast below. In Nelly's absence for a few more days, he had taken from her room a sheet of her pink writing paper, and had meticulously cut off the vertical heather sprig, using the official scissors with which every postman is theoretically equipped.

'Linger no longer,' he wrote. But that sounded like one of his mother's songs, and Robin cut away a horizontal strip also.

'Come away at once.' At times like these, Robin, as everyone else, proved not to have been taught Shakespeare for nothing.

'Come away at once. I await you respectfully. Here is the address. Take a taxi, if necessary. Act now. Have trust. POSTMAN.' Robin knew that a woman in Rosetta's position would fly more readily to the protection of another woman, even an unknown one. He had therefore fully particularised Mrs Gradey's identity and whereabouts. He could not offer a telephone number, because Mrs Gradey could not manage a telephone. However, there was plainly no telephone at Rosetta's house either: nothing but a wisp of greenish smoke, tiny but undying; that and silence. Robin subjoined no little cross. The moment was too serious for that.

He folded his letter into its matching pink envelope, but made no attempt to stick it up, as he might easily think of something to add. Since it was even possible that he might wish to rewrite the whole thing, he also helped himself to a spare sheet. He put the cut-off heather into the pocket of his shirt for good luck. It would lie near to his heart until Rosetta came to him.

He tore downstairs, now rampant for breakfast, albeit belated.

'Your father didn't come home last night.'

'Nothing new about that.'

Robin's mouth was full of scrambled egg, bacon, half-a-beef-sausage, grilled tomato, pigsfry. On such a morning, what did it matter that piping hot was meaningless? All the easier to get down as things were.

'I sometimes worry about him.'

'Nelly will be back soon.'

'I sometimes worry about all of you.'

'No need to worry about *me,* Mum.'

Robin's mother glanced quickly at him as he fed. He should have been on his bike ten minutes ago; clean out of Brusingham; pedalling hard; remembering his round. Robin's mother began to weep.

She was always doing that, but, when, infrequently, they were alone together, just the two of them, he loved her none the less because of it.

'Oh, Robin.'

He chucked down his knife and fork. He had almost cleaned the busy plate, in any case; surely with record speed? He laid aside his heavy cup, not bothering with the saucer. He scrambled round the faded but familiar room, and pressed himself against his mother's deep bosom.

'*You're* mine, anyway,' said Robin's mother, crying all the more profusely. 'Mine. Mine.'

Robin laid his left cheek, newly shaven as the regulations stipulated, against his mother's bare throat and front. He looked downwards at her tight black petticoat.

'It's *such* a struggle,' said Robin's mother, dissolving anew.

'One day you'll get away from it all.'

She stopped crying for a second, and looked at her son hard and seriously.

'Do you really think so? Do you believe it?'

'Of course I do, Mum.' He gave her an extra hard and special squeeze. 'Now I must go. All those letters. All those parcels. Etcetera.'

Before finally releasing him, she gave him a serious and deliberate kiss. Tears were rolling all over her. She said nothing more.

'Bye, Mum.'

He raced to unlock his bike. Every moment, his left hand was on the packed but unsealed letter, and on the spare sheet of heathered paper beside it.

When the time came, it seemed the merest trifle to wander off course and make his delivery. Who cared that morning about the cracked old telescopes, half rusted-up and with whole lenses missing; about the battered Brownie cameras; about the hearts dry as boleti when their season is over? All were well lost if this were love.

Robin strode along the fragmented path as if he had every right to be there, and official business to do. He struck up his letter and persuaded it through the idiosyncratic flap as if it had been a Last Demand. For the first time, nothing dropped out as he did so. He gave hardly a look to the house as he rode away, though he did check the timid green effluvium. There it was, and there, he could not but suppose, was the snail on the thorn, and all things like it! Quite unconsciously, as he pedalled he began half to sing another of his mother's favourites: 'Dreamy bridegroom. Dreamy bride. She's the sweet one by his side. Father's darling. Mother's pride.'

Four days later Robin was sitting alone in the room he had rented.

He had managed to take in Rosetta's abode each morning, but each morning he had gently tilted the funny flap without result. He did not need to be told that Rosetta must be in inner turmoil. He no longer even noticed her skipping blithely from shop to shop in Lastingham. She was facing the crisis of her life. There might not be another such crisis for her until he himself had a sudden heart attack or total nervous breakdown. If all went well, that is.

Robin was not merely alone in his room. He was alone in the house. Mrs Gradey and all her brood were out scavenging. They seemed to do it every evening, when the weather permitted. They brought back objects amazing in their variety, which Mrs Gradey spent much of each day sorting through and rendering marketable.

Mrs Truslove had told Robin that the old man had died the day before. Something fearful had set in finally, and the end had come as a release. 'When people begin to go, they crumble like trees,' Mrs Truslove had remarked poetically. She had been sorting out postal orders as she spoke.

The bell rang: long and loudly. Robin remained fairly calm. Mrs Gradey had visitors at many hours, and so did her two

Intrusions

eldest daughters, and her eldest son, whose name was Laegaire. Robin was schooled already in discounting all expectation.

However that might be, he was greatly surprised this time. At the door was Nelly, back from the coast, brown as a seadog (or female equivalent), firm as a rock.

'I'm coming up,' were her only words at that stage.

Robin stood in the middle of the carpet he had rented, partly fawn, partly woodnut. Nelly wore a flowered travelling costume.

'It's all I can afford,' said Robin, smiling around. 'For the present, that is.'

'I hope she's got short legs,' said Nelly, looking at the bed, which might well have been in fumed oak.

'I don't really know,' said Robin, smiling still.

'Who is it, Robin? Better come clean with me. Then we'll be in it together.'

'Her name is Rosetta Fearon. It won't mean anything to you.'

'Won't it just! She's that piece who prances round Lastingham getting in everywhere first.'

Robin's heart, and much else within else, turned right over. Only then did he realise how very far from sure he had so far been. It would take two or three minutes for him to regain confidence. Still, yet again the old and invalid postman and fisherman had been confirmed in his words.

'You *are* simple!' said Nelly; much as she had addressed Robin from his very earliest days.

'You won't tell people, Nelly?'

'No. But you'll never get that one into bed. Not into this bed or any other.'

'It's not the point, Nelly. It's not the only thing there is.'

'No,' said Nelly. 'Not the *only* thing.'

Robin glanced at her. She was at such an advantage with everybody, and always had been; starting with their mother, let alone their father. Nelly had simply been born like that.

'Sit down, Nelly,' said Robin gravely, 'and please tell me just what you mean about Miss Fearon.'

Instinctively, Nelly seated herself on the only chair that was fully sound. She had not needed even to shake or test the others. Nelly pulled down her skirt sharply, as if she were with a stranger. There was a sense in which Nelly was always with a stranger. Robin sat upon the floor, drawing up his legs to his chest.

'She's not the kind for anything like that,' said Nelly. 'For one thing look at the way she's dressed. Clothes like that aren't meant to take off.'

'I think she dresses beautifully.'

'A woman knows,' claimed Nelly. 'Besides, there's something funny about her.'

'Such as?'

'She knows nobody and doesn't want to.'

Robin let his legs stretch themselves a little. 'Nelly! Can you honestly blame her?'

'And nobody wants to know *her*. I can tell you *that*.'

'They wouldn't know what to say.'

'She holes herself up and no one knows what she does.'

Robin stared upwards at Nelly from the floor. 'Nelly, how can you or anyone else possibly know, when no one even speaks to her?'

'I'm talking to you, Robin. You can take it or leave it.'

Robin reflected for a moment. 'Tell me,' he said. 'How did you find out about me? About this place?'

Nelly smiled for the first time—and quite affectionately, Robin thought.

Intrusions

'Everything *you* do or think about is an open book to me, Robin. Always has been, and always will be. You must know that.'

Robin reflected once more. Nelly had not even set eyes on him since he had moved in.

'There are times when I'm frightened by it all. I admit that.'

'Robin,' said Nelly earnestly, or seemingly so, 'I advise you to give it up and return home.'

'I think most chaps are frightened for some of the time,' said Robin, following his line of thought, and remembering his chums, squared up in memory, jumbled together in the break.

'It's not for you, Robin,' said Nelly; softly, and therefore perhaps even more in earnest. 'Come back home.'

'I've not left home, Nelly.'

'Then what's all this?' Nelly's gesture would have comprehended the entire long guest wing at Sandringham.

'This is something additional. That's all.'

Nelly looked hard at him. 'That's not possible, Robin. I tell you. It has to be one thing or the other.'

Robin lowered his knees and intersected his legs in the supposedly Turkish manner. 'I can't go back now,' he said. He was trying hard to seem at once resolved, unmoved, and in control.

'You certainly can't come back with me,' said Nelly, as if he had been speaking literally. She had risen to her feet and was examining the state of her tights, first one leg and then the other. 'I've got to go and help Mother, and Mother would only wonder if you arrived with me. No doubt I shall see you later. If you're not interrupted first, that is. I've said what I have to say.'

'It's nothing like as desperate as that, Nelly,' said Robin, smiling again; which this time required an effort. 'Of course you'll see me. My stomach's beginning to gnaw. How did you get here, anyway? Are you on your bike?'

'Boulton gave me a lift from Trapingham. He's waiting for me now.'

'Where is he waiting?'

'In the Peck of Peas. He's another reason why you can't travel with me, little brother.'

Boulton Morganfield was from outside the region; basically from near Coventry. He looked unlike anyone else.

'Are you gone on Boulton?'

'Not in the least, Robin. Not one little bit. Not one tittle.'

That time, Robin managed almost to laugh.

'Take care of yourself, Robin. Do try.'

But all that happened after this necessarily disturbing talk, was that Robin gave things another half hour by his official watch, and then bicycled slowly home. Though he was very hungry, it would be no good hurrying. The preparation of the evening meal always took his mother and Nelly a long time, because the task was always being interrupted by confidences. There had been no sight or sound of the returning Gradeys.

On the very next morning a letter fell at Robin's feet as he tipped Miss Fearon's flap. He unbuttoned his jacket or tunic before reading it.

> 'I can suffer no more. I throw myself upon you here and now, certain that you will treat me with respect. ROSETTA.'

And there were two crosses; this time larger.

All day Robin had difficulty in remembering the order of the different structures and shacks; in not wheeling leftwards at crossings where it behoved him first to wheel right. At about half-past eleven, he almost ran down a Mrs Watto, who wrote books for older women, and who always wore a full smock, concealing who-knew-what.

'You have quite broken my train of thought,' murmured Mrs Watto, her eyes glinting, her lips parting.

In the late afternoon, Robin bicycled over to Jimpingham. Naturally, it was at the earliest possible moment; though Rosetta had not been able to specify a very precise time. At some distance from the homestead, Robin perceived that the Gradeys were already out and about. There were manifestations which one had learned to interpret from quite far off.

Robin locked his bicycle, and slowly went upstairs. He opened his door cautiously, as always; it being necessary structurally.

The beautiful Rosetta was seated within. Like Nelly, she had found the one dependable chair.

Rosetta rose upon her lovely legs. 'Are you my postman?' she enquired in her musical voice, higher than Robin was used to, but rippling like a cascade in the sun. She held out her hands. She was holding her gloves in the other hand.

'My name is Robin Breeze,' said Robin quietly. 'I am only a provisional postman. I think I should say that right away. I shall be doing something else soon.'

He would not have expressed himself so positively even three minutes ago. Rosetta's voice had inspired him; her hand, so precisely right in warmth, texture, and grip, had already strengthened him.

'So shall I!' said Rosetta, and laughed like tiny pieces of purest silver falling into a sunlit pool. She resumed her chair.

'Do sit down,' said Rosetta; very much the hostess, receiving. Robin thought it wisest to sit on the bed. He had first shut the door, though it was close in the room.

'Where is everybody?' asked Rosetta.

'Out at work. It's a family named Gradey. A mother and some children. I hope you don't mind.'

'I shan't be here for ever,' said Rosetta.

'I've arranged for Mrs Gradey to cook for you, if you would like that. Pretty simple, I'm afraid. Rather like we get at home.' Robin thought it well to make clear as soon as possible that he had no idea of himself moving in on Rosetta immediately; not even into another room in the cottage, supposing one to be free. Besides, the way he had spoken should lighten the tone of their conversation; make it perceptibly more familiar and intimate.

'I've not been eating very much for some time,' said Rosetta, dimpling a little. 'I've been through rather an ordeal, you know.'

'So it seems,' said Robin, aiming at an air of mastery. To his delight, Rosetta could not be much more than ten years older than he was, even now that he could closely examine her, at about four feet distance, in sunlight, and newly relaxed. 'How long have you lived in Lastingham?'

'I was left the house by my uncle. In his will, you know. Mr Abraham Mordle. Perhaps you have heard of him?'

Robin shook his head. As it happened, he had indeed heard of Abraham Mordle. He was known to all the kids as the Spook King. It seemed best for Robin to shut up on the subject.

'And you moved in?' he asked politely, though he had been slightly shaken.

'There seemed nothing better to do,' said Rosetta. 'I found plenty to occupy myself, though it is an easy house to run. You know it used to be called *Niente*.'

'What does that mean?' asked Robin.

'It is the Italian for Nothing. The name fell off and before I could arrange for it to be put back, Paul was there.'

Intrusions

'Couldn't *he* put it back?' Robin asked; facetiously no doubt, but more and more familiarly, which was the real point. Every second second, he was glancing at the subtle neckline of Rosetta's dress; every intermediate second, at the perfectly placed hemline.

'Paul could do *nothing*. Have you heard of H.H. Asquith?'

'Just.'

'Asquith's wife—his second wife—said: "Herbert who couldn't strike a match!" It's the one thing everyone remembers about Asquith. Paul was like that too.'

'He didn't *look* like that,' said Robin. 'I saw him once, you know.'

'Paul was very different from his looks. That was something I soon learned. *One* thing I learned.'

'I had to deliver a parcel,' said Robin. 'It was addressed to you. Did you ever get it?'

'I expect so,' said Rosetta. 'Parcels were always coming along.'

Robin managed somehow to stop himself from saying 'They were *not*.'

'Paul did what he thought best with them. He *was* my husband, remember. Not that he was inconsiderate. I told you he was not.'

'You told me things I couldn't quite follow,' said Robin. 'I suppose you didn't feel like going into details. Perhaps you could tell me more now? I don't want to ask, if you would rather not talk about it.'

'There's little to tell,' replied Rosetta, again dimpling, and this time completely. 'One day I woke up and found myself married. Just like Lord Byron. I have never understood how it happened. It was like a dream, and yet not. You say you saw Paul for yourself. No one could just dream up Paul.'

Letters to the Postman

Robin nodded. He had no wish of his own to talk about Paul. 'We had better think more about the future, hadn't we?' he suggested.

Rosetta laughed her sunlit pool laugh. 'How practical you are!'

'That's best, isn't it?' asked Robin, somewhat at sea.

If he himself wished to be practical, it was, he thought ruefully, in a quite different way. He tried to take in the complete glorious totality of Rosetta, from cornfield hair and mignonette eyes to slender feet and figment shoes. Suddenly he wondered how ever she had made the journey. He could not see this vision gathering peat. There at least the old man had been mistaken.

Rosetta spoke definitively. 'I think I had better just remain here for several weeks at least. Incommunicado, you know. Except sometimes to the postman.'

Robin caught her eye.

'But only sometimes.'

'We could plan what to do next,' Robin said, trying to turn her proposition to account, though feebly, he felt.

'I shall use the time for resting, and then perhaps I shall go abroad. You must understand, Postman, that I have no money. Only what's in my handbag. Paul was very stringent. It was one reason why I left. One among several. I *had* to leave. I had no choice.'

Robin felt that he had turned paler with every sentence of this confusing narrative.

'But—' he said; without entirely knowing what words he was proposing to use next.

Rosetta spared him. 'It is best for me to tell you this quite clearly, Postman. Of course I shall repay you every penny in the end. When I am strong enough, I shall go abroad. I can make my way there. Not in England. But for my uncle's legacy, I might have starved for all my so-called friends and rotten family cared. There was a little money from Uncle Mordle, as well as the house. You have no idea what people are really like, Postman. At least I hope you haven't. I shall let no one near me ever again. Paul was the last.'

It was a speech with elements of bitterness, to say the least of it, but Rosetta spoke it gaily, like the middle-distance chiming of medieval bells.

'I shall do everything I can,' said Robin; though by now he had no idea how he could do anything much. It was much as when, through inexperience, he had swallowed an entire lemon sorbet at one of his father's professional banquets—the only one that either of them had attended. Like every worthwhile young man, he had supposed that romance would provide its own mysterious wherewithal. At least to the true believer; he who had faith. No young man who supposes otherwise deserves consideration.

Rosetta was regarding him with a smile in her blue eyes. 'I shall pay you interest as well,' she said. 'Of course I shall. In the meantime, I throw myself upon you.' It had, of course, been the expression she had used in her last letter.

But the Gradey family was back. Robin had been hearing their miscellaneous rattlings and crashes for some time, though hardly listening to them. Rosetta had of course made no remark. The dialogue between her and Robin had been of great intensity.

There was a tap on the door.

'Enter,' said Rosetta. It was the first time in Robin's hearing that she had spoken as perhaps a foreigner speaks. At home, his father said 'Come in' to each patient alike.

Mrs Gradey entered, still spotted with rust and dung. 'How are you, my dear?' she enquired sympathetically.

Letters to the Postman

'Fairly well,' said Rosetta, remaining in her chair. 'Tired after my ordeal.' She smiled; as it were, bravely.

'I knew well you had arrived. It is a gift that I have. Robin will tell you that.'

'You were quite right about it,' said Rosetta.

'My children have the gift too,' said Mrs Gradey.

Rosetta nodded slowly and graciously.

'Did Robin tell you about my children?'

'Yes, of course. I am sure I shall make friends with all of them. Have they got bicycles? It's so good round here.'

'Bicycles they have, but some other things they have not.'

'I must see what each of them most wants.'

'That's very thoughtful of you, my dear. They are quiet, good children. You'll not hear one sound as far as they are concerned. You'll sleep in peace. I promise you that.' In fact, there were still thuds and clankings outside, but Mrs Gradey's eyes were roving round the simply appointed room, comparing it with the simply elegant Rosetta. 'If there's anything you'd want me to buy for you, I'll send the eldest into town for it.'

'Thank you. I'll make a list.'

'It's not a steak you'll be wanting for your supper! What about a nice plump guinea fowl? And a bottle of fine French wine from the Peck of Peas? They've surely a splendiferous off-licence at the Peck.'

'Thank you,' said Rosetta. 'Between ourselves, Mrs Gradey, I am quite hungry for the first time since I can remember.'

'Call me Maureen,' said Mrs Gradey, breaking out into a broad simper, albeit her face was still filthy from toil.

Rosetta smiled back, though she did nothing more.

'And will Robin be staying for everything?' asked Mrs Gradey.

'No,' put in Robin, 'I can't. I can't possibly.'

Intrusions

There was a long and curious pause among the three of them, as in *tableaux vivants*. It could not be said that there were little crosses in the air at the moment, though one could perhaps hope.

'I have to go home,' said Robin. 'I'm expected. I shall come round tomorrow evening at the same time or a little later.'

How desperately and confusedly he wished that he could have added 'with a thousand pounds in banknotes'—even if only to himself!

But, he reflected in his bedroom that night, it was not only money that was a problem and a question mark. Romance was singularly lacking in everything that had happened, and practicality all too intrusive. At the evening meal, Nelly had noticeably shown no further interest in him, and had applied herself entirely to organising the morrow's tasks with their mother. Arrears had accumulated in quantity during Nelly's absence. Their father had turned the pages of the evening paper back and forth, as he often did; spent by the day's struggle with intangibles and intractables.

When Robin reached Jimpingham the next evening, Mrs Gradey was awaiting his arrival, in order to hand him a bill for thirty-nine pounds odd.

'A few little extras to brighten up the room,' she said.

Then she handed him a second bill, for forty-seven pounds exactly.

'I don't entirely know the nature of that,' she said, 'but I think it's all right.' She was standing expectantly; intercepting Robin on his way to the delights above. Robin was more than forty minutes later than on the previous occasion, in any case.

Letters to the Postman

He was in no state to assimilate or analyse the financial details. 'You want the money now?' he asked. It was all he could ask.

'Sure and I can't give credit,' said Mrs Gradey, with a new thread of militancy in her tone.

How had the cash been found to pay the different shops and businesses and the fares for Laegaire or Emer to reach them, probably absenting themselves from school for the purpose? Doubtless from Mrs Gradey's strongbox buried deep beneath the praties and watched over by little people.

'I'll bring it tomorrow, Mrs Gradey.'

Fortunately, he had as much as a hundred and eighteen pounds invested—naturally, in the Post Office.

'Or I'll bring as much as I can. I have to give three days' notice to get the rest.'

Mrs Gradey said nothing. Robin could hear the children playing Micks and Prods in the garden. At previous times they had made only noises connected with their business.

'I think it's three days.' Robin was finding it difficult to be certain about anything.

'Sure, and she's a charming lady,' said Mrs Gradey enigmatically.

'But don't you go buying anything else for her,' said Robin. There was more of fear than of firmness in his voice. 'I can't afford it.' In the hope of a little understanding, even fellow-feeling, he did his best to smile at Mrs Gradey.

'Slim purse never bought fair lady, don't they say? Up you go, Robin, while still you can.'

Tapping at Rosetta's door, Robin noticed how much his hand was once more shaking.

'One moment.' That lovely voice was unlikely to quell Robin's tremor.

Intrusions

He waited. Mrs Gradey was taking up tiny tasks immediately below. All the time, she could see him standing there.

'One moment,' said the lovely voice a second time.

Right away, Robin would very probably have dissolved into nothingness for ever, had the opportunity been offered him.

'You may enter now.'

Rosetta was in a different lovely dress, as always when he saw her in Lastingham; but the odd thing was that he could see no change to the room at all, nothing added, nothing subtracted. Not even the air seemed to have changed.

But there was a small dog trotting up and down the room on business of his own; a fluffy terrier, putty-coloured.

'Where did *he* come from?' asked Robin; trying not to make his meaning too obvious.

'I found him in the room when I woke up,' said Rosetta. 'First Paul, and now a puppy.' She laughed. 'I'm not much better with a pet than I was with a husband. I wonder if you could do something with him?'

'I can't take him home,' said Robin quickly. 'My father won't have a dog in the house. He's a doctor.'

'Then *don't* take him home,' said Rosetta.

Rosetta had not as yet suggested that Robin sat. They stood looking at one another with the terrier darting about between them and among their legs. Probably it was only because he was so young. Robin knew it was what people would say.

'I don't think I could take him to the vet either,' said Robin slowly.

'Perhaps he'll turn into a handsome prince,' suggested Rosetta.

'I'm your handsome prince,' replied Robin; after only a few silent seconds had passed.

Letters to the Postman

He could only hope that this time he had chosen the right moment for the boat-burning that was at intervals essential.

'I *have* a prince,' said Rosetta. 'You never seem to realise that, though surely I made it clear in all my letters?'

'No,' said Robin. 'Actually you didn't. Where is this prince?'

'Abroad. I'm on my way to him. I told you.'

Robin continued to gaze at the scrubby carpet; far too familiar after perhaps six sightings. The dog crossed and recrossed his field of vision.

'So that's all there is to it?' he enquired.

'There's no need to be disagreeable,' said Rosetta, rippling with reasonableness. 'I told you from the first. Anything else is entirely in your own imagination.'

'What about Paul?'

'I shall divorce him. I have grounds enough. Though you don't really need grounds nowadays.'

'What about me?' Robin was improvising blindly; gaining time and extenuating reality; unlikely to achieve.

'I'm very grateful for all you've done and I hope you'll continue doing it for a few more weeks. Of course I don't expect you to visit me every day. I said that too. The Gradey children will go between us, if necessary. They are fine kids. I've given them all machine guns. Girls don't like being left out nowadays.'

'*I* don't like being left out much,' said Robin, without one leg to stand on, not one toe.

The little dog seemed busy as ever, though what the business was no ordinary person could tell. Robin was sure of that.

'If you'll sit down for just a moment,' said Rosetta, 'I'll tell you exactly what to do.'

Of course the very last thing that Robin wished was to go, so he seated himself; naturally upon the bed, leaving the good chair to his hostess.

Intrusions

Rosetta came at once to the point. 'Give up all the wild ideas that buzz round you like wasps. Or like bluebottles. Oh, yes I know. I know all there is to know about men. I can read them through a brick wall. Find a nice, ordinary girl, not too attractive or you'll be jealous all the time, not too bright or you'll be anxious all the time, not too rich or you'll have nothing to strive for, not too original or she'll upset people. There are plenty of them, and all of them are available to a young postman like you. Those are the terms offered.'

The terrier had come to a sudden standstill, as if he had been a white gun dog on one of the estates.

'*You* don't live like that,' said Robin from the bed.

'I don't live at all,' replied Rosetta. 'Haven't you realised?'

'Perhaps I have.' Now Robin was staring at her: momentarily still that muggy evening; for seconds rigid as the dog.

Rosetta smiled. 'I am the person every postman meets in the end.'

'I'm a provisional postman only. I told you that clearly,' remarked Robin, starting once more to relax.

'Do what I tell you. What else is there for you? Only wasps and bluebottles.'

'It seems that I have to meet the bills, none the less,' said Robin. He could feel them at this moment in his jacket or tunic pocket.

'Only till I can repay. And with interest.'

Robin must have looked in some way sceptical, though it was not with intent.

'I promise.' Rosetta even leaned towards him. The dog too had recovered mobility, and had begun to lick Rosetta's ankles.

Robin made a second supreme effort in the course of that short meeting. 'Take off your dress,' he said; hoarsely in the still, worn air.

'All right,' said Rosetta, quietly but immediately. Her eyes were on his.

She went to work at once. Robin continued to sit on the bed, affecting calmness, convincing none.

Rosetta had removed the lovely blueish dress, and it lay there, with the little motley dog now sniffing round it. But she was wearing a dress still; a lovely pinkish dress.

'Take it off,' said Robin, now almost growling with masculinity.

Again she went to work, and a second dress lay before him, near the first dress, and with the dog pattering interestedly and indecisively between them. Rosetta now wore a lovely dress that was greenish. She was smiling placidly. She reseated herself in the sound chair. For the first time, Robin noticed her green earrings, long but light.

'Postman, I'll write to you always,' said Rosetta. 'I promise.'

He would have to borrow; but from whom could he do so? Only from Nelly that he could think of; who was likely to have ideas of her own. It had to be remembered that rent to Mrs Gradey would have to be paid too, for as long as Rosetta cared to remain, though Mrs Gradey might well be among the least of his prospective creditors.

'Always?' enquired Robin.

'Always.'

Now he could stand up. It seemed hardly right merely to shake hands, as when yesterday they had met; and Robin suspected that Rosetta's kisses were strictly and exclusively epistolary.

'I'll not say Goodbye then?'

'Never say Goodbye.' Rosetta was standing too. The dog was looking up at them, from one to the other, half interested, half apathetic, and with its tongue beginning to hang out.

Intrusions

Mrs Gradey was lurking below.

'Tomorrow then?' she demanded. 'With some of it? As much as you can manage? I'm not the Queen of Tara, you know.'

'You are the queen of my heart,' responded Robin jauntily; 'which is far better.'